ADVANCE PR/
ALWAYS GR(

C000071489

★ ★ ★ ★ ★

"Both a sharp rebuke of where humanity is and a dire
warning about where we may be headed."

—*Foreword Reviews*

"Lawless's debut turns a satirical eye toward the
voyeurism of reality television and the future of
augmented reality."

—*Publishers Weekly*

"Lawless' clever novel reflects the present day's digital
media voyeurism and *Survivor/Big Brother* exploitation…
with an ultimately dark outlook on the amoral peddling
of schadenfreude."

—*Kirkus Reviews*

"I was blown away. And oh man, it couldn't have ended
more perfectly! I'm still giddy about it."

—James Dashner, author of
THE MAZE RUNNER

Explore more of the ΛLWΛYS GREENER universe:
LawlessAuthor.com

Follow the author:
Facebook.com/SpaceLawyerSF
Twitter.com/SpaceLawyerSF

For more great science fiction and fantasy novels:
UproarBooks.com

Follow the publisher:
Facebook.com/UproarBooks
Twitter.com/UproarBooks

ALWAYS GREENER

J.R.H. Lawless

Uproar
Books

1419 PLYMOUTH DRIVE, NASHVILLE, TN 37027
UPROARBOOKS.COM

ALWAYS GREENER

Published by Uproar Books, LLC.

Edited by Rick Lewis.

Cover illustration by Khristian M. Collins.

Printed in the United States of America.

ISBN 978-1-949671-04-9

First paperback edition.

To the original Gig

<u>Fun Fact</u>

The words *entertainment* and *religion*
share the exact same etymological meaning:
"that which binds together"

1

RedCorp agent rank 57005

ARGYLE, Liam (age 41)

Status: Unattached

Summary: Weather presenter for 24-hour newsfeed on Stream 2. Ratings above par (marginal).

Highlights: Top "likeability" scores among current workforce from feeder synthetic personality testing. Second highest "mockery" scores.

Psych assessment: Repressed intellectual identity. WJ VI standard score 112 (High Average), Exner FABCOM1, PSV1. Mild depersonalisation disorder (DPD) under stress. Light anti-social tendencies. No medication required as per last medical inspection.

Employment history: Telemarketing ("summer job"). Unemployment post-grad. Directed to Stream 2 by unemployment algorithms (2053-present).

Education: Master's (Philosophy), University of London (see "known associates," Schedule A)

Personal notes: Former alcoholic (relapse perspectives: moderate), Mild Gaming addiction, Compliance level 4

Extracted - 08:23 13/01/2072

Ms. Heath stopped reviewing the AR[i] personnel file and moved it to the background of her heads-up display. The Chair, Ms. Preston, was about to open the board meeting.

"First point on the agenda. The ratings for *Reality Shock* are down for the fourth quarter in a row."

The stout and sharply dressed matriarch at the head of the conference table didn't have the usual AR profile floating in front of her. No title, no position in the corporate organigram, no family ties. None of the personal background and preferences that became the Corporation's property—and, in a large part, the Corporation's creation—the moment you signed on.

Everyone knew who Ms. Preston was. She didn't need any display. And ramming home the difference between "Management" and "management" was a side bonus.

"We had to make a tough decision, but we cannot wait any longer. It's time for a change. We're bumping *Reality Shock* back to daytime and launching a new feed for the Spring line-up. Mark?"

A squat boulder of a man squirmed in his chair. The words "Mark Underhill, Marketing Director" scrolled at the top of his display. He tried to draw himself up to a height he did not possess, making him look rather like a startled hippopotamus. He coughed and launched into his overly rehearsed spiel.

"Thank you, Ms. Chair, members of the Board. Our department has been hard at work over the past few months fabricating the next big thing. We decided the best way was to go back to the source and evaluate our past successes. Why did so many people tune in every night to watch *The Eliminator*?"

As he spoke, free-floating AR windows popped up to the left side of his ear. They showed a desperate, half-naked man running from unseen pursuers through a jagged metal jungle.

---

[i] Mere *Augmented* Reality, which is to say, "made bigger," as opposed to full *Virtual* Reality, from the Latin for "manliness, manhood." Etymology proves once again that technology is size compensation by other means.

"How did a podfeed like *The Daily Diary* manage to topple local governments on three different continents?"

More windows appeared to his right. The newsfeed footage showed people, young and old, brandishing old-fashioned ink pens in the air. Confused and worried officials looked on from the windows of official-looking buildings.

"Why did viewers start watching the old, so-called 'reality television' programs in the first place?"

He paused, daring anyone to venture an answer to his rhetorical questions. Or even worse, to suggest he and his department only wanted an excuse to watch old vids of half-naked young men and women walking around flats. No one suggested any such thing. Satisfied, or close enough for management work, he continued.

"I'm not trying to give you a history lesson here. What we've been seeking is nothing less than the source of the terrible attraction of realpod. And we found it: voyeurism. The need to watch, observe, love, despise, scorn[1] and—above all else—judge."

"Today's society belongs to the individual, not the community. It no longer fulfils that basic human need to judge our peers. With realpod, we wrap all this up into convenient daily doses. Ready for consumption from the comfort of home, office, public toilet, or anywhere else you can catch the feed."

He paused, taking a sip of water and enjoying every second he made them wait. But the Chair, Ms. Preston, stared at him the way a dog stares at a fallen scrap, *i.e.*, not for long. He coughed and resumed in a rush of words.

"We already knew all this. And to be frank, as the Mirror's troubles show, we've run the concept dry." At his words, the previous two clips faded into the background. An animation appeared instead, showing the show's ratings over the past two years. It was like something out of a ski adventure sim.

---

[1] "to rip off someone's horns": graphic food for thought

"So, how can we make it fresh and powerful again? I'll tell you how." He started to pause for dramatic effect again, then glanced at the Chair and thought better of it. "The sources of realpod's historical popularity are more potent than ever today. Literacy reaching beyond a fast-food delivery menu has become a joke. People are more isolated from one another than ever before. Everyone is a victim.

"Not only is everyone a victim. Everyone's part of a world-spanning shouting match to get everyone else to recognise them as a victim. Children are suing mothers. Mothers are suing children. Psychoactive over-the-counter drugs are popped on an hourly basis by people of all ages, colours, classes, and creeds." He couldn't help but pause again, preparing his audience for the home stretch.

"So, what we asked ourselves was this. What if we gave every poor slob in the world the opportunity they've been begging for all their lives? A chance to have their unjust suffering recognised by all? What if we created an arena where these unfortunate souls would compete for our pity? What if we let the whole world watch them humiliate and reveal themselves, then vote on who has it worst?" He grinned, and his eyes gave a firm flick to the left.

"Ladies and gentlemen of the Board, I give you the Red's[i] greatest triumph to date. I give you *The Grass is Greener*."

You could hear the boldness.

The lights dimmed in response to the command. A tense hush fell over the assembly like a woolly comforter. A retro techno beat started up, with sound fed through bone conduction into each participant's inner ear. The walls disappeared from everyone's AR-enhanced

---

[i] Cultural integration and the desire for generational distinction being unstoppable, it was only a matter of time before someone realised "red" was both a brandable colour in English and the word for *network* in Spanish, and it became the new fashionable term for the ever-growing interconnectedness of all things electronic, replacing the old *internet*. At least, that was the official story. The millions put into advertising and product placement in popular media by the RedCorporation may have had something to do with it as well.

view. Instead, there were vast expanses of nothing, spotted with rare pinpoints of bright light.

A disembodied emerald-green hand appeared above the centre of the free-floating boardroom table. It snapped its fingers three times in rhythm with the beat, with unmistakable tactile cheer. Then it gave way to a slightly squished blue-grey ball, rotating with ponderous grace.

The planet—for such it was—fell through the void, spinning upon itself as its moon spun around it, and both spun around the distant sun. As all this happened in dizzying precision, the table and viewers fell ever closer. Bits of brown, green, and black started popping up amongst the grey clouds and the blue sea. Soon, the screen broke through the cloud cover. It soared over a landscape of vein-like maglev tracks, huddled vegetation fighting a doomed rear-guard battle, and a triumphant conglomeration of urban sprawl.

"Earth," boomed a deep voice, perhaps out of charity for the slower viewers. "Our home. Since the dawn of humanity, we have lived in society, ever striving to shape our world to meet our needs. All this time, a single question has dominated human existence like no other: 'Why am I here? Today was supposed to be my day off.'"

The view merged with a random piece of sprawl. People milled about, as hard at work as the proverbial ant. The music's beat sped up with reckless abandon.

"We all have our load to bear, and the real question behind the human condition is this: Who has it worst? Is it you? Is it your neighbour?" Everything paused at this. Maglev trains stopped halfway around a bend. Ground vehicles paused in traffic. The rare pedestrians froze mid-stride, forever awaiting another leg to stand on. The camera swooped and soared, making a show of trying to take it all in.

"Let's find out, shall we? New on Red this season, the realpod feed that will become a legend. Together, let's see who has it bad, who has it worse, and find out where—" dramatic pause— "The Grass is Greener. Now taking applications."

The AR display faded to opaque silence. Both lights and walls returned to feed upon the gory aftermath. The only sound was a gulp as one executive, somewhere in sub-Saharan Africa if her display was correct, took a tentative sip of water. Everyone sat in what they no doubt hoped to be thoughtful poses.

A seasoned veteran, the Marketing Director allowed everyone their moment of posturing before he spoke. "As I'm certain you have already realised, the title *The Grass is Greener,* which we ultimately retained at the end of extensive synthetic target-response testing, allows us to clearly describe the voyeuristic nature of the feed while avoiding any of the more... unfortunate connotations. With '*The GiG,*' as we've taken to calling it, we can give the main theme a positive spin, reducing guilt issues amongst feeders."

"Would we be looking at similar scheduling to *Reality Shock?*" asked a balding sprig of a man. An animated "Programming" logo played across his AR display in a misguided attempt at quirkiness.

"This would need a constant, twenty-four-hour broadcast as a base, but with a couple of novelties on top. Testing has shown moving the weekly feature broadcast from Friday to Sunday would reduce feeder turn-over up to fifteen percent. Our socioanalysts think this encourages 'religious' feeding behaviour. Our psychologists say it appeals to feeders trying to counter the imminent Monday dread and suicide rate peak. And the computer people running the simulations say, 'That's what the computer says.'"

As he continued, the Programming exec's bald pate shone like a small, hair-fringed moon. "Then there's the bit we're most excited about. Legal has figured out a risk-free way for us to force contestants to have our new eyeNet lenses implanted for the show. We're looking at full, first-person perspective coverage, all day, every day."

The matriarch butted in with one word: "Fred?" Nothing else needed saying.

Fred turned out to be a short woman sporting the kind of pink bow that's only appropriate on the head of a bear riding a small bicycle.

She righted herself to attention. The sober word "Commercial" bobbed along with the display in front of her, the only one not animated or scrolling in any fashion.

She frowned in concentration as columns of data appeared before her eyes only.

"First projections show annual advertising revenue of some eight-point-three billion fids[1]. A net growth contribution of one percent after advertising, supplies, maintenance, and personnel losses."

"Which brings us to the second item on the agenda," said Ms. Preston, not only hammering the point, but nailing it. "The success of this feed will hinge on finding the right kind of person to host it. Someone under our control; someone people can relate to, and maybe even 'like,' while still being able to condescend to him."

She stopped, considering what she had just said. "Yes, we need a male for this one. A woman could never fit that bill. Does anyone within your units seem suitable?"

Some young thing sitting behind Fred—half a continent behind, in fact—let out an involuntary "Umm." It earned him the terror of Ms. Preston's undivided attention.

"Sorry, Ma'am. I was only thinking, sorry, wouldn't it be better to hire someone who is, you know, famous, to draw people in to watch the feed? Sorry," he punctuated again.

No hint of a smile broke the Chair's countenance. "Don't be a fool. A poorly trained lemur could host this feed and become a worldwide superstar overnight. We don't want some video-enhanced diva already loaded up with an ego the size of a planet. And even bigger pay expectations, no doubt. This isn't a celebrity gossip feed; this is about the nitty-gritty of life."

---

[1] Fids is the common abbreviation of Fides (pronounced "fee-dess"), which is itself a contraction of Financial Determinant of Sale, the international monetary unit born in the direct aftermath of Market War One. Nobody had ever used the thing to buy or trade anything, but it was still handy for comparing the obscenely large sums of money bandied around by the elite corporations, mostly just to show off.

A sharp young lady halfway down the table let out a tactical cough. Her display read, "Ms. Alyson Heath, News and Weather," in prominent but sober font. "Stream 2 currently has in its employ a young man who seems suited. Liam Argyle, our evening news weatherman."

"Him?" scoffed the Marketing Director through the folds of his chin. "The tall guy with the stubble and the jug ears, to host our flagship primetime feed?"

The Human Resources manager drew up Argyle's psych profile and let out a loud "Hmm."

"His profile also says he is educated—in philosophy, of all things. Clearly, this was some time ago. Yet is he not a bit... mismatched for a host position such as this?"

"He does have a nice smile, though. Sort of authentic, you know?" This thought came from a Human Resources middle manager who might not be a resource himself much longer unless he guarded himself better.

"Yes," cut in the matriarch, addressing all comments at the same time. "And it is precisely because he gets such reactions that our Mister Argyle will be the perfect host for *The Grass is Greener*."

She turned to the burly man with a red tie sitting on her right. "Les, get the full personality and background assessments started on him straight away. Make sure any of that high-horsed nonsense has been squashed out of him over the years. If he checks out, I want him on the job starting next week. Can you take care of the details, Alyson?"

"You can count on me, Ms. Preston," replied the younger woman, her face stonier than the cliffs of Moher.

"Well done. On to more pressing matters," said the Chair. As she scanned the faces around her, a scrolling list of items and prices appeared behind her head. "What are we having for lunch?"

2

Sunk deep within the embrace of the automated vehicle taking him home, Liam couldn't believe his luck.

The whole experience seemed alien. As removed from reality as letters to the North Pole, news of floods in eastern Kazakhstan, or the eternal feasts in the Halls of Valhalla.

The sheer impossibility of it all had been gnawing at him since the call on Thursday. Liam had braced himself for disappointment, fully expecting the ground car to fail to show up to take him to the Heath estate. Things like this didn't happen. Not in reality.

And yet, there the car had been—five minutes early, of all things. And off he had gone, stepping into the world of his betters. Hearing the offer again straight from the mouth of Ms. Heath, the goddess of his own personal pantheon.

His own show!

And not just any show, the network's flagship feed! He hadn't dared to ask the question that seemed to loom over the whole affair like an elephant behind the settee.

Why him?

Liam didn't think of himself as ugly. Not in so many words. But the face in his mirror didn't belong to a Sanchez-Oda, or whoever the latest androgynous flavour-of-the-season was. Neither did the belly, added the deriding voice of integrity.

Liam almost slid into the abyss that was his despair over a four-year absence from the female front[1], but caught himself. He was fine as he was, he convinced himself once again, before wrangling his thoughts back to the day's events.

Why him?

He wouldn't risk breaking the charm cast upon an otherwise sane and uncaring world by uttering the words out loud. And in any case, what was he supposed to do about it?

He'd tried to remain as composed as possible during the brief meeting. But it was clear he was no longer in control of anything. Refusing the offer was not only unthinkable. It was on par with one of those primordial Words of Power. The true name of some Great Old One, which if uttered would sunder the very fabric of reality beyond the skills of any passing cosmic Penelope to repair.

What's more, it was a silly notion.

How could he refuse? It wasn't a once-in-a-lifetime opportunity. It was, from his experience of the universe, a never-in-a-lifetime opportunity. Or at the very least, never-in-Liam-Argyle's-lifetime. It was an astounding chance to finally take his rightful place with the movers and shakers of the world. To help the company make the world a better, richer place.

That was the problem with the covering the weather, of course. Weather affected everyone—it was far and away humankind's single greatest topic of conversation. But a weatherman didn't, contrary to popular belief, affect it.

You put words to data other people, using expensive chunks of metal zipping through space, had worked out about what it might do next.

You gestured at the maps and diagrams some other people displayed on AR lenses around the world.

---

[1] Among other fascinating sides of the female anatomy

And yet, people reacted as if he were the weather's trainer in some great elemental circus. They blamed him when it broke loose, escaped, and took a member or two of the audience along with it. It must be true, after all—it was on TV.[1]

This show would be a chance to have an impact. To make a difference in the lives of so many people.

His own, first and foremost.

What did he have to show for his life up until now? A Philosophy diploma still stuffed down the side of one of the boxes from his last move. A second-rate job, a beer paunch, and a liver the size of a small bowling ball. They'd taken pleasure in showing him the MRI after the stomach pumping, on the night he'd decided to recognise his drinking problem.

And imagine everything he could do to help the poor slobs he'd be interviewing. To bring their problems out of the shadows and into hi-res nanoparticle light across the two hundred seven states covered by the Red. He could give them legitimacy. And along with RedCorp, he could bring them hope, he could help them better their conditions, while making a tidy profit for the company to boot.

Ms. Heath had been adamant about these possibilities, some-where around the third glass of heady port. As a result, it all seemed a little hazy, but the heart of the matter was clear. Could he let nagging doubts about losing control over his own life get in the way of this sanity-rending opportunity?

A firm cough came from the front of the vehicle, where the human driver would have been, were such things not laughably obsolete.

"'Ere we are, mate," came the disembodied voice, oozing synthetic "personality."

---

[1] An archaic expression that had somehow lasted long after the last "telly-vision" had been stripped for its rare earths. In terms of anachronism, it ranked right up there with "it's written in black and white."

There's nothing else for it, Liam realised with dread, marshalling[i] his thoughts.

He'd have to give her a ring.

"William," mothered his mother in her motherliest of tones, you know you've always had issues with commitment. DPD isn't a personality flaw, you know. It's an illness, something you can cure."

Her picture, floating in the air before his eyes, was slightly distended. Liam's cheap AR lenses couldn't quite compensate for the alcohol messing up his iris reactions. But her frown of maternal concern came through loud and clear, nonetheless.

"Yes, Mother." She was the only one who ever called him William, now that his dad was gone. By the gods, he loathed that name with every quirk and quark of his being. And Willy, Billy, or anything of the sort.

"You've only just come to terms with that drinking problem of yours—"

"The rehab finished over a year ago, Mother. That's all over with."

"—and I know you think you're living comfortably now," resumed the monologue, thoroughly devoid of heed. "But you've always had so much potential, and we could use the extra income. My pension doesn't go far these days, and your father's benefits are running out in another year."

"I know, Mother," he said, surrendering to the inevitable, but doing his best to tune her out nonetheless.

"And you know I've never liked that hovel you're living in, William. You'll need a proper home soon if you ever plan on building a family of your own. Oh, speaking of which, I'm organising a get-together this Sunday with a friend from the horror movie club.

---

[i] Or, more accurately, *mare*-shalling — yes, as in a female horse. Etymology is both weird and revealing.

Her lovely daughter is coming along too. About your age and with a promising career in interior design. She happens to be single and I'm sure would be most charmed to—"

"No, Mother, we've been through this before."

"I'm not getting any younger," she carried on, regardless. "And you do know how I'd love to see my grandchildren before I follow your poor father."

"Yes." Ye gods, how he hated being an only child. "Listen, Mother, what I called you to talk about was what you thought of this job," he finally managed to get in edgewise.

"Oh…" She paused, rallying with the ease of an accomplished nag[i] as he derailed the freight train of her rant. "Well, it sounds like the opportunity of a lifetime to me, and you'd be a fool to turn it down. But you know I'll be here to support you, whatever you decide is best."

"Yes, Mother. Love you, Mother."

This is the way the world ends. Not with a bang but a simper.

---

[i] Nothing to do with female horses this time. Through Scandinavian etymology, "to nag" originally meant "to gnaw." Food for thought.

3

Liam peered at the card, turning it over between his fingers. He stared, mesmerised[i] by the gleam of sunlight on the plastic edges. He just wanted to avoid facing the full reality of what he now held in his hand. For another few seconds yet, at least.

He wasn't certain whether Corporate had sent the short, suited man next to him to give him a tour of his new workplace at the unfashionable end of the Thames or to act as his boss. But the man carried on with his speech, either unaware of, or uninterested in, Liam's fugue state. "Now that we've got the card template on file, you can order them by the box from Corporate. Ask me for the form anytime you like. The tag inside is set to load the contact info into any local AR networks. Right then, let me get this open."

The bright AR-enhanced green of the show's "outstretched hand" logo shone brighter than anything else on the card. He stood staring at the words printed in bold and inescapable clarity underneath:

The Grass is Greener

The AR copy of the card in his hand popped up at the corner of

---

[i] The term is the linguistic legacy of Franz Mesmer, 1734-1815, who conned the Paris elite into believing in an "animal magnetism fluid" that could be used to impose one's will an another. In hindsight, that's basically shooting fish in a barrel.

his eye like an unwanted proposition, broadcasting his new lot in life to the whole world.

A good name for a show, all in all.

"Ah, here we are," said the little man, as if the matter were up for grabs and reality needed convincing on the subject. With a flick of a hand, he triggered some element in his AR overlay. The imposing warehouse doors clattered and raised at a nonchalant pace, bordering on spite. In a professional building like this, a lens somewhere would be capturing every detail of his face and anatomy, cross-checking them against his Corporate file. He'd stopped worrying about one of the machines getting it wrong and causing trouble for him ages ago. It never happened, despite what you heard sometimes.

That typical bizarre warehouse non-light bathed the space inside. The sort of light designed to make things harder to discern than actual honest darkness. In contrast, the address on his new card leapt out from his AR display. Was it some sort of typo? Surely nobody in their right mind would name a place...

"Mr. Argyle," boomed the man with the AR display identifying him only as 'The Editor,' "welcome to Tantamount Mews[i]."

Liam looked up. Doors loomed out of the non-light at him like suspects in the mythical police line-up. Embedded AR tags flashed their names, somehow resentfully: 'Networking,' 'Studio 1,' 'Studio 2,' 'Field team,' the improbable 'Lounge,' 'Agency Storage,' 'Editor/Producer,' and, last and most probably least, 'Host.'

Well, that's it then. Attributing emotions to doors. I've finally lost it.

Best to follow Emperor's-New-Clothes wisdom and avoid pointing out how ridiculous calling this place 'Tantamount Mews' was. The little boy at the end of that story can't have made many friends by laughing at the powers that be. Or by dispelling the collective illusion.

---

[i] Common throughout the UK, the term "Mews" designates a row of buildings converted from stables, named after cages designed to hold hawks while molting, and ultimately after the Latin *mutare*, "to change." Also, cat sounds and a bunch of legendary Pokémon.

The story doesn't say he lived happily ever after. Or lived at all for that matter.

"It's a bit rough still, I'll be the first to admit," said his new Editor. "We've had to get this old archive warehouse emptied out and geared up in a matter of weeks. But here we are, two weeks before filming starts and ready to go. I think the name also gives it a bit of a homey touch, don't you?"

"Oh, yes. A homey touch. Quite so."

On that note, the Editor ushered him over to 'Networking.'

The door opened, and the non-glare went from sickly yellow to actinic blue. A large man swivelled around inside, hauled himself to his feet, and lumbered over. He extended one greasy hand in greeting, the other nervously adjusting the professional-grade computer interface wrapped around the palm.

"These are the backbone of the whole operation," began the Editor, before pausing. He turned from the miscellaneous machinery banks lining the cramped room and stared at the room's occupant for a moment. He treated him to an expression both as fogged and as empty as a city sky by night. As Liam took the man's proffered paw, the Editor apparently succeeded in remembering what the man was doing in his studio. "Ah, yes, Liam Argyle," he resumed, with a cough. "I'd like you to meet our, um, Infrastructure Technician, Mr…"

"Barry Fletcher, sir. You can call me Barry," said the man, going so far beyond beaming he must be forming his own closed rictus circuit. "Watch your feed every night, I do, and you've never led me wrong once. Well, except for that one time, what was it, three years ago now? But who could have seen that heat wave coming anyway? Pleasure to work with you, sir, a real honour."

"Likewise," replied Liam, out of get-rid-of-the-weird-weatherman-fan instinct. "So, err," he fumbled, sensing the uncomfortable silence stalking the conversation amongst the eaves. "What is it you do here exactly, Barry?" He didn't rank high enough in the corporate food chain to have any organigram info in his AR display yet.

The man couldn't have smiled further if he had been the victim of a particularly sadistic medieval torture involving cheeks, cables, and easily excitable horses. "Well," he began, hooking his thumbs into the belt loops of his insulated overalls. "I take care of these here beauties." He followed this with the inevitable wink, jerking his head over toward the back of the room. Banks of eye-watering lights, humming metal, and jumbled cables sprawled along the walls like so many walruses enjoying a mid-afternoon bask upon the floe. "They're what makes all this possible now, aren't they?"

"Yes," added the Editor. Liam made a mental note. His new chaperone was the sort of man who couldn't stay quiet while people gave out information he wasn't controlling. Or at least taking credit for. "As I was about to say, these devices are the backbone of everything we do here. They're linked up to the Red central broadcast pod downtown, of course. They'll broadcast everything we produce here, after proper Editing,[i] of course. They'll also let us receive instructions from headquarters and keep contact with the field teams."

Barry grinned. "Yep, they may look old, but through these beauts, we'll be feeding onto every AR lens in the civilised world."

"Well, not quite directly," corrected the Editor, with a little sneer. "But the principle is there. In any case, Liam," he added, taking him by the arm and steering him toward the door. "You won't have much to do with this part of our set-up. It's important to know it's there. Comforting and so on, I'd imagine. But you needn't concern yourself with it *outre mesure*."

He opened the door and then turned to give a curt nod to Barry. The man nodded back, sliding back into his chair the way an avalanche might settle within a valley.

"We'll leave you to your own devices, then…" The Editor trailed off, realising his unintentional pun with an expression of horror.

Barry let out a deep belly laugh as the Editor retreated into the non-gloomy entrance hall/warehouse, pulling Liam along with him.

---

[i] Audible capitalisation, naturally

Liam thought it was a good laugh though. Maybe this wouldn't be so bad after all.

His treacherous optimism was proven wrong the instant they breached the 'Field team' door, next along the line. A small metallic-sounding blur ricocheted off the doorframe and buzzed toward them before they had the chance to enter. Or even, as the case were, duck.

The blur and Liam's left ear entered one of those struggles typical of two objects convinced of their right to occupy the same space at the same time. Pain blurred his vision, and a fleeting smile of relief crossed his features.

There was the universe he was used to. He'd been starting to get worried.

4

"Zing!" came the complaint from his ear nerves. But his brain soon hushed it to a low grunt of discontent. It didn't have time to deal with such nonsense from mere extremities. Particularly such unbecoming ones as Liam Argyle's earlobes.

Inside the room, a clutter of faces not so much swam as bobbed before his charcoal grey eyes. He had either stumbled into a support group meeting for very flat acrobats or else someone had loaded AR mugshots into every open spot of air. The same someone had vandalised most of them with bright red virtual markers.[i]

There was a gasp, and two of the more substantial faces pierced through the AR curtains.

"You idiot!" snarled a plump-faced Asian woman in her early thirties. She stared at him for a moment, during which the only sound was the wet flap of something broken in the overhead air-conditioning. Then she jerked into motion and rushed toward him, her extended hand rending the air and clutter like the prow of an icebreaker vessel. But a tall, shaggy-looking apparition barged in from the far right to cut her off.

"Very sorry!" gushed the hairy, hulking form of the newcomer. "Didn't see you coming there. Lucky that didn't do too much damage,

---

[i] Though one would be hard pressed to earn any serious historic accreditation for the idea that Vandals may have acquired, and furthermore employed, such instruments as marker pens during the Sack of Rome.

eh?" he added, pointing at the metal cup rolling across the floor. Given the man's size and pilosity, Liam was surprised he was hearing words and not a sort of bear-walrus grunt. If movies were any guide, he should be making nonsense noises everyone else would respond to as if it made perfect sense, making Liam feel like a pillock.

Liam also reflected that people often had a different definition of 'lucky' than he did. Even a nice plain not-having-things-thrown-at-him would have been luckier than "only" getting his ear nicked.

Wait a second, was that an 'Eh?'

"Ah, let me guess. You're Canadian, yes?"

"Yup," said the shaggy man, for lack of a name. "Well, to be fair, I'm mostly Italian, what with my name being Carpentiere and all. But it's also true my gran, his wife, you see, was from a second-generation Iranian family, so that must count for something. And I'm also one eighth Algonquin, on my mother's side, so…" He paused. Everyone around him was mouthing the words out, trying to catch up. Or, in the case of the Editor, staring into the distance, probably waiting for the moment to insert the conversation back into his reality.

"Err, so yeah, Canadian. You betcha. It's all explained in my profile anyway," he added in a mumble Liam was sure was for his ears only. As if he could read anything in anyone's display through this augmented mess.

"Ah," said the Editor at long last. "Mr. Argyle, I see you've met our field team. Field team, this is Mr. Argyle. Our 'host[i],'" he added, chuckling to himself. "Feel free to mingle and so on, as you'll be spending a fair amount of time working together. Just remember we want diversity and candidates within easy travel distance of the studio. You lot can sort that out together. I'll be back in a bit."

He seemed positively mirthful as he left and closed the door with an excited, "Hoho, oh yes, that's rich." His voice trailed away down the hall.

---

[i] Amazing etymology there. Look it up, but consider this your spoiler warning!

Action overcame the dam of awkwardness and seeped back into the room, roughly as fast as defrosting molasses and twice as stickily. "Coffee?" suggested the massive Carpentiere, by way of a peace offering. Liam took the proffered foam cup with a sigh of gratitude and relief. As the distinctive pitter-patter of caffeine crept down his spine, he was finally able to focus on the room, its contents, and its occupants.

"There's rather quite a lot of stuff in here, isn't there?" Liam said, with the mental equivalent of a wince, when he could no longer bear the silence.

"Yes," replied the short woman in an over-firm tone, having succeeded in negotiating her way around her massive co-worker. "We've received thousands of applications since we put the adverts out last week. We were just, err, discussing which tags to remove from the wall, to make way for some promising new ones that came in today."

"Discussing, were you?"

"Energetically," added Carpentiere.

"So," Liam said, bending down to scoop up the offending cup, "this was part of said discussion?"

"A mere contundant argument addressed to my esteemed colleague here," said the scruffy giant.

"One still awaiting a fair rebuttal, if I'm not mistaken," replied said colleague. Her tones were as calm and collected as the growing shadow of a freefalling anvil.

"Now then, Norma, there's no need to—"

"I told you not to call me that!" shrieked she-who-was-apparently-not-to-be-referred-to-as-Norma, her hand darting to grasp a handy silver letter opener. "That's Ms. Lee to you, buttmunch!"

"Ms. Lee, Ms. Lee, alright!" stuttered (Buttmunch?) Carpentiere.

"Yes, and I'm Liam Argyle, pleased to make your acquaintance, alrighty then. Well, that's done, and well done might I add."

He desperately tried to conclude the topic at that, fighting, in vain, against the question on his lips. "So, if I followed that tantalising exchange correctly," he couldn't help but continue, turning to stare into the scythe-sharp eyes of the letter opener-clenching woman, "your full name would be—"

"Norma Andrea Lee, most pleased to meet you," she replied through gritted teeth. The knuckles grasping the metal implement had already crested egg and were making their stolid way toward the purest angelic white. Where his personal resolve had failed, his sense of self-preservation kicked in. Liam somehow found the strength to cut back any attempts at a pun, at the last second.

A sudden wave of misplaced compassion seized him at that moment. *So this is what life as an editor is like.*

In any case, his new co-worker seemed satisfied for the time being. "Maybe you can be the arbiter of our little dispute about these applications."

Her tone didn't seem open to discussion, and Carpentiere nodded in agreement.

"Err, alright then," Liam said, in an utter failure of both prudence and eloquence.

In a bustle of activity as violent as it was sudden, the two set upon the room. They reached out to manipulate bits of the AR clutter here and there, gathering bits together. Then they stood facing Liam with the lot.

"What about this one?" asked Ms. Lee, thrusting forth an RFID displaying what looked like a CV to Liam. It even had a little picture of a droopy-looking middle-aged man in the upper right-hand corner. But it had the strangest entries:

Full Name: Richard Blaine Fields

Age: 42 (my gods, already?)

Place/Area of Birth: Tool shed, Nr. Quarry Road, Cradwell (mother in transit to nearest hospital, after borrowing neighbour's car)

Work Experience (Previous): Plant Worker, Unemployed, Textile Worker, Unemployed, Telemarketer

Work Experience (Current): Senior Surface Technician (H-mart all-purpose Janitor)

Overall Work Experience: Dreadful - Duration: 12 years, 7 months, 16 days

Hours: potentially 24/7, never the same hours two weeks in a row

Conditions: Aggravated and dangerously rushed customers (on the store floor as well as in their vehicles in and around the building), draining and polluted setting, chronic depression and suicides among co-workers, falling items and appalling sanitary conditions in food storage and packing (part of duty being minimizing contagious disease risk from vermin and human wastes), harassment by robotic delivery drones

Health and Safety Issues: see above

Failed Ambitions: Ecologist, Veterinarian

Habits / Medical Conditions: Social drinking, Medium strength Valnex (psychiatrist prescription, no longer under therapy), regular use of painkillers at night for back troubles

Extraprofessional Activities: Had to give up bowling and then gardening because of back pains. Feed watching in chiropractic chair (game shows, Realpod, nature shows).

Last Meal: Fried Chicken

What insanity was this?

"Yeah, some of them had a bit too much fun with their applications," said Carpentiere, misreading Liam's reaction for amusement. "That's what we get for asking people to submit 'anti-CVs.' Still, as a marketing gimmick, it worked rather well, I suppose. They're good at that at Corporate."

"Too good, if you ask me," said Ms. Lee. "We need to trim this lot down to twenty-or-so applications by next week. And we already got rid of over half of them. We've got the rejection letters ready. We just need some help setting some guidelines for what needs chucking out." She turned on Liam with enough force to make a sledge-hammer rust with envy. "So, what did you think of that one?"

"It's, err, that is to say, I thought it was, umm, a bit... plain?" Liam finally replied. He watched their faces with all the painstaking attention of an obsessive-compulsive portrait artist at a discotheque.

"Plain." The giant swayed a little in the predominant breeze of uncertainty.

"Plain..." A frown crept up Ms. Lee's petite features like Saturn's ring rising over Titan. Something small yet fundamental deep within Liam quivered in abject terror.

"Sounds right to me," said Carpentiere, against all expectations.

There is much to be said for that overwhelming force behind human actions that is laziness. Humans need a damn good reason to do something. Especially when someone else has removed the need to do anything other than agree. Passivity is the cement making society possible. Liam felt a sudden surge of gratitude and love for his fellow Man, so encompassing that he had to privately blame the air conditioning for making his grey eyes water.

But it is at one's own peril that one underestimates the drive to compete, even in matters of laziness.

"Right, too plain," added Ms. Lee. "Or not enough. Whatever. We need people so plain their platitude will make the commonplace seem extraordinary." She sent the application to the virtual bin.

By this time, her colleague had already forced two more disembodied sheets full of intimate facts to the forefront. They danced before Liam's eyes like indiscreet ballerinas. "Which of these two do you like?" he asked in a voice like a foghorn. "The dog stool texture and odour analyst for KibbleCo or the suicide hotline night shift lady?"

"Umm, I'd have to go with the dog poo guy..." said the erstwhile weatherman. "But they both have real pathetic potential," he added, eager to be helpful.

"Right, we'll keep her as backup then." Carpentiere added another layer to the vertical filer.

"What about these?" said Lee, pouncing into the opening. "I've got a disabled 50-year-old fast food branch assistant manager." She waved a poorly presented AR form in her right hand. "There's also this live support technician at SelectSat, who has a lisp." This, presumably, was the sad AR face she was waggling in her left.

"I'll take the support technician, any day," Liam was quick to say.

Surprised to find himself enjoying the exercise, he sipped his coffee as he examined at the next pair proffered by the candid Canadian.

"The career shoe salesman, I should think."

He took another sip.

"What? A desperately single monkey mating expert? Please, let's not turn this show into a farce. We'll go with the amusement park ride tester." He gesticulated in an excess of emphasis, pushing the coffee beyond the limits of the cup's tolerance and scalding his hand.

"Let me mop this up first," he grunted through gritted teeth, reaching for a few sheets of used stationary. He dabbed, then resumed. "Right then, let me have a look." And so he did, looking, then closing his eyes and looking again.

A pained look, not to be mistaken with a sudden attack of internal plumbing issues, squeezed his face. Suppressed memories pushed their way through the crowd to sock his consciousness a good one. And a well deserved one too, for that matter.

I've seen people like this before. Those guys in the construction jackets who ram people into commuter trains at peak hour. I've always wondered if they were actually paid to do that or whether foul people stepped up to do the work pro bono.

Context sprang back to meet his conscience like a bungee jumper. "Yes, he's a good candidate for the show. Who else do you have?"

Liam smiled to himself, thinking he could get used to this. Then a muffled clamour started up at the other side of the cheap plaster walls. There were shouts there, growing more and more insistent.

Curiosity may be a known felicide, but its many other crimes are wholly unaccounted for. Liam decided to take his leave and put it to immediate investigatory use.

"Belay that, I need to get going," he said, making for the door.

"No problem, we have a good feel for the type of application we're looking for now," said Carpentiere. "Thank you for your time."

"And for taking an interest!" added Ms. Lee, not to be surpassed. "Looking forward to working with you!" With that, she shut the door behind him.

5

Outside, the voices reaching him from the next room, along with its dubitable "Lounge" name tag, couldn't have been louder if their owners had been holding a firearm to Liam's head.

"I'm sorry, sir," said a defeated feminine voice.

"Sorry isn't good enough! We don't pay you to be 'sorry.' We pay you to do your job!" shouted a voice Liam recognized as the Editor's.

"Sorry, sir!" the first voice replied, tears audible, if perhaps not yet visible. "It's just that—"

"Just that what?" The Editor's voice wore an audible sneer.

"It's just," the female voice paused, swallowing, "just that in the outsourcing contract it says that we're entitled to—"

"Entitled to loaf about in the staff lounge on work hours, hmm? Is that what you're entitled to?"

"It says we're entitled to ten minutes break per day, sir!"

What am I doing? Liam asked himself, somewhat hypocritically, yet without making the slightest attempt to move on or stop listening.

"Yes, ten minutes a day, to go to the bathroom or something, or to have a cup of coffee to keep you going, not to sprawl on Red property,[i] having a bit of a ten o'clock snooze!"

---

[i] Rousseau says civilisation, and with it, differences between Men, was born with the first delimitation of private property, the Latin "proprietas," which overlaps with the moral judgment of *propriety*.

"I'm sorry, sir—"

"And fancy[i] that, what a coincidence, me strolling in for a bun just as you were sitting down to 'rest your eyes'... Do you think I'm a fool? Do I look like a fool to you? Answer me!"

Liam pictured the Editor's brown-specked bug-eyes popping out of their sockets as if they were mounted on strings, and had to fight to suppress a guffaw.

"No, sir!"

"You've probably been asleep here for the past hour already, haven't you?"

"No, sir! I swear!"

"Oh, you swear, do you? Guide's honour? By the gods, woman, what is this, preschool? I've a mind to cancel our contract with Mobile right now and let some other agency do our outsourcing from now on!"

"Please sir, no. I'll make sure it never happens again, sir."

The fear in her voice was, as they say, palpable.

"You can be certain of that." Liam could hear him gathering his smugness before delivering a dismissal all the more devastating since it had been introduced by that most desolate of clichés.

He couldn't let this happen. He barely had the time to register that the hand opening the Lounge door was his own before he found himself being stared down by the combined glares of a wiry-looking woman of some forty years of age, her eyes puffed slightly red within their sunken sockets, and a petulant Editor, flustered at least as much by the interruption as by the realisation of the identity of its author.

"Err, Argyle, yes. Come in, and shut the door behind you." The Editor scanned Liam's face whilst composing himself. "As you may have heard, I was in the midst of disciplining this... agent of ours, after having caught her napping in the employee Lounge, here."

---

[i] *Fancy* is a contraction of *Fantasy*, and most often used sarcastically, when there isn't the least bit of fantasy involved.

Liam sat down, with assurance that surprised no one as much as himself, beside the woman on the imitation leather sofa which must have been someone's gravely mistaken idea of a happy marriage between taste and budgetary reason. It was the centrepiece of the supposed Lounge, thought Liam, who was of only slighter-than-average build, would have been hard-pressed to actually succeed in doing anything even remotely resembling lounging in the squeaky little two-seater.

The thrum of the central air conditioning unit above his head did not add to the room's appeal, either.

"Liam Argyle, pleased to meet you, ma'am." He smiled, extending a hand which, after a reflex moment of wary inspection, was shaken.

"Mary, Mary Artworthy, sir."

The Editor turned a livid pale green, and Liam decided to press his advantage.

"I'm new here and just getting my bearings. So, what is it you do here, Mary?"

He could have drawn up her profile, but there was a lot to be said for the human touch, especially in a situation like this.

"Err... I'm an agency worker, sir," she said, looking as one who has just realised the reason something looked too good to be true was because it, in fact, was.

"I see. But what do you do?" he repeated, before the Editor could butt in without breaking the form of things.

"Well, I mostly do the cleaning up, and writing mail, and fetching parcels, and repairing a few things when they break down and so on, catering, odd jobs... You know, agency work." She gave him the sort of shrewd stare generally reserved for things found under shoes or stuck to the underside of tables.

Liam remembered meeting agency people before, or at least bumping into them in hallways. A furtive lot of people of all shapes, colours, and creeds, doing just about any menial job conceivable and only identifiable as a group because of their tendency to fade into the background, despite the bright yellow safety bands Health and Safety made sure they always wore on their arms.

But never before had he actually sat down and spoken with one, beyond wishing them a vapid "good day," motivated in equal parts by the overriding urge to distinguish himself with a bit of civility and the perverse desire to see whether this agency worker was the sort of person that would freeze in surprise at a demonstration of politeness, which often came across as an attack in this rigorously calloused world, or the sort that would rally and return the gesture with a profound dignity that would leave both parties elated.

Now, however, and in reaction to the Editor's obnoxious assault upon the poor woman, he somehow found himself going beyond mere genial toying with these people and considering one as, well, a person. It was evidently a new experience for them both, through which they floundered like dolphins brought aboard a tuna trawler: nobody had expected them to be there, nobody had the foggiest idea what to do now that they were, and it was all just a big public-relations nightmare as far as the head honchos were concerned.

"Erm, that's quite a lot, isn't it? How many of you are there working here?"

"Oh, just meself in the day, and Taylor who does night security and maintenance. It isn't really big enough a job to warrant the agency sending another person." She glanced up at the frowning face of the Editor as one might dare glimpse at a looming crimson moon before adding, "But we're all grateful for the opportunity to be part of such an important endeavour!" This, she spouted in the same tone as children spout poems that in other circumstances they might have quite enjoyed but that they were forced to learn by rote.

"Yeeees..." said the Editor, "and such an important part it is. I am certain that you will not be lax in the execution of such a fundamental contribution again." He seemed to take great pleasure in staring her down.

"Oh, certainly not, sir!" Her wide-eyed innocence and eagerness[i] were picture perfect.

The Editor studied her face for what seemed to Liam like just a moment too long, then gave a curt nod, turned, and made for the exit. "Argyle, if you would join me in my office." This was unquestionably a command, spoken with his back turned as he opened the door.

"Right behind you," Liam replied, rising off the sofa and making to leave, but not without turning to give... Mary, he forced himself to remember, a smiling wink. The exasperated eye-roll she addressed to the Editor's retreating back lifted Liam's heart and spirits in an entirely unexpected measure.

He made his way through the non-gloom past the "Agency Storage" cupboard and over to the final door, with its "Editor/ Producer" AR sign, which played through the non-light in the warehouse entrance hall much better than any of the previous ones. The door stood[ii] open.

Inside, Liam blinked. The light was so soft he was forced to pause at the doorstep to let himself adjust and focus. Shelves of books lined the walls on either side, greeting anyone entering the room. Actual paper books! The collection might be worth a fortune, if the books weren't simply solid imitations, as he strongly suspected them to be. Such a collection would be enough to make a sizeable museum proud

"Do close the door behind you and draw up a seat." Buried in the depths of his desk's padded chair, the Editor could have been sold off to the nearest aquarium as a rare new species of hermit crab. "It's a bit early for a tipple, but can I get you anything to drink at all?" he offered, listless and monotone, as Liam took in the rest of the room. The overall impression was that someone had put a great deal

---

[i] Interesting how both innocence and eagerness to comply with whatever someone else expects of one should command the same sort of facial expression and refer to the same child-like image. But then again, so does a deer caught in the headlights.

[ii] As opposed to laid down open, which would have suggested something else altogether. Not that "stood open" doesn't, necessarily.

of effort and money into creating an inescapably imposing caricature of a classic gentleman's study. Even the obligatory desk podscreen blended into the polished imitation stone surface in order to be nigh on invisible, unless you knew what you were looking for.

"Yes, err..." said Liam at last, experiencing the mental equivalent of running to catch, or at least make desperate hand signals at, the retreating rear of a bus. "Water would be fine, please."

The Editor smirked. "Still or sparkling?"

"Sparkling."

"Glass or bottle?"

His defences finally depleted under this sustained assault of solicitude, Liam crossed the room, flopped into the padding of the offered seat, and answered with a resigned, "Glass, thank you."

A smile crossed the Editor's pudgy face like a freight train accident waiting to happen. "Chilled?"

"Please." The cocky bastard.

The Editor focused for half a second, and a deceptive panel in the imitation woodwork at Liam's side slid open to reveal a glass of gently frosted carbonated water. As he took it into hand, he couldn't help but boggle at the man across the desk, which visibly delighted said man to no end.

Liam glared at him.

"It only does a small selection of drinks," came, at length, the Editor's concession, borne upon the back of a thunderous pause.[i] "The secret," he whispered, leaning in over the table toward Liam for no purpose other than effect, "is that every idiot says water."

"What?" started to protest his victim, before realisation hit. "Err..."

The man's smirk grew wilder. In revulsion at being made the butt, as it were, of yet another awful joke,[ii] Liam clutched onto the

---

[i] Not to be confused with *paws*, though potentially just as sharp and hairy.

[ii] "A jest, sport or pastime" in the original Latin, from the Proto-Indo European word root for "word" or "to speak." Hence, "the whole word's a play." Shakespeare missed it by a letter.

oddity that the man's public profile didn't contain his actual name, just his job. This was gross discourtesy, bordering on illegality in certain jurisdictions.

"Tell me... err, hmm, I don't even think you've told me your name yet."

"You don't want to know my name," said the Editor, looking more or less exactly as serious as a mime doesn't.

"Try me." Liam made a lacklustre attempt at a winning grin.

"I'd rather not," said the as-of-yet nameless one, his voice as dead as a pan.

"Oh, but I insist," said Liam with a voice like saccharine, which is to say, somehow managing to sound both sweet and horrible.

"Well, it's just that, err... my name is..." His eyes darted here and there, seeking an escape with equal parts of desperate determination and inevitable futility. "... Ed," he grunted.

Ugh, complained both Liam's sense of good taste and his faith in humanity, joining forces in revolt to violently seize control of his jaws, tongue, and vocal cords, before collapsing back into the silence of a black hole.

"But wait," rallied his synapses and vocal chords. "You would have obviously known your name and what it would lead to as you were choosing jobs..."

"Fate!" said Ed the Editor, with a helpless lift of his hands.[i] "There just wasn't a thing to be done for it." He narrowed his eyes at Liam, waiting to pass judgment on his response.

As usual, whenever confronted with an awkward social situation, Liam fell back on literature and popular culture. "Sort of like Hook in *Peter Pan*, then? Or Scar, the lion in that old Disney movie."

The Editor grunted with apparent satisfaction, and Liam counted himself lucky for choosing references so old that the man hadn't noticed both were villains.

---

[i] An ancestral gesture meaning, "Bugger this, you take this load off me;" first use attributed to the mythological Atlas, if Ayn Rand is ever to be believed.

"You look like a fate-bound man yourself," the Editor eventually said in solemn judgment. "And you're certainly an intelligent[i] man."

Liam eyed him in much the same fashion as a mariner eyes the oncoming storm. The Editor seemed to be sizing him up and could only, Liam assumed,[ii] come up with the result "big," what with the man being a good three heads shorter than him and built like a hot dog.

"Tell me, Argyle... What do you know about etymology?" asked the Editor in unwitting horror house voice parody.

Liam sputtered like a proton frozen at absolute zero, or close enough for practical purposes. "What? You mean, words and such?"

"Indeed." The Editor's voice creaked like the first defrosting of a primeval glacier.

"Well, I suppose I know a bit... Words, they can be pretty interesting and all that. I've never really given it that much thought."

"As one only does at one's great peril." The man in black drew himself straight, ready to deliver his sermon from behind his desk. "Take the word 'editor,' for instance. Damn interesting word, editor. Where do you think it comes from?" The man's glare would have made a prison yard searchlight pale with envy.

"Well, the verb 'to edit,' I'd say." The only response Liam received was a scowl, which for some reason reminded him of his kindergarten teacher, Mister Saunders. "Err, that is where it comes from, isn't it? Person who edits?"

The scowl deepened like a valley. "Yes, yes, of course, but where does it actually come from? What does 'to edit' really mean?"

Liam's mind raced upon a circular track. All he could come up with was "to choose what stays and what goes," and he was convinced this would not be to the man's liking.

---

[i] *Intelligent* meaning, here, "marginally more civilized than a chimp and naturally far, far below my own level of intellect."

[ii] And, indeed, when you assume, you make an ass of you and me. Or Liam and the Editor, as the case were.

Instead of risking sounding like a fool again, he remained silent, and shrugged.

The pontiff in the Editor came back to the surface. "To 'edit' is, literally, to 'say out.' Such is the essence of my function: I say what goes out and what remains."

Liam nodded in a gesture of understanding that was met with barely covered contempt.

"Of course, it shares the same origin with the word 'edict,' which opens whole avenues of richness to the texture of the word." The Editor chuckled. "The point is, if you don't know what a word truly means, then how can you ever hope to know the essence of the object it describes?"

Liam's baffled silence was taken for assent.

"Well then, it is getting on, so it is my regret to have to make literal use of my named function and now say: Out."

Liam sat making sense of this. As he was making no visible attempt at moving, the Editor urged him on with a curt nod, and he eventually got the message, fitting form to function and turning the Editor's jumbled words into actual communication.

"Oh, err... alright then." Liam stumbled to his feet, knocked his chair out of place, righted it, reached the door, turned in complete bafflement, and managed to utter, "Well, err, g'bye then."

The Editor dismissed him without looking up from some display or another he had just opened upon his table top screen. "Farewell.[i] And I'll be seeing you bright and early on Monday for our first feed."

The door drew shut with surrealistic silence.

[i] Of course, as *Hobbit*-era Gandalf would have been prompt to highlight, had he been ambling past, the Editor's meaning here was the absolute opposite of "fare you well."

6

Among the crinkled corn chip packets, demolished cheese board, and spilled remains of three of the most expensive bottles of wine they'd had at the H-mart, the heavy gaming-spec physical screens loomed like the half-excavated walls of some lost city of old, redolent with hidden threat and mystery.

Or maybe he was just in one of those moods, having been thoroughly thrashed by Kyla, his best friend since University, and the rest of the old gang in the opening sci-fi RTS game of their usual Friday "Wine and Warfare" gaming session. His mind just wasn't on the game—might as well rip the band-aid off and break the big news.

"What, you mean that new big feed they've been harping on about all day and night all over the Red?" Steve managed to cover both his beard and the table in cracker crumbs as he spoke.

"That's the one," Liam said. "The Grass is Greener".

"How the hell did that happen?" he scoffed. Only good friends can expect to show this sort of callousness and still get invited back next week.

"Well… They just called me up and offered me the job." Liam didn't think he was convincing anybody, and least of all himself.

"Liam," Hank said in the calm, reason-filled tones of a well fed Hank, those self-same tones which would make the Archangel Gabriel hirself moult with envy, "the Reds must have armies of weathermen working for them... Legions! Not to mention the news anchors,[i] hair stylists, office clerks, and mail boys who'd make just about as natural a host for a feed like that as you would. Hmm..." He bent down to serve himself another hefty slice of cheese from the moribund board. "I'm happy for you, don't get me wrong," he said through the dairy mush with the confidence of someone who knows, through experience and much training of his audience, that they'll be understood anyway. "But why you?"

Following Kyla's cue, they sat there watching him like drying paint as he thought this over. He hadn't really had the time to stop and think about why they'd chosen him. It was hardly much of an assumption to think there must have been plenty of other candidates who had been interviewed as well. There must have been... but surely a board bigwig like Ms. Heath wouldn't have taken the trouble of seeing them all.

He tried to view himself from their perspective. Looking at himself through the mirror of his friends' minds, he had to admit that the perplexed-looking man before him seemed nice enough, in a non-assuming sort of way, but he certainly didn't cry out as being prime star material. If anything, he was the plainest, least assuming of the lot of them. Kyla, with her ever-changing hair currently coloured a rebellious orange, would have made a much more natural choice. Or a more interesting one, in any case. Even Hank or Steve were at least as good at speaking in public as Liam.

So why him?

Had there been some sort of covert testing done long before that call from Corporate? There'd always been rumours about the darker sides of Red-based personality testing, but it only made sense to keep an eye on your people to make sure they were getting along alright, and to weed out the nutters. So he'd never really given the rumours much stock, despite the questionnaires that popped up on his display

---

[i] **Often submerged, sometimes beached, yet never truly at sea, if they're worth their salt.**

ever week, just like everyone else. Had something like that happened here?

"Well, it's awesome, whatever the reason is!" said Steve, rising to slap Liam on the back, much like a whale does the open sea. "Our Liam, a podstar! The world won't know what hit it! I'd say this calls for that bottle of champagne we've been saving in the cupboard, what say ye?"

He was off before anyone had answered with anything more than a half-smile or, in Liam's case, a half-objection that he hadn't told Steve or anyone else about the bottle of champagne at the back of one of his cupboards.

Nonetheless, he was glad that he'd told them about the show, he indulged in telling himself as he studied the freshly formed bubbles on the side of his champagne flute. He'd been worried about how they'd take it, he now admitted to himself, worried that the news would cause some barrier to come between them. He had worked himself up so much that when he'd finally told them, it had seemed over almost before it had started, the memory being little more than a blur. Such was often the way the mind coped with moments of focused stress, or it was in Liam's experience of the world, at least.

They'd taken it very well, he had to concede to his essential optimism. They were all drinking and eating and chatting away, on that and any of a plethora[i] of other random topics; all was well with the world. Only Kyla seemed, to Liam's attuned eye, slightly subdued behind her good-natured grin—he had known her since they were teenagers, and he could tell.

"So, how do you feel about all this?" she asked him in private, as they cleared the debris off the table some hours later.

"Well, it's a lot to take in, you know, all at once, but it's an incredible opportunity. I feel very good about it." The fact that he welcomed

---

[i] Originally, an excess of bodily fluids. Thanks to the advances of medical science, our overflows are usually less physical these days, but they still need to come out *somewhere*.

the following intrusion of Hank with the thoroughly polished cheese board compounded his unease with a vague feeling of alienation and shame.

"We're still on for next week, aren't we?" Kyla asked as they made their way back into the waiting taxi shuttle.

"Definitely," said Liam, but not without a quiver in his voice. "Wouldn't miss it for the world."

7

Showing up at the show's outer London Tantamount Mews head-quarters for the second time, Liam received his first taste of his new routine. It tasted a lot like grapefruit.

Before they left for their first interview, he eyed the copy of the first potential contestant's AR anti-CV over crappy instant coffee in the Lounge: Finn Oldman, 34, single, and something called an "accounts facilitator" with Health Services.

A large vehicle was waiting outside to take him, Lee, Carpentiere, and most importantly, their expensive equipment down to the main Health Services offices in the northern suburbs of the city.

It was a long bumpy ride, and judging from the worn feel of the suspensions, the flashy Red logo nano-paint job with its constantly shifting patterns and colours had probably cost more than the vehicle itself. Liam gazed out at the criss-crossing maglev shuttle lines packed with an undying ebb and flow of commuters at all hours of day and night. Anything to avoid having to talk with the other occupants of the vehicle. The idea of having to open that social can of worms and, once conversation was started, having to find subjects to cover the entire drive thereafter seemed to be a terror shared by all present. None dared break that primeval ice for fear of what might lie beneath.

It didn't even make sense that the suspensions would be bad. He hadn't been in a vehicle with suspension problems since he was a child. Everything was made from self-maintaining nano-materials these days. It either worked well or gave out altogether when the nanites reached minimum levels and shut down. You just couldn't get something that only worked half-assedly anymore, and yet these suspensions were unquestionably doing exactly that. If his AR encyclopaedia was to be trusted, for that to happen you'd need to somehow modify the basic nanite programming to drop all the safeguards and then keep running the parts down as they literally crumbled apart, burned out nanites dropping away like dead skin cells...

He shuddered, closing the AR search window. *Weren't we all supposed to have flying vehicles by the time I was an adult, anyway?*

The idea was certainly good for a distraction, but it was also something he was truly passionate about. The promised future from his childhood stories was supposed to be the present now, surely. The technology seemed to be there, with superconductors you could fry eggs on. So why the hell wasn't this damn thing zooming across the skies to land gracefully on a roof-top platform? Why was it "too expensive for any practical use," as the media always said, when at the same time, the residential and commercial playgrounds of the corporate rich had private flight lanes into the urban centres, paved entirely with room-temperature superconductors? Was gross inequality the only way to realise the dream of flying cars that humankind had defined as "the Future" for so long?

The Health Services building, which eventually provided Liam with a welcome excuse to stop thinking about such things, was indescribable; not merely indescript, which simply underlines a certain laziness on behalf of the describer, but quite literally indescribable, in the same way that the mind cannot truly describe things it cannot grasp, be they too vast, like the yawning chasm of the country sky above a city-bred child's head, or too horrible, such as the limitless potential of that self-same sky at night. One could say the building was grey, one could say it was bleak, one could say it was tall, but that would not be actual describing; those same words could apply to just about any building in a fifty-kilometre radius and, indeed, were in essence already contained in the word "building" in this setting. Those qualities[i] which made this specific building "Health Services" lay elsewhere. Somewhere elusive, beyond the merely physical and into a realm of quickly silenced despair and routine little bureaucratic evils that both beckoned and repulsed the mind of servant, subject, and onlooker alike. Nonetheless, inadvisably to Liam's mind, they entered.

Liam tried to ignore the obvious scene they were offering with their professional-grade pod-cameras[ii] and sound recorders (sets of three eye-sized lenses to be positioned around the room for best feeding effect and, in a noteworthy demonstration of anachronistic conservation, referred to in the business as tripods) as they made their wary way across the desolate lobby, past the terminally unmanned reception desk and, after some debate and on the directions of a grimy and manifestly outdated AR directory, into the eventual elevator and up to the fifth floor, left wing, "User Relations."

A man whose AR ID introduced him as "Agent 1215084 – OLDMAN, Finn – Accounts" was waiting for them by the "employees-only" water outlet.

"I wasn't sure you'd really be coming," said the man, putting an end to a seemingly millennial state of relative inertness in order to gush forward to shake their hands, without taking the trouble to introduce himself any further than his ID already had. "It's not much, but here it is," he said, waving his arm in the general direction of the mess of meter-wide and long cubicles that honeycombed an office floor entirely devoid of proper walls, or even windows, for that matter. "Hey, is that thing on?" His gaze fixed upon the lit pod instruments in Lee's hands, his hunger evident and unabashed.

"Yes, but don't worry about it, just doing some preliminary light

---

[i] For a given value of the word "quality"

[ii] The "chamber," a little space designed to capture a moment, lock it up, and keep it safe and deathly still forever more.

and sound tests and so on. Don't mind them," said Lee in the consecrated formula dear to seekers of "candid" footage[i] since the birth of the graven image reel.

"Shall we go have a look at your workstation?" asked Carpentiere, to general, if not particularly fussed, assent.

They seemed to expect Liam to lead the way, so he did. Finn's cubicle was, quite precisely, three and a half walls, the patch of plastic floor they delimited, a chair, a small physical filing cabinet, a folding table that did not deserve the title its obvious function as a desk bestowed, plenty of bare wall for AR window display, and a mess of paper scraps. Writing implements were apparently at a premium, and the waste basket was out in the space between sets of, for lack of a better word, walls. One could only resist against dignifying this space with the title of "hallway."

Finn took his place at his chair, casting constant glances at the lens, while they stood next to him, outside the cubicle. He would occasionally burst out and say, "So is this going to be in the feed? Is it?" to which they'd calm him and tell him to just go about his business while they made certain all the settings were right.

Liam knew for a fact this was an outright lie because he'd half-listened to them discussing the matter toward the end of that interminable ride from the Mews to this wretched place. The feed had been live from the moment they'd left the van, and what they were doing now was trying to get the more-or-less candid work scenes that would be the filler for Finn's preview spot.

He wasn't all that comfortable with the idea of systematically lying to the applicants right from the get-go, but he couldn't deny that the only way to get people to look properly natural for the feed was to make them think it wasn't on. Since there was nothing to be done for it, he decided to let it go.

At length, Carpentiere broke the silence. "Alrighty then, I think

---

[i] The imperial measurements will live on in etymology long after the metric system inevitably replaces them in all practical uses.

we've got it. Mr. Oldham, could you please start by telling us what it is you do here." The man looked up from his podscreen, where, ostensibly at work, he had been frowning and sighing at an open file for a good five minutes now, and started.

"Oh, well, I work in accounts, see. When users sign up for HS coverage, they're filed, and we start up an account for them. Any treatment they undergo is billed to that account, where we validate any deductibles and bill the rest back to the users on a monthly basis..." Here he paused his rehearsed spiel, looking hesitant, maybe even fearful. When he spoke again, it was in the lowered tones of a conspirator[i], or perhaps of a man who, faced with the choice, preferred to part with some of his throat rather than his cigarettes.

"The problem is, our 'users' are by definition the dirt-poor people who can't even pay for perfectly affordable private health coverage, like Medicalc™." Liam was reminded of an advert he remembered from some train ride or another. "So they can barely ever afford the seventy or eighty percent of the treatment cost that isn't covered. And then there are the incentives: Health Services gets a fixed envelope every year to cover all expenses, and that's not just to cover the basic treatment coverage for the users, but also everyone's salaries at HS. The budget is tighter than... well... it's very tight, so anything that doesn't get paid by the users ends up coming directly out of our pockets. That's why we need guys like me. Our job is to follow up on the users and make sure they pay every cent they can... even when, really, they can't."

Liam looked around him as he listened to the man. The cubicles around him were filled with women, men, and enbies who were ordinary enough, judging from the backs of their heads at least, and yet here they came, day after day, pushing society's most unfortunate to the brink of survival—he wouldn't allow himself to finish that thought to its logical conclusion.

"Take Fred Watson here," Oldman said, lifting his podscreen to

---

[i] "Breathing together." Ultimately, we are all conspirators.

face the lens. "I really shouldn't be showing you this, so don't go putting it on the feed now, but it really shows what I'm talking about. Fred here has two kids he only sees every other week but still needs to support, a second mortgage he can't really afford, and a budding thyroid cancer that should have been diagnosed years ago, and it's my job to make him pay up for the meds that will only postpone the inevitable at this stage anyway." Liam returned his full attention to the man. "Sometimes, that means using threats: repossession of the little flat he inherited from his mom, letting the Family Services in on his financial difficulties, that sort of thing... I suppose you could call us something of an uncivil service[i]." He chuckled, not so much balefully as like a literal long-forgotten bale of rotting hay. "But the thing is, Fred here is just so damn typical it's tragic. I deal with hundreds of Freds every day."

Liam examined Oldman's flabby lines, his receding hairline, and his nose hair in turn, and in mountingly horrifying detail. The man seemed to take the silence as a sign of expectant interest, for he continued.

"I have to study these files, take in all the details, and then go about my job making sure they pay up. Let me tell you, it's not an easy job, emotionally or psychologically."

Always one for compassion, or so he liked to believe, even in the face of congenital antipathy, Liam had to cut in. "Why don't you just get out of it then? Find some other job? Maybe we can help."

Finn raised an eyebrow. "Change jobs? What good would that do? I've been here a while now. I'm starting to get some decent benefits at last. I'm not about to give that up on a whim, and a man's got to eat, you know. No, what we really need is to have the psychological stress involved in the work taken into account by the Services and properly compensated. At the very least, we should get some coverage on our psychoactive medication. If you really want to help,

---

[i] To be translated into French as "dysfonction publique," en français dans le texte.

you can put this in the feed to give us some media attention and force the Services to do something for us. That's why I sent in the application in the first place. So..."

"... this'll all be in the feed, right?"

The large AR projection more-or-less tastefully thrown again the walls of the Editor's pseudo wood-panelled office froze on the man's eager expression of hope and greed.

"Perfect! This is precisely the kind of thing we're looking for. Despicable and pitiful at the same time." The Editor beamed like Pharos rebuilt. "We'll take out that last statement and cut straight to the scene at that hovel of his, with the indefinable mutt. People always root for the underdog[i]. It'll be pure synthetic pathos gold."

Liam knew the Corporation had to be right. That's why they were the Corporation, after all. But an odd thought trotted through his mind and past his lips. "Won't that make him seem... better than he really is? We spent about five hours filming with him, and it only took five minutes to see he was a pretty despicable guy. I don't know if I feel comfortable with the idea of making him seem almost sympathetic with a pitiful home life scene."

The Editor's first reaction was a quick glance at his desk's security-shaded podscreen. "Argyle, my dear boy," he said. His tone irked Liam to no end, as he knew very well that the man had all of five years on him, regardless of his obvious efforts to make himself look older. "What we are doing here is a service to the public. These kinds of situations need to be brought to the light if we're ever going to make a difference. You do want to make a difference, don't you?"

"Well, yes..." Liam said, in earnest. In a display of the sort of obliviousness that had earned him his job in the first place, he wondered when the callous Editor had become such a master of empathy, to be able to read into him so openly.

---

[i] The one who's getting it in the rear, that is.

"Then what's a little doctoring here and there? The ends justify the means, and we could hardly honour the little git with an integral display of his lechery, could we?" Liam certainly agreed there. "Don't let it get to you. It's all for the greater good." He closed the conversation with what was undoubtedly meant to be a wise nod. Liam didn't know what to say, so he stuck to what he knew.[i]

"That's that then," said the Editor. "You and the crew had best go grab a sandwich from the trolley in the Lounge. You've got a busy afternoon ahead of you. In the meantime, we'll start shaping this up for upfeeding back to Corporate." The subsequent silence made Liam think he was dismissed, but the Editor must merely have been pensive since, as Liam was making his way out to find the trolley, he added, almost as an afterthought, "Oh, and Argyle. Keep up the good work."

---

[i] *i.e.:* nothing

8

"That's your actual name?"

If Liam hadn't taken such an instinctive liking to the next potential contestant, he would never have believed him.

"That's right," said the chipper young man, spreading good cheer like some sort of jovial plague carrier as he sat on his pub stool. "Usnavi. I know it's weird and supposed to be degrading, somehow, being named after the U.S. Navy because of a Cuban thrice-great-grandmother who didn't have any other name for her child's father. But that was my grandfather's name, and his grandfather's before him. It's become a bit of a family tradition by now."

Smuggled into the country as a newborn by parents who were denied refugee status but came illegally anyway, there was hardly a thing in his voice or mannerisms to give away Usnavi Musibay's Cuban origins. Certainly, his accent was no worse than every other East Londoner's.

He seemed to laugh in the face of his ridiculous name, the withered right arm he made no effort whatsoever to conceal, and the world in general. It was difficult not to like the young man instantly, and Liam saw no reason to fight the impulse.

"Have you been, you know..." Liam gestured at Usnavi's arm. "Like that since birth?"

"Oh, aye. 'Upper Limb Reduction Defect,' the doctors call it, which is medical lingo for, 'You've got a withered arm for some reason and we can't do anything about it.'" He laughed. "Not that I want them to. This arm here is just like my other one, it's part of what makes me who I am. It's just one of them things, you take them as they come."

He shuffled a bit on his stool and took a swig from the pint glass gripped in his good hand.

"Of course, it's just as well that I look at things that way, since I certainly can't pay for any of the fancy prosthetics that might make it look like I have two good arms. Maybe someday, right? Especially if I make it into this big show of yours."

He drained his glass and set it back down on the gleaming engineered hardwood bar top.

"Until then, I'll just have to be like the Earth itself, in that Hitchhiker book. Not 'armless, but mostly 'armless."

Usnavi cracked up laughing at his own expense, and Liam didn't know whether it was appropriate to join in or not. He was very much in terra incognita as far as his political correctness charts were concerned. He decided to just go with it for a bit, then bring things back to business.

"So, Usnavi—if you don't mind me calling you that—what is it you do for a living?" Looking over at the young man, past his shrivelled arm, Liam realised how crass the expression "for a living" truly was.

"Well, for a long time, it was illegal to hire me, being here without paperwork and all, so I'd try my best to get a bit of manual labour now and then that pays under the table. But, of course, even that's hard to come by if you've got half the arms as everyone else begging for work. Then my family got rounded up and threatened with deportation back to post-war Cuba."

Usnavi paused as the server came back with a refill for his pint, ordered in perfect silence through his charity-bin AR lenses as he was talking. He rubbed the right side of his chest, beneath his worn

Star Wars T-shirt, a reflexive action by all appearances. Liam encouraged him to carry on.

"We all thought there was nothing for it but to live on the street in what's left of Havana. Then, at the last minute, the immigrant app offered the only work visa it said I qualified for. I think the official title is 'Clinical Investigation Agent.' Sounds grand for a human guinea pig, doesn't it?"

Liam nodded. Obviously, new products and research needed to be tested on people before they could be opened to the public. It was one of those things you knew must be happening somewhere in the background noise of society. It certainly was strange to meet a human test subject face to face, though.

"What kind of research have you been involved with?"

"Oh, all sorts, but they've only started offering me the ones that really pay the bills this year, since I had my full medical and genetic details done up." He wiggled his withered arm for emphasis. "Other than this, it seems I came up pretty clear. Odd, really, since I usually feel like shite warmed up—excuse my French. But one of the doctors even said that I was a perfect test subject, whatever that means."

Usnavi put down his glass and lifted his good hand, ticking off the fingers. "New drugs, medical nanotech, cosmetics, all the classic stuff. You name it, I've done it. Right now, I've got a sweet deal trying out some new bacteria-fighting ninja virus strain. It's great, because I have go to lots of public places to expose myself to as much disease as possible, and they pick up the tab." He took another swig of lager, sighing in satisfaction. "Tastes all the sweeter when you know someone else is paying for it, but I suppose that can't last forever. There's another cool gig I've applied for, I'm just waiting for them to get back to me. All very hush hush, but it's definitely interesting. Maybe something the people watching your show might like, do you think?"

Liam couldn't stop himself from grinning at Usnavi's naked enthusiasm and resolved to make sure the young man made it onto the show, one way or another. This was the perfect example of a life that needed to be heard and seen. A chance to really change the world for the better.

They followed him around all the rest of that day as he gave them a first-hand tour of his life, from his favourite street Cuban *empanada* food truck down in Brockley, to the tiny little room he shared with three cousins in a lean-to extension around the back of the family's grey plastic labourer prefab, one of the thousands crammed onto the old parks in Redbridge.

When Carpentiere's drives started running out of room for footage, they realised they'd already stayed two hours longer than scheduled. The *Grass is Greener* team took their leave, with Liam promising to get back to Usnavi as soon as possible. Carpentiere loaded the podcameras and sound equipment back into the vehicle and, noting Liam's good spirits, matched the host's grin with his own.

"If you liked that one, Liam, wait until you see the plan for tomorrow morning. I hope your passport is in date, because we're flying to Hollywood."

9

At first glance, Liam thought they had taken a wrong turn and ended up in a clothing exposition room, the kind overweight people went to out of fear that their shopping app might get their sizes wrong again. Everywhere, manikins[i] in various states of dishabille loomed like fashionable gargoyles.

Again, it was one thing to know that all pornography these days starred the robotic descendants of the humble vibrator. It was another to be confronted with a studio full of the things.

One of the super-humanly buff male figures in the centre of the room stepped forward and reached out to shake his hand. Liam rallied his runaway wits and smiled as best he could, finally recognising the figure from his profile pictures.

Spike Bighorn, the last flesh-and-blood porn star in Hollywood.

Towering over Liam, Spike—yes, that was his actual birth name; Liam had double checked the file before he could allow himself to believe it—wore a skimpy "Indian" brave costume that should have looked both racist and ridiculous. Spike somehow managed to make it look authentic.

Torn between curiosity and deep-grained moral dislike of the whole business, Liam stood there, hesitating to even take the proffered

---

[i] "Little man." Also used for robots in early sci-fi, before Čapek coined the truest possible term.

hand to shake it. He eventually decided to shake the hand anyway, before the situation got even more awkward[i] than it already was. Spike didn't seem to mind.

"Boy, am I glad to see you guys. They need me for another shoot, and I was starting to think you had gotten lost on your way here or something. Did the AR take you the scenic route?" His voice boomed, full of imagery of tomahawks and calumet pipes.

"Just a bit of hassle getting our luggage at the airport. They mixed up the tags on our case with the luggage of some South African tourist family, and the systems refused to release any of the luggage until we could get a supervisor to override it. I suppose that's what they call progress, right?"

Spike's laugh could have brought down a fighter drone at eighteen hundred meters. "It's the same here, friend, I can tell you. So, do you want to do the interview here, or would you like me to find an unused set for us?"

"No-no," Liam replied, a bit too fast for his own liking. "Here will be fine. I wanted to ask you about your relationship to your... co-workers, I suppose."

Spike let out a slightly less military-grade laugh.

"What, the Erobots?" He draped an arm around one of the nearest male manikins, reminding Liam that he had taken Spike for one of them just moments before. "Beautiful craftsmanship, by all accounts. Skin like silk, and let me tell you, that's one hell of an improvement over the sandpaper they used to cover the first generation of these guys in." He let out a sigh, not intended to be dramatic, but coming from such heights and depths that it almost had to be.

"That's all just appearances though. Obviously, the adult entertainment industry is all about appearances, so that's only to be expected. Between the design improvements and advances in AR enhancement, you can hardly tell the difference between a real person and an artificial performer anymore—and that's the whole

---

[i] "Turned the wrong way"

problem, really. How are we supposed to compete with perfect tools who make a Turing test sound like a come-on, and will never mess up a take, miss a cue, or make a funny face?"

All around them, the mecha-pornstars stood in silence. Surely, it was only Liam's imagination which made it seem like they were listening? He had to break the silence. "It says in your application that you're the last human actor left in the Hollywood... adult entertainment industry. Was that just a figure of speech?"

"Nope, I am the very last real person working in front of the cameras. I hear they're not quite as mechanised yet in Krung Thep or Bollywood, but the last other guy around here was Harry Balzac, and he got his retraining orders over a year ago now. Last I heard, he was working as a sports presenter. Of course, the female co-workers were the first to go, what with power tool burn."

"Power tool burn?" Liam tried not to ask, he really did.

"Sorry. That's the term for muscle strain caused by piston-driven artificial members. It's been around for a while. Mostly affects the female performers for obvious reasons, through us males have not been spared from that ourselves. But at least I get to take turns."

Liam somehow felt that he should be taking some form of offense here, but Spike was just so damn natural and open about everything, as if android bisexuality were the most common conversation topic in the world. Liam liked the man.

They carried on with the tour of the set, but Liam knew it was a done deal. The Editor had been adamant about wanting Spike on the team, and Liam could see his point—so to speak. Who would resist the temptation of taking a peek through the eyes of the last human porn star in Hollywood? Imagine the ratings...

Following Bighorn through the set, between rows upon rows of frozen Erobots and boxes full of other tools of the trade, Liam began thinking about the viewers who would be watching all this, once the show finally started. What sort of person would they be, to be attracted to content like this?

10

One crammed and cost-effective transatlantic flight later, Liam and Carpentiere were back on the hunt for their elusive contestants. After a flop with an abattoir "surface technician" who had suffered from a terminal lack of charisma, they were more than a little antsy as they waited at the curb outside a residential unit in Chiswick for their next candidate.

"Where the hell is she?" asked Carpentiere, rubbing his hands to fight off the late fall chill. "We managed to get here on time, even though we only got the address at the last minute. Isn't this supposed to be an emergency service?"

A crash from inside shook the fronting of the building behind them. Both Liam and Carpentiere turned and looked up out of instinct, before shielding their faces with their arms as shattered glass fell down upon them both.

Liam brushed the bits off his jacket sleeve. Neither of them seemed to have been hurt. "Rough neighbourhood," said Liam, in a failed attempt at lightening the mood.

"I say we give her another five minutes and then we write her off," replied a nonplussed Carpentiere.

"Come on, man. This could be good."

"Ten minutes, then," said Carpentiere with a grunt, leaving them both waiting at the curb in silence, each lost in their own AR displays as their breath condensed to mist before them.

They shifted to one side as a heavyset lady stormed out of the residential complex's front door, bearing a case. She passed Liam, Carpentiere, and their equipment case before stopping and whirling around on them. The effect was terrifying and made them regret any sins they may have or may not have committed. The apparition was uglier than imagination cared to allow for.

"It's you, isn't it? From the Red reality show?"

Despite his sudden and profound desire that it not be them, Liam managed to stutter some form of confirmation. The lady, whom Liam could only induce[1] was their potential entrant, a Ms Juliette Binns, put a fist on her hip.

"Have you been waiting out here this whole time? You've only gone and missed it all, then, haven't you?"

Liam presumed they had.

"Just as well, though, I suppose," carried on Ms Binns. "It got a bit hairy in there today. You must have seen it when the guy broke the window, yeah?"

Liam confirmed that, sadly, this had indeed been an obligation, while scolding himself for getting into one of those distant moods again and trying his best to bring himself fully back into the moment.

"Well, the clients can get like that sometimes, in my line of work. There's a reason why all the AR service providers have to offer emergency on-site technical support teams, and that's because people freak the fuck out—can I say that?" she asked mid-sentence, addressing Carpentiere, who had already pulled out his podcam and begun recording. Liam found it highly interesting that the one holding the equipment was the one people turned to out of instinct, and noted that in an empty corner of his psyche for later.

---

[1] Yes, "induce," not "deduce." This is induction, a probabilistic hypothesis based on what facts are available, as opposed to deduction, a strictly logical and necessary consequence of those same facts. Sherlock Holmes never deduced anything!

"Feel free to say anything you want, ma'am," came Carpentiere's reply. "We want you to be as natural as possible."

"Well, I can do natural," said Juliette, with a smile. "So, yes, people freak out very fucking badly indeed when their AR systems fail. Whether it's due to a software crash in the operating system or some kind of hardware failure, the result is always the same. People are used to living with AR constantly editing the world around them, adapting how they see and experience it, and formatting their interactions with the rest of the world. When that protective layer disappears suddenly—well, naked, unaugmented reality can be a pretty scary place. They had us experience it ourselves as part of training, and it sure gave me the willies."

Juliette shook, and not from the cold.

"So I guess I can't really blame the poor bastards who lash out at us when the service interruption flag goes up and we arrive to sort things out. Some of them can get a bit nasty though, like that guy today, with his meat tenderiser."

She paused, a pensive look crossing her features like the shadow of a cloud passing over a particularly disturbing mountain range.

"Of course, it does seem to be a lot worse for me than for most AR emergency techs. I suppose that, well, this," she said, gesturing at just about everything from her collarbone up, "doesn't help things very much. The poor bastards are getting their first look at unfiltered reality in ages—probably in their lives—and they see this face coming through their door."

At this, Juliette hefted her case and shrugged.

"Well, nothing to be done for it, I suppose, and it just means I'm probably the most qualified tech around when it comes to handling panicking clients. Speaking of which, do you gents want to come back to the response centre with me and wait for another call? I could show you around the place."

Liam tried to hide his resigned sigh and failed miserably. "I suppose so, Ms. Binns."

The last thing Liam wanted to do was follow this lady any deeper into the world behind the comforting illusions that kept people entertained, informed, and sane. But orders were orders, and he needed at least another two hours of footage before he could run back to the Mews for a cup of tea and a sandwich.

Still, he mused as he followed the woman down the street to the Tube, a frontline soldier in the battle between reality and artificial paradise? The woman would certainly bring a unique perspective to a show like *The Grass is Greener*. He wondered what she'd make of their new lenses.

11

The next day was a Saturday, but that had little meaning for Liam and Carpentiere as the official-looking DMPC vehicle stopped in front of them. With a contented little pneumatic hiss, it opened its seating compartment door and they entered.

Liam smiled at the other passenger, a broad, muscle-bound man in a crisp uniform, and waited for Carpentiere to finish setting up the podcam surround system before speaking. The car was already heading at full tilt toward its own ends by the time he was done.

"Right then, Mr... Leigh, is it? Or is it Brad?" Their host acknowledged with a nod as stiff as a two-by-four, his hand resting on a case taking up the entire seat next to him, but remained silent.

"Excellent," Liam lied. "Could you please tell us a bit about what you do, then?"

"Brad Leigh, Disease Monitoring and Prevention Corps number 2599401-51," reeled off their potential contestant, like a combatant resisting interrogation, "assigned to the fast-reaction target interception and vector pacification task force, sir."

Surprised, Liam double-checked the profile in his AR display. Looked like the right guy, and surely there couldn't be two people with a mug like that, even though his facial recognition app seemed to be having a tough time getting a lock on his face. "There must have been some mistake. I thought you were a Germ Bouncer?"

The man's stony facade broke into a rare smirk. "I have heard civilians refer to the task force that way before, sir."

"So, if you don't mind me asking, what's with the military get-up and all of the official symbols on the car? You'd think this were some sort of military police operation or something."

The smirk disappeared, to be replaced again by an utter, disdainful absence of features. Impressive control, and far more insulting than any anger might have been.

"As I am sure that you are aware, sir, the Disease Monitoring and Prevention Corps works under public tender in application of World Court jurisprudence and laws transposed in every State. We look like a military police operation because we act for the public good with the full weight of military status and police authority, sir."

"Oh, I meant no disrespect, of course," Liam was quick to back-pedal. "I've always had the highest respect for the boys and girls in khaki. I was just surprised you needed to advertise it, though. Is that something you find helps in your day to day work?"

The atmosphere in the tight compartment relaxed a bit.

"Well, it never hurts to show our colours to the vectors, sir—the disease-bearing people, that would be in layman's terms, sir." Leigh seemed to relax a bit, and carried on. "You know, most of them still resent us and try to resist treatment. Some even act as if it were optional and they had any say in the matter! Between ourselves, that's why the brass decided we needed a contestant in this new reality show of yours, to make people fully aware of what we do, how we operate, and how important it is."

"I couldn't think of a more deserving cause," said Liam, wishing he were brave enough to make it sound as sarcastic as he felt it should. "But why would that be you, instead of any of the other agents, do you think?"

Leigh shifted a little on his seat. "Well, that would probably be because of my little... problem."

"Sorry, it doesn't say anything in the file. What problem is that?"

"Well, if you must know... it's my face, sir. It's common."

"Common?" asked Liam, with a blink. "I don't think any of us are winning any Mr. Universe pageants, you know."

"Not like that," growled Leigh, a red flush creeping up his neck. "Common, as in difficult to distinguish by the damn face recognition apps that seem to be everywhere these days." He sighed, and seemed a different man for a moment. "You know, when people say they have 'one of those faces'? Well, that's me. It's always been the same, ever since I was a teen and public buildings started using facial recognition security doors. If I had a cred for every time I've been pulled for interrogation because my AR ID tags don't match who a door says I am, I'd be rich enough to retire." He paused a moment, pensive. "It's a bit of a hindrance in our line of work, of course. Vectors tend to resist even more when their AR display tells them I'm not who my badge says. But then again, without all of those problems, I might never have felt the call to serve in the Corps. It showed me just how little the individual matters when it comes to public security."

A shiver ran down Liam's spine, and it wasn't one of the good ones. He was desperate to change the subject before he had to think about it too much. "So, do you think we'll get to see one of your.... interventions, today?"

"Of course, sir. I have an average of twenty interventions per day. Even more so on a weekend, when the public toilets are in full use and their sensors send all manner of viral and bacterial alerts our way. Public toilets count for a good half of my intervention workload on a day like today, sir—so I hope you don't mind getting your hands a bit dirty, so to speak."

Liam balked. "What do you mean, get my hands dirty?"

"Well, things can get a bit hectic with this sort of intervention, sir. Our response times are fast, because they have to be. We need to get to the vectors before they leave and start spreading their disease among the unsuspecting public. This means the vectors are usually still in the middle of their business, such as it is, when we arrive and commence treatment. Entitled pricks think they can keep us waiting, too. Selfish bastards."

"Wait, so you actually do barge in on people wherever they are and force medical treatment on them? I thought that was just an urban myth!"

"It is a necessity, sir. We do what we have to do, sir, however surprised the disease carriers may be to see us arrive."

"Well, why don't you let them know you're coming beforehand, give them some time to prepare?"

Clearly, this was the funniest thing, or perhaps just the most ridiculous, Leigh had ever heard. "What, and give them time to run off before we could possibly get there? Oh, that would certainly be one way of making my job easier, that's for sure! I didn't realise this was a comedy program!"

His laughter was interrupted by a flash from the car's interior lighting, clearly matched by an alert on Leigh's AR display.

"Buckle up, boys, we've got a live one. Influenza in the colon— looks like we'll have to bring 'em in to camp to apply enema treatment. Are you boys ready?"

Damn the Editor and his inescapably clear instructions.

"As ready as we're ever going to be, Mr. Leigh," Liam replied, trying his best not to sound as horrified as he felt. "Unless you think we'd get in your way. As you say, Corporate has pretty much secured your place in the show anyway. You can just drop us off anywhere here, if we're going to hinder you in your very important work."

"Nonsense!" said Brad, dashing Liam's meagre hopes. "It's hard out there, fighting the good fight, day in and day out. We need all the publicity we can get! And I've yet to meet the sicko I couldn't handle on my own after a good lick of the taser."

"Oh, goodie," Liam sighed, turning to stare out of the car window at the blurred grey buildings speeding by. He would have been happy to walk all the way back to the Mews, through the slums, if it got him away from Mr. Brad Leigh any faster.

12

Their next interview was only a short ride away from the Mews, but it felt like an alien planet. Liam sat in the sad little academic office in the unfashionable end of his old alma mater, the University of London's Birkbeck College, and wondered what he was doing there. Perhaps the equally sad-looking man sitting across the desk from him had the answer.

"Professor Fourka, if you don't mind me asking, sir... Why did you send in an application for *The Grass is Greener*? You do realise the point of the show is to see who has the worst lot in life?"

The professor, Dr. Ali Fourka according to the profile in a corner of Liam's AR, smiled a little and shrugged his tweed-clad shoulders. "Of course. However, if I remember the advertisement correctly, it mentioned 'all walks of life,' yes? Surely, this means you aren't just looking for the destitute[i], the sick, and the maimed. 'All walks of life' includes all of those who have suffered the most from the... let's say 'evolutions,' to remain polite, of modern society. Since they shut down LSE to replace it with in-house Corporate government and business directorship programs, I'm the only political science academic left with a position in all of the UK. Even that, I sometimes fear, is only an overlook. Once they get around to auditing the books and see that they still have a Professor of Political Science on the payroll, I'll

---

[i] Etymologically: Abandoned, put away.

be queuing up for reassignment by the employment algorithm as well. Already, they're reducing my classes and giving me the worst time slots. The students are gently encouraged to mock me, when they show up at all."

Liam thought he remembered crossing paths with Prof. Fourka, as they both ambled about the corridors of Birkbeck. He certainly hadn't seemed dangerous or undesirable, and probably less offensive than some of the other faculty. Perhaps he was just being paranoid, which had been known to happen among academics after reaching a certain age without obtaining tenure.

"Why would the College want to get rid of you, specifically, Professor Fourka?"

"Isn't it obvious, Liam? If you don't mind me calling you Liam, that is. It's quite simple. These days, nobody wants a political scientist around providing critical thought about the abdication of the political sphere in favour of the world of private business. Not when we're all so busy living it."

Liam had thought as much in private himself, but the podcameras were rolling, and he felt it was part of his job to play devil's advocate.

"I'm not certain it is quite that simple, Professor. You speak as if we no longer had a political system and everything was decided in Corporate boardrooms, but we still elect our politicians. We still have Countries, Parliaments, Governments, Councils, Mayor—the whole lot. Certainly, the Corporations now have their own extraterritorial Courts and their own Law system, but that doesn't mean we've sold our political decision-making power to them."

Professor Fourka tilted his head somewhat, considering Liam before he responded. "What sort of people do you find in these elected positions, these days?"

"Yes, I see where you're going. Most of them are business people and have business ties, but that doesn't mean Corporations are running everything. That's just the people's choice, since the business world is where all of the most talented people work. People were fed up with the old crew, the professional politicians. They want elected officials who know how to make money, who will get rid of the bureaucrats and get the job done."

"Ah, yes, getting rid of the bureaucrats. They've certainly done that. Let's take a look at the core prerogatives of the State. Do you know who runs the Police service and the Tax system in our own country, these days?"

"Well, the Government and Parliament, obviously."

"Really? So, when you receive your income tax notice, or if you are taken in for police questioning, then you are dealing with State-employed civil servants, are you?"

"No, all of the actual hands-on management is outsourced nowadays to companies like RedCorp and the Revenue Corporation, obviously. But all of the actual policy decisions are still made by the elected politicians."

Across the table, the smile on Ali Fourka's face contained less actual cheer than a clown's wake. "Are they? I think you'll find that the first thing an elected official will be keen on 'outsourcing' to a third party is the responsibility for an unpopular police enforcement measure, or tax hike. Deniability is the main goal of the government outsourcing program, Liam, not efficiency or cost reduction. That can happen sometimes, certainly, but it is entirely coincidental, and the outsourced services are usually more expensive than the opposite. Private business exists to make profits, after all, and the taxpayer has to pay those at some level."

Liam glanced over at Carpentiere and the podcams, whirling away to provide a full, three-dimensional recording of the discussion. Damn it all, he didn't want to be arguing against this man, he wanted to buy him a drink! "Very interesting theories, Professor Fourka. So, if I understand correctly, you think your treatment here at Birkbeck justifies a spot on *The Grass is Greener*? Presumably, you would use this to expound upon these ideas of yours?"

"The way I see it, your show is a bit of an epiphenomenon, a frontier where control may not be quite so tight. With a bit of publicity, maybe I could make myself more trouble to get rid of than to keep. I'm not holding my breath, but I've got to try something. I'm sure you understand."

Poor bastard. They followed the Professor in silence as he gave them a tour through the worn-down University halls. Professor Fourka had a snowball's chance in a fusion reactor of actually making it onto the show, Liam told himself, so at least he'd be spared the public humil-iation. The Editor would never let the show turn into a platform for these kinds of ideas.

13

Back at the Mews, the Editor beamed at Liam from across the empty, polished surface of his desk.

"Thank you for coming straight in to see me, Liam. I just wanted to congratulate you on the excellent job you've been doing. We are well ahead of schedule regarding the candidate interviews and selection. I've been reviewing the footage you uploaded, and there are so many good candidates there, we are embarrassed for choice. I'm confident the last few interviews already lined up for next week will provide us with the final two contestants, giving us a full complement of eight in time for the live weekly première next Sunday."

Liam's brain did a couple of mathematical gymnastics flips and did not like the scores he came up with. "Sorry, sir, but did you say two more contestants? I'm not certain we have six definite contestants after the interviews so far. You aren't counting the abattoir cleaning lady, surely? We could have congealing porridge as a contestant and it would be more interesting to watch."

The Editor made a show of looking pensive. "No, my count is correct. With Professor Fourka, that makes six."

"Professor Fourka? But... well, I had assumed that..."

"What? That RedCorp wouldn't want that sort of anti-Corporate opinion voiced through our show?" He actually laughed at this, taking the caricature beyond breaking point.

"Liam, my dear boy, you have so much to learn. Would you like a drink?"

"No, I'm fine, thank you," Liam responded by rote. His alcohol rehab conditioning had been worth every penny, even though he suspected it might be put to the test over the next few weeks.

"Very well, then." The Editor steepled his fingers and leaned forward across the desk. "Tell me, Liam, did you know that Bedlam[1] Asylum was one of the biggest entertainment venues in Georgian London? Toffs would pay quite handsomely to go view and mock the inmates, the insane, and the political activists alike. Ninety-six thousand visitors in one year alone! It was quite the popular and commercial sensation."

Liam had no idea where the Editor was going with this, and wished things could remain that way.

"So, as you see, *The Grass is Greener* has a proud heritage and is only the latest iteration of an old tradition—probably as old as humanity itself. People have an instinctive need to see, and to mock, other people. Our contestants are the inmates of our own little asylum, and will be treated and interpreted as such by the viewers. Professor Fourka will be a grand bit of fun when he airs those crazy ideas of persecution, especially when put alongside the life of someone like Usnavi Musibay. Nobody will take a word he says seriously—quite the contrary! We will make sure of that."

Liam felt sick and regretted not accepting that drink after all—at least he would have had an excuse for feeling sick, then.

The Editor carried on. "But, of course, it is our viewers who hold the power and will vote to decide the ultimate winner of our little bit of entertainment, so who knows? Maybe even Professor Fourka will have a chance. But none of that will matter if we don't get the final two contestants lined up. So, once again, keep up the excellent work, and I look forward to seeing your interviews."

Dismissed like a pop-up ad, Liam skulked out of the Editor's

---

[1] Originally, Bethlehem

office. Standing in the non-gloom of the Tantamount Mews central warehouse area, he shuddered to think that, in a matter of days, he would be broadcasting from this same cavernous room to networked eyes and minds around the globe. He felt lost, dwarfed by the enormity of what lay before him.

Sucking it up, he grasped onto the only thing he could, the job in front of him. All he could do was deal with this task, and then the one after that. He would just have to see it though, come what may in the end.

Steeling himself, he set off to grab a bite to eat from the trolley. If he were quick, there would be just enough time to wolf down a sandwich before they had to leave for the next interview.

14

Liam hoped it was just a trick of the light and the podcams would see things more objectively than he could. To him, the dark-skinned woman leading them up the stairs looked and moved like she were at least twice the age of thirty-five, which was listed on her profile, under the name Azar Acquah.

"People always make fun of me when I say I'm a Dumb Squad freelancer, but it's not my fault the company decided to call itself that way," she said, panting slightly as she reached the landing at the top of the stairs. "It's not that bad a name, after all. Everything has been made 'smart this' and 'smart that'—we just make them dumb again."

After checking they were still following, she made her way down the corridor and over to the apartment door at the far end of the hallway.

"Don't worry," Azar continued, and Liam was unsure whether she was talking to them or to herself. "The clients always set up entry authorisations for me when they want me to come treat their house while they're out, which is most of the time."

She stood in front of the door and waited for the security system to pick up her AR network ID. A loud click confirmed the system had decided it liked her enough to disengage the bolt, and they entered the apartment.

After the dark corridor, the light streaming in from the tall windows blinded Liam a bit, and his AR glasses just made the glare worse. Still, he had to admit it was a very nice apartment, if you were into that centre city style of living. He stood, appreciating the retro-swing era decor that was so fashionable these days, and Azar must have noticed his interest.

"Yes, the clients have some pretty swank places. They're the ones who can afford to have their devices disconnected." She laughed a bit, and the creases at the corners of her eyes only served to draw attention to the glassy lifelessness of her left eye. "It's funny, really. You would think it would be easier not to put all of the connected chips into all of the products in the first place. Does your toaster really need to communicate with your wallpaper and your socks? But even with all of the medical proof now of how bad that constant EMF soup is for your health, no one is willing to buy a product that isn't so 'smart' it should know better than to sell itself in the first place. Hah!"

She pulled out an EMF scanner, as well as what looked like a long pair of tweezers, attached to a bulky battery at her hip. Leaving Liam and Carpentiere to their own devices, she walked over to the living room sofa and started slowly running the EMF meter across its surface.

"No, apparently it's easier to cram everything full of smart chips anyway, and then have those who can afford it hire the Dumb Squad to manually go over each and every consumer item in their house, to hunt down and deactivate every non-vital bit of electronics. Nice for some..." She sighed, but never paused in her painstaking work, even as she crawled along the base of the sofa. "Still, it's what keeps me in work, and at least I know I'm doing something useful. The gods know I could have used something like this when I was a girl."

At this, Liam cleared a knot in his throat and spoke up. "Yes, your profile says something about an illness?"

"If I had only one illness, I'd be a much happier lady today. I've been sick for as long as I can remember, and they say it's all down to the early AR implants my parents gave me for my seventh birthday. Of course, we all know now that those things had less EMF-shielding than a box of cardboard and were basically see-through cancer coins. But my parents had no way of knowing that. They were sold on the idea of being cutting-edge and offering me a leg up in the Augmented world of the future. Since then, I've also come to realise that, for a relatively well-off couple of busy professionals, AR implants may have seemed a lot cheaper than employing a Nanny to keep their only daughter calm, entertained, and traceable at any time."

She prodded the sofa with her tweezers and sent a crackling discharge into the fabric, lighting her features up like a Cinco de Mayo mask. The podcam lenses twinkled and twirled as they recorded every glimmer.

"That was before I started getting seizures and they finally took me in for testing. Eye cancer, brain cancer, the whole shebang. Textbook case for these first generation AR lenses, and far too late to do anything about it by then."

Azar broke into a coughing fit at that point, leaving Liam to wonder how much of that was dust and exertion, and how much of it was psychosomatic, given the topic of conversation. Either way, she soon pulled out of it and lifted herself from under the couch.

"Maybe it would have helped to get my lenses upgraded. Those new ones are supposed to have much better EMF shielding than back in the day. But what would be the use, even if they weren't so damn expensive?"

"Wait, you mean you still have the lenses?" asked Liam, baffled. "Even though they gave you cancer, and are probably still making it worse? Why didn't you just have them removed?"

Azar paused, halfway between the living room and her next targets in the kitchen area, and turned to face Liam. Her expression was one usually reserved for things found crawling under stones. "What, just remove my lenses altogether? Without replacing them?

Frankly, I'd rather live with the cancer, so to speak. I don't know what I'd do if I didn't have my shows to distract me from the work and keep me going. I'm re-watching one of my favourite old comedies right now, if you must know."

She gratified Liam with a little smile, as if asking for forgiveness after her outburst, and resumed her walk over to the kitchen linen drawer. Pulling out one kitchen towel after another, she scanned each one and zapped them whenever necessary, talking all the while.

"Of course, it hasn't been all bad. If I hadn't gotten sick, I would never have heard about the Dumb Squad. After all the medical bills, my parents couldn't afford that sort of thing, but they took me right in when I applied for a job there. It's funny how it all works out in the end, isn't it? As if everything has a purpose."

She paused, kitchen towel in hand, and turned her smile upon Liam once again.

"It's just like your show, really. I just happened to see the advertisement, and when I read the application paperwork, I learned you'll be offering free, latest-generation lens implants to all of the contestants! Now there's a sign I'm meant to be part of the show, if there ever was one."

For all of his scepticism regarding lazy, superstitious reasoning, Liam couldn't bring himself to disagree. As he followed busy Azar from one luxury apartment to the next, he realised there were lots of ways of doing good, big and small. Maybe helping someone like Azar Acquah get the lenses she could never afford otherwise was the realest kind of good he could hope to do through the show. And, at the end of the day, probably the one that meant the most.

15

What a week! he informed himself, nursing the remains of his second gin and tonic. *I know, I was there,* came his own surly answer, and this made him snort slightly in laughter. If he hadn't been safe in the comfort of his own seedy armchair, he might have felt embarrassed. But he deserved to let loose a little. They'd gone through three more applicants that afternoon, and out of those, only one had turned out to have any real potential for the feed.

Of course, it had to be the bitch of an inner-city Post-Top[i]. He tried to repress the shudder this thought provoked, and failed. The woman had been utterly terrifying, a raging monolith with a bone to pick with the entire world, preferably one supporting some vital organ. He poured himself a well deserved third as the memories rose unbidden, in a sort of mental acid reflux.

"Where do you come off, thinking you can barge in here, hide behind your little machines and pretend to judge me?" she began to

---

[i] In a world where "topping oneself," the most common euphemism for suicide,* had become so routine it had a dedicated and specialised service industry, post-suicide cleanup companies, or "Post-Tops" in common speak, were in high demand.

* There also used to be "Human-Caused Delay," specifically used in PA announcements after a suicide on public transport rails. However, the term fell into disuse after new laws removed any obligation for the trains to clean up or gather any remains until after they arrived at destination.

rant as soon as the light on the recording lens turned on. There was no bullshitting that one. "People aren't some damn insects for you to study. Trying to profit off people's misery by making a spectacle of it. You make me sick." She physically spat, missing the nearest lens by a finger's width.

"And YOU!" she continued, pointing an index at the lens, as if warning it, just in case it thought the worst was over with the saliva's near-miss. "Watching all this in your underpants, on your settee, in bed, or possibly on the damn bog! Have you no shame? Have you no dignity? Have you truly nothing better to be doing? So, you think we're pathetic? Pah, what does it say about you that you don't have anything better to do but sit there like the idiots that you are, gawping at US?"

At that point, she grunted and pushed them out of what she had just decided to be her way, knocking the lens to a tilted angle as she clambered into the passenger cab of her service vehicle, with all of the cleaning equipment—and the mind hesitated to consider what else—stored in the rear cargo section. The heavy-duty engine gunned like hell's doorbell, and the door swung open. The post-tops' ugly mug leaned out to haunt them.

"I've got to get this load to the crematorium and then sluice the truck down by sundown. Are you maggots going to come along and have a chat or are you wimpin' out?" she asked them, with high expectorations.

The others had been struck dumb. "Err, no, that's okay. Our camera in the cab will give us plenty of footage. We'll just use that, and get back to you," Liam eventually said, mainly just to bridge the gap, since nature abhors a void.

"Har!" had been her only reply as the door shut and the engine left them wallowing in a cloud of fumes as thick and dense as the woman had made him feel. He took another swig of gin, but was shocked and desolated to discover the glass was dry. Can't be having with that, now, something located at the top of his spine told him in irrefutable terms, and the arm already pouring another healthy dose of gin seemed to be in agreement.

Well, it was all done and dusted, now. Eight contestants, all lined up to receive their implant lenses at the first live show on Sunday. He had asked why it was on Sunday, and the Editor had spouted some nonsense about religion and suicide and something or another. These managerial types really had far too much time on their hands. And the editing! He was happy enough to put it down to the stress of the approaching deadline, but surely it couldn't be right to distort all of the initial interview footage like that. The way the Editor was putting together the intro sequences for the first live feed, he would be turning the real-life people, and their honest stories, into either heroes or villains. It wasn't a proper show anymore. It was a Frankenfeed, and Liam shuddered into his gin at the thought of the monsters such a soulless construct would beget. *Ugh, watch out,* he caught himself. *You were slipping into one of those moods again.*

It was a shame he'd had to cancel the Wine and Warfare meet this Friday. The Editor had scheduled a major screening meeting that evening. He'd sent a com message to the gang during the subway ride back, and he hoped they weren't too disappointed about it.

Still, he had to admit, the GiG team had done a pretty good job, really, especially given the circumstances. Now that they were done with the selection process, he'd be able to keep a closer eye on the editing process, to make sure they didn't stray too far from the truth. They'd be ready for the première, no problem, and he'd be able to keep the show on track. He was going to make certain that the feed stayed focused on helping people, on making a difference. Yes, everything would work out just fine... And on these soothing notes, he lulled himself to sleep, fully dressed and marinated, among the debris of his living room.

16

He hated make-up[1]. He used to have to go through the ritual caking of orange muck every night back at Channel 2, and he'd been looking forward to only having to do it once a week from here on in. Once a week... how odd that seemed, minutes before the première. He needed to get through that first, preferably alive, before he allowed himself to indulge in the soothing waters of routine.

Mary was doing quite a professional job on the make-up, though. She was a lady full of hidden resources, and he made a point of telling her so.

"Oh, go on. You are too kind." The woman blushed and scolded him as she continued to apply the bright goop, a smile on her face.

"You deserve it, Mary. This place would fall apart in a matter of minutes if you weren't around." And it was true. She was always zipping about, tending to something or another, cleaning, doing maintenance, posting AR notices, sending memos to everyone, pushing her little trolley... Her sandwiches were satisfactory, nothing to write home about, even if there were anyone at home to receive such, but better fare than a lot of work food he had tasted in his life. Mary simply smiled and went on with her work.

Liam didn't have time to push the pleasantries any further, in a

---

[1] Something that sounds like having to apologise after an argument simply can't be good.

doomed attempt to avoid having to confront the looming trial by fire. It came back with a vengeance when a figure he only vaguely identified as Carpentiere came to tell him that it was "fifteen minutes to feed time" and that they needed him on set. Shock clouded his mind like water cast upon a campfire.

"Five minutes!" shouted Barry Fletcher, from the depths of his plasma-lit lair. At these words, what he tried to think of as a battle calm descended upon Liam, as would a well aimed ball of catapulted glue. He took in his surroundings with the eyes of a newborn.

The gaping warehouse entrance had undergone, since his first non-glimpse of it all those days ago, the kind of plastic surgery that could open up wide avenues of future crime and profit for even the most actively sought-after menace to law, order, and morality.

Where darkness and shipping boxes had once reigned, there was now a caricature of a sterile, gleaming medical operating room. Doctors, nurses, orderlies, everyone was present—and some of them weren't even bit actors called in for the evening. The decor was only skin-deep and didn't go any further than the immediate area of the operating table, but that hardly mattered—the rest would be edited in for the full, AR experience.

Behind the scenes, Mary shepherded her little flock of contestants, and her presence helped calm Liam somewhat. She was certainly a lady of many resources.

The little blinks in the darkness were the tell-tale signs of so many active pod lenses, ready and undoubtedly raring to feed his every movement through Barry's fortress and the Editor's live scrutiny to Corporate, and from there all the way to the hearts and minds of nearly a billion screens, AR lenses, and glasses, around the globe. A fair amount of these would probably even be in use at the time by their owners, and that was the part Liam was still having issues with.

His lingering doubts about the final applicant roster chosen for the première did not help in the least. He was quite convinced they'd gotten the best of the applicants they had been to interview over the past two weeks, and he had no qualms whatsoever over the quality of the work he, Lee, and Carpentiere had put in, under the circumstances. However, he couldn't help but wonder about all the evident candidates who had lives far worse than the blue collar fools they'd spent most of their time interviewing, but who hadn't seemed to enter into account at all for the feed.

Where were all the down-and-out hobos he flicked AR charity coupons at every other day in the subway stations? Surely, they were the ones who really had it bad, who needed the help and attention the feed could provide, more than anybody else. Where were the terminally ill? Where were the Fourth World poor? Surely there were enough of them about to find at least one to include in the feed. He had broached these concerns with the Editor only the day before last, and the response left him perplexed.

"Argyle," he said, the rainbow reflects in his eyes betraying the fact that he didn't even take time to put his AR display into standby before answering, "you don't seem to grasp the fundamental resource we're tapping into here. To put it bluntly, people watch these feeds because they need someone to pity, and you can only pity someone you identify with. Feeders just wouldn't see enough of themselves in a hobo or in some damn Fourth World ghetto child for them to be of any practical use for the feed." He raised a hand, anticipating a swelling tide of indignant protest. "I don't have time to explain it to you properly." The Editor tossed him something the size of a pebble. "Here. Why don't you take this and copy it onto your drive."

Liam caught the tiny bookchip in wary silence.

"It's Rousseau's *Inequality between Men*. It'll tell you everything you need to know. You'll find the important bits bookmarked. Just leave it in my box when you're finished copying it."

The shape weighing gently against his suit pocket lining reminded him that he had yet to indulge the Editor in his strange new fancy, but he had a feeling that he might do so once this première was over with; he could already feel the need for a good read wax bountiful within him, like the harvest moon.

Still, they were an interesting crowd, these candidates of his. He was glad they would all get their contractually guaranteed two weeks of fame and annihilation of privacy before the first elimination session was scheduled. Eight lives and only two preliminary launch feeds in which to expose their pathetic daily antics to the world. He diagnosed some bizarre paternalistic emotions stirring within him, and he wondered how he would deal with having to part with the losers.

He dismissed this as the resounding call "One minute to feed!" shook his mind like an Etch A Sketch, wiping away any stray grains of thought.

17

The contestants milled about in a vague sort of line, like poorly disciplined schoolchildren. Liam had no mental energy to spare for them as he stepped into the neon-lit, AR-enhanced studio simulacrum of an operating room.

Who were they trying to fool, anyway? Every child over the age of four knew AR implants were easier to install these days than having your ears pierced, and certainly didn't call for a full operating theatre. But perhaps that was the point, after all. It was all a theatre, all a show, and sometimes the props, the clichés, are more real than what they're meant to represent. So be it, then. Liam would do his part, however meaningless it may be.

Was that truly his own voice, trying to pontificate[i] about how simply and utterly *ecstatic* he was all these viewers had tuned in to join in what would undoubtedly be the "greatest live feed of the century," whatever historians and marketing directors may have to say on the subject? He was no longer certain. Everything around him seemed to take on a strange new colour—something on the far side of the spectrum, a sort of blacker-than-black. With each passing heartbeat, his glands pumped more and more stress-induced cortisol into his system, completely upsetting his natural diurnal rhythm,

---

[i] "To build bridges"

effectively tricking his body into thinking he was actually in a dream-state, which was a comforting thought.

The contestants seemed just as stunned as him as they made first contact with the world at large, but at least they had the protection of the group. For that one brilliant moment, they were all equal before the invisible hundreds of millions of viewers. Soon enough, if the Editor had his way, which he naturally would, cocky Brad would be throttling the weaselly Finn, and a terrified-looking Juliette would no doubt clash against Azar, who looked as if she had found a winning lottery ticket inside a fast food fortune cookie at the idea of getting her shiny new top-of-the-line AR lenses. But, for now, they were all equal before the ophthalmic micro scalpel, and it pained Liam to be the one who would have to burst that bubble.

Something was beeping behind him. His body seemed to know something he didn't, and turned to face the blinky-whirly contraption on the far wall which he barely recognised as being called a camera. The camera lights were the only bright points in the ambient gloom of the stage. The blinky-whirly stopped blinking and simply sat there, watching his body gesticulate and talk in a frantic, whacked-out on life sort of voice he hoped to the gods was not actually his.

It might just have been his depersonalisation disorder talking, but as he ushered Usnavi, his first little volunteer lamb, to the Augmented Reality slaughter, he kept telling himself that he must have misheard Barry. There was no way that there were actually one-point-five billion viewers for tonight's feed. One with nine zeroes, with an extra five and eight zeroes thrown in for good measure? They always made sure you spelled out the number in letters when signing documents, it made it more real that way... But these weren't zeroes, they were people.

An insistent cue appeared in his AR view and, mechanically, he waved an arm in a grand sweeping gesture. The nervous smile on the face of the Usnavi strapped into the operating chair was soon replaced by the genuine smile of the Usnavi in the new, free-floating

AR video window. As the pretend doctors and nurses descended upon the real Usnavi, chromed instruments gleaming with all desired dramatic effect, the viewers were free to look away—if they so desired—and watch the sequences filmed the previous week, introducing Usnavi and exposing his life to the world.

Liam couldn't help but feel a tingle of pride at the idea that he was doing his part to bring injustices like Usnavi's to the light, to redress some of modern society's wrongs.

And yet, with flawless timing, the interview sequence faded to black at the very second when the operation was finished and the new AR implants came online. The AR video feed now twitched, and a blurred bar appeared down the middle. The bar widened and soon showed a first-person perspective chaos of blinding lights, blue surgical scrubs, and himself—Liam—half visible in a corner and looking off someplace else entirely.

Liam took no pleasure, despite his rehearsed[i] tones, in vaunting to the world this amazing technology which would now allow them to view the world through Usnavi's eyes, night and day, whenever they so desired, between now and the end of his participation in the show. Liam hoped Usnavi would be among the last, and maybe even the winner. He certainly had more to complain about than most of the rest of them.

Jill elbowed her way in next, seeming to dare the assembled actors and medical personnel to lay even a finger on her. They did, nonetheless. When Jill's own flatteringly edited intro sequence was replaced by her first person live feed, she immediately returned into the ranks of her fellow contestants and put her new advantage to good use by capturing the most unflattering close-up footage of them possible. Liam would have laughed at how obvious these antics were, but he was still front and centre, escorting the next contestant, Azar, to the operating chair.

---

[i] Is that what the the expression "death warmed up" means? When you are "re-hearsed"?

Azar wouldn't stop thanking him, which made him feel even more of a hypocrite than he already did, but at least she was thanking everyone else around her as well, as they sat her down and came at her eyes with sharp, gleaming instruments of ocular doom. When her own intro sequence had finished and her live feed came online, they thought there must be a problem and started to adjust the lenses, before realising that the blur was simply due to the tears of joy cascading down Azar's worn ebony cheeks.

Spike took his eye shot next, not seeming to mind big things looming in close to his face. Ali Fourka seemed to take it all with stoic resignation, as opposed to Finn Oldman, who sweated and threatened to sue the Network if they messed up so much as one of his eyelashes. He obviously hadn't bothered to read the extensive liability exclusions in his contract when he signed on, or even looked up the definition of corporate extraterritoriality, for that matter.

Brad scowled at Juliette as she urged him to go on before her, and stepped forward to do his duty for the Corps, as he took great pride in declaiming at every opportunity. This left Juliette as the last contestant to submit to the surgery, and she proved the most difficult by far.

"Is this really necessary for the show?" she seemed to not so much ask as plead, as if oblivious to the fact that one-and-a-half billion people were listening to her every word and no doubt enjoying her discomfort immensely. "Can't there be one contestant without the new lenses? Just to shake things up a little?"

It pained Liam to have to be the one to remind her of the obvious, but at least he could try to sound caring and sympathetic about it. "Juliette, you knew what you were getting into when you applied for the show and when you signed the contract."

"Signed the contract?" Juliette lowered her voice, as if whispering would prevent the viewers from hearing her. "You know what AR contract systems are like. All I did was look a bit too long at the accept button and my interface thought I had clicked to accept. I was probably going to say yes anyway, but I didn't get to look at any of the fine print."

"Regardless, you have an obligation now, and I really don't understand what the problem is. You work with fixing AR implants all day, and I would have thought that, of all people, you would have no problems with our little broadcast setup."

"That's part of it. I know what an AR implant can and can't do, and these new twenty-four-hour broadcast implants have done away with so much EMF shielding, they're bound to—"

"Now, now," cut in Liam, in response to an urgent prompt from the Editor over his AR display, "I'm beginning to sound like a broken record here, but do I need to remind you of the non-disparaging clause in your contract regarding Corporate products and intellectual property?"

Juliette scowled at Liam. "There's no need to get vulgar. I get the message. And that's not even the real problem." She sighed, and went silent, as if deciding whether she should say whatever was on her mind live on the show. For her own sake, Liam wished she wouldn't, as he couldn't see a single scenario where this turned out well for her. But if wishes were fishes, there'd be no such thing as industrial devastation of fish stocks and, accordingly, she carried on. "It's just that, well, I don't like the idea of having strangers looking out through my eyes. And not just one stranger, but millions of them, man, woman or child, anywhere around the world, looking out of my skull and seeing everything I see. It makes me feel dirty."

"Juliette, that is a perfectly understandable response, but really, why overthink it? Surely you can see that it makes no real difference to you, not so long as you continue acting naturally and don't let it affect you."

Liam thought this was utter shite, but it was what he had been trained to say and he could spout crap with the best of them. On the spot, Juliette seemed unable to point out the gaping flaws in the official logic, so Liam pressed the advantage. "And it's all for the good of the show, really. We want to make the best show possible, don't we, and I'm certain that you want to do well in it."

With a visible shudder, Juliette steeled herself. "Let's get it over then."

Five minutes' work later, Juliette reopened her eyes. The complete set of eight first person perspective feeds were live and available for browsing by anybody with an AR interface. It was entertainment history in the making. Why, then, did Liam feel like he needed a shower so hot it could scour his soul?

18

The Editor was in his office, with one of the live feeds displayed in high resolution on his new, ostentatious physical display screen. Liam was hardly surprised to see it was his friend, Suicide Jill. The Editor had been adamant they keep her on the show, and he was now fawning over her picture as she spat her contempt at the world and all its lodgers.

"She is so ultimately precious. Look at how her sneer reflects off the mirror... Listen to the beautiful harmonies underlying her snort..." The man then stopped and simply stood upright, swaying slightly, and with a dazed look. "She's... she's perfect. Perfect, I tell you! There's nothing to edit! Nothing I could remove could make this any better!" He paused before the monumental[i] realisation. "By the gods... I think I'm in love."

Jill tactfully, or perhaps out of some little-known quantum sense of self-preservation, chose that precise moment to expectorate violently and launch into a rant about "those booky wimpling types who wouldn't know a good lay if it came and hit them in the frontal lobe with a maglev carriage."

The Editor allowed himself only the briefest moment of registered shock before editing this out as well and declaring, "Well, nobody can be *perfect*, of course."

---

[i] From the Latin *monere*, "to warn," specifically of the presence of a grave.

He coughed, adjusted his tie, and carried on as if nothing had happened.

"That's precisely why we need to keep a tight rein on everything that happens in these so-called 'live feeds.' As you interact with our contestants during the weekly features, please keep in mind that any slips or unfortunate comments will need to be edited out, by myself or one of the team here on those rare occasions when even I must sleep. I do not plan for there to be many of those, not with so much riding on this show being a complete success, but nature will out."

Liam had managed to remain quiet and just nod up until now, but his impish nature got the best of him. "Nature will out what, sir?" he asked, his grin conspicuous by its absence.

"What?" The Editor seemed astounded that part of the furniture of the room had just called him out on his phrasing. "Oh, Argyle. Shouldn't you be out there rounding up the staff to go have a drink or something? I'm sure I'll be along shortly."

If everything didn't still seem so distant and so unreal to him, he was sure he would have found that funny.

The gin did him a world of good. He could feel his senses returning, watch things sharpening and becoming whole again. It was odd, and slightly disturbing, how moments of stress seemed to put his consciousness into a sort of sleep mode while his instincts dealt with the situation. He gulped with relish.[i] Still, his little semi-fugue state had seen him safely through the first big show, and everyone seemed pretty pleased with the results.

After the première had finished, and the fully armed and operational contestants were sent back to their various conflicting realities, the GIG team had migrated, at the behest of their native guide, Barry Fletcher, to the nearest watering hole. For some reason, Liam was amused to see that it bore a superimposing AR sign

---

[i] Not literally, thankfully.

identifying it as The Hive. He was now coming back out of the feed haze at last, amidst a dream of steel-topped bars, an orange dance floor, soft lighting, and ancient classic rock music. The stucco and mirrors at ceiling level were a rather nice touch though, he felt.

He ordered a second gin without a thought and turned to find himself alone. Eh, good riddance. Everyone had been crowding around him, eager to clap him on the back, which he hated, and trying to bask in the reflected glow of his new host status like some media-minded lizard, which he hated even more, since he didn't feel any such glow himself. They didn't even have the decency to leave him enough time to have a proper drink and gather his wits. Other than this largely unwanted attention from his crew, he'd been receiving glances from random people in the bar, some of their eyes still shot with the reflected rainbow glow of their AR pods.

How odd. It must have been the first time in, well, ever, as far as he could recall, that he actually took notice of the podjockeys sitting around the place. People crouched over podscreens or reclined with eyes twitching had always been there in the background of his life. They were as much a part of the scenery as road signs in the city or the horizon in the rare open country areas which remained. Yet now, for some reason, they stuck out in his mind like the sore cortical homunculus of a thumb.

As he was entirely occupied by the task of securing a second refill for his gin, he did not notice the woman's reservedly grand entrance, nor the hushed silence that fell over those parts of the bar which were not already silently basking in an asocial flickering light. In fact, he did not register her presence at all until she strode over and tapped him on the shoulder.

"Argyle," she said in a voice as sharp as the crease of her suit, "I must congratulate you." Somehow, the "must" sounded less like emphasis and more like the statement of a necessary chore.

Liam turned. "Ms. Heath," he managed to get out between sputters. Gin and nasal passages do not make good barfriends.

"I followed the feed tonight, of course," she continued, having the good grace to pointedly ignore his floundering, even in the face of all evidence. "Well done, all in all. You held up your end of the affair quite well, although of course, we knew you could, and would."

Liam could have given an early "moving picture" a run for its celluloid in an Olympic speechlessness event.

"I won't keep you from your just revels. I simply wished to let you know that we at Corporate are all behind you, and are keeping a keen interest in how the feed evolves. Rest assured that you can count on our support every step of the way. We'll be watching," she added, without even an attempt at the smile that a lesser person would have allowed circumstance to dictate.

As he watched her leave the bar in the same wraith-like fashion in which she had entered, Liam was somehow far less assured than before the intervention. Resting was entirely out of the question. Nope, sullen drinking was all there was for it. Such desperate times called for desperate measures, and preferably generous ones too, of something single malted.

In the end, it was only the sheer horror of a well lubricated Editor in a *good mood* which brought him straight out of his own depths and into frenzied flight, in the general direction of where his shiny new car had parked itself.

19

Success.

He was a success.

The show was a success.

He had the attention of the entire world.

The attention of the woman in front of him, however, seemed far away. Kyla sat across from Liam in the new, deep plush chairs in his sitting room and frowned into her barely touched glass of gin. "Being host of a show like *The Grass is Greener* gives you a unique perspective. No doubt about that," she said, breaking the silence.

But deep in the combined comfort of his armchair and his own third glass of after-supper tipple, Liam merely smiled and nodded. "You're right. The show is so unique." He grinned, loving the thought of it.[i] "It's such a privilege, to be in a position to look into the lives of so many people."

"Yeah, lives all lined up for everyone around the world to see," muttered Liam's best friend in the world. Her hair, dyed an uncharacteristically subdued mauve for the occasion, dangled lankly, half-hiding her face. "Sounds like hell to me."

Anger flashed through Liam's merrily intoxicated mind. Kyla was the only one of the gang who'd answered Liam's invitation to come over, so they'd just watched a movie and ordered a curry in instead

---

[i] Or, in other words, becoming philosophical.

of playing. He was grateful she was there. After the première, he felt he needed some grounding. But if all she wanted to do was rain on his parade, she might as well not have come at all.

"Hey, I don't make the rules, okay," Liam said, bits of spittle flying from his lips. "People's lives are the way they are, and that's just the way the world is. All I do is make sure they get the recognition they deserve!"

Kyla raised her head, sadness filling her stark blue eyes as Liam took a deep, angry swig from his glass. "I wasn't accusing you of anything, Liam. I'm on your side here. But you must know what I mean. Seeing all those lives laid bare. The chains and dependencies set up to keep people firmly in their place: education[1], health, work, mortgages…" Kyla paused as a shiver ran through her, head to toe. That only made the anger roiling deep inside Liam flare higher.

"But that's just the natural order of things, Kyla. The right order of things. It's just like they taught us at back at school, like Hobbes said. People left to their own devices would destroy each other and them-selves. That's why we need the Corporations, right? To bind everyone together and make us better than individuals, so everyone ends up better off."

Liam chuckled at the thoughts pouring from his own mouth, and stopped to crack open a fresh can of mixer. His glass was empty again, and this philosophising was thirsty work.

When he looked back up again, the sadness was gone from Kyla's eyes, replaced by sharp steel. "Is that what you really believe, Liam? That the Corps are doing those poor people in your show some kind of favour? That your show is actually helping them?"

"Hey, they volunteered, didn't they?"

"Do you think they had any actual choice? Next time, have a good look at your contestants. At all the innocent little factors which, stacked up, become a structure more secure and more unbreachable

---

[1] To educate is "to lead out of." It says nothing about "into what or where," "by whom," or "to what end."

than any physical prison ever built. Do that, and then tell me that they had any other option, any other hope, than to sell their souls to that show of yours."

Liam chuckled again, swirling his fresh glass to get the mix just right. "So now we're talking about souls, are we? What is this, the Bible by Foucault?"

"Yes, exactly!" said Kyla, a fresh flush of hope rising in her voice. "It's Foucault all over again, Liam. *Discipline and Punish.* But now, the all-seeing prison warden is every single one of us, with our displays and our podcameras. Ten billion wardens paying for the privilege of watching over ten billion prisoners, all dancing to the tune of the Corporations, just because they're the ones who give us the chance to act as our own jailers."

"Never thought you'd turn out to be a modern-day post-structuralist, Kyla."

"There's no such thing as a modern-day Foucault, Liam. There can't be. Nothing of note ever comes out of the Universities nowadays. It's all been said and done as far as the world is concerned. And nobody would read a scholarly publication anyway, even if they bothered."

"You know, that reminds me of something my boss said." Liam lifted an arm to flick through his interface, then let out a choice swear as he knocked the glass over and emptied its contents onto his new Persian rug.

With a cry, both he and Kyla sprang into action, all philosophical debate forgotten for the time being. Kyla pulled some tissues from her pocket while Liam ran to the kitchen for the paper towel roll, and by the time they were done soaking most of the junipery mess out of the beautiful scarlet rug, they were both giggling at the incident, best of friends once again.

It felt good. So much so, in fact, that Liam almost wished Kyla hadn't remembered he was about to show her something before he knocked the glass over.

"The Editor RedCorp has saddled me with at the show is an odd bird. The sort who'd read Foucault's panopticon like a Do-It-Yourself manual. *Domination for Dummies*," Liam added, with a chuckle. "So I'm not sure how I'm supposed to take this. But he transferred me this, before the show."

On the new wide podscreen mounted on the wall of Liam's sitting room, the Editor's book-file loaded up: "*Discourse on the Origin and Basis of Inequality Among Men* by Jean-Jacques Rousseau" read the title on the front page.

"Wow, that's old school," said Kyla, leaning in toward the screen. "And surprising. I read this one ages and ages ago, but from what I remember, Rousseau is all about man's natural pity for his fellow man. And that's not exactly what your show and your employer are known for, is it?"

Deep in the plush comfort of his chair, Liam bristled. "Isn't it? The show is all about pity for your fellow man."

"Liam, that's not pity," said Kyla, sadness flooding back into her voice. "That's exploitation. Social jockeying. Exactly what Rousseau hated about man in Society, taken to lengths the world has never seen before. It's dangerous."

Before he realised what he was doing, Liam was up on his feet, looking down at a cringing Kyla and nearly shouting. "Dangerous? I'll tell you what's dangerous. Hiding behind ideas and the so-called spark of 'nature' to justify selfishness and laziness. That's a dangerous spark, Kyla. In an instant, it could burn away everything humanity—organised, orderly humanity—has managed to build."

He paused to catch his breath.

"You know, I think that's what the Editor was trying to tell me, and damn if I don't agree with him. It's no coincidence that the old nation-states have surrendered all the really important decisions to the Corporations. They're the only ones who have the skills and the leadership. Who aren't tied down to a bit of land and can see the big picture."

"Even if they aren't accountable to anyone?"

"Without having to pander to a million competing interests and to election cycles, you mean?" replied Liam, adding a scoff of punctuation. "The Corporations are more accountable than any government ever was. And not just to their accountants," he added, leaving Kyla alone as he started pacing across the room. "But even more so to the women, men, and enbies in the commuter train. To their customers. If they stop seeking progress, the best new product that creates the maximum amount of happiness for the greatest amount of individuals, then the next Corporation in line will do it instead. They'll eat them up, without remorse or hesitation, because competition is fierce. And competition is right, since that's the only way to guarantee the most important thing always comes first: the best results, at the best price, for the greatest number of people."

It was Kyla's turn to stand up, but without any of Liam's anger. "People used to have a name for what you're describing, you know. Do the words 'corporate state' ring a bell at all?"

Liam stopped mid-pace and spun to face Kyla once again. "And what if they do? The Corporations aren't just pretending to serve some meaningless 'common good.' It's not just lip service. They actually do make things better for everyone. They don't have a choice."

"So that's it then. That's what you see around you, is it? One happy world, united under the almighty profit?"

"It beats the alternative," spat Liam. "Local politicians who say they stand for accountability and against corruption, but are just a bunch of clowns, surfing on the fact that people know the old system is broken. Even if they were serious about accountability, how could they possibly do anything about it using the tools of the past?"

Taking a deep breath, Liam turned away and retrieved his empty glass, to fix a fresh drink and replace his lost one. The system was right, he fumed. And he was right to be part of it.

Kyla stayed silent the whole time, gazing at him with an infuriating pity in her eyes, and waiting for him to speak.

"Look," Liam said at long last. "The main thing is that I'm in a unique position to be a force for good. And I'm going to use every opportunity[1] the GiG offers me to help my employers and make a difference in the world."

Kyla nodded, but not so much in agreement as confirmation. "Well, I'd better get going if I want to catch the last tube train. You just make sure you don't forget what's important, you hear?"

"Never," Liam promised, meaning it with every drink-sodden fibre of his being. He went over to give Kyla a big hug, holding her small, tense frame against his for an instant, before escorting her to the door.

"And don't forget, I'm always here if you need me," Kyla added, before closing the front door behind her.

A smile on his face, Liam headed back to the sitting room, picked up his glass, and flicked through the Rousseau on the wall screen. A minute later, with a profound sense of well-being, he slumped deeper into his comfy armchair and fell fully-clothed into the sleep of the self-assured just.

---

[1] Literally, "every prevailing wind coming toward the port."

20

Why does everything have to start so damn early? He fought a losing battle against his brain as it tried to get back into working order. He so desperately wanted to preserve that delightful worriless slumberfuzz numbness which could so easily become all a man could ever want. His first rational thought of the day was that he'd probably stumbled onto the reason why chemical paradise-inducing drugs are known as narcotics. On that note, he eventually set about squirming out of bed and grabbed his bathrobe from off the floor.

He commiserated with his reflection as the bedroom mirror gave him the unadulterated damage report. It was a long-standing oral tradition amongst free-thinkers and celebrity interview podfeed hosts that a man or woman's thoughts in front of their mirror, first thing in the morning, were their most honest ones of the day, and revealed much about who they were and where they were going. Liam stared into the deep grey of his own eyes, searched deep, and thought how much he needed to use the bathroom.

This task took a mere few blissful seconds, but as it was trickling to an end, Liam realised that other organs were seizing the opportunity to demand their fair share of use of the facilities and, always one to recognise willingly that the king of the body is indeed an asshole, Liam sat down to business.

He had to make sure his resolve to act remained intact, rose the thought, above the supremely physical yet cathartic strain. The previous night's resolutions, everything he'd said to Kyla, were fundamentally right. He should be doing everything in his power to make life better for his contestants, and through them, for the world as a whole. But just saying it wasn't the same as getting it done. In practice, it could take some time before he was in a position to do any real good. In the meantime, he needed to play my cards well. He finished, then stripped and clambered under the steaming shower. His thoughts dissolved under the assault of heat and the touch of the water, before slowly recomposing.

The best he could do for now was to play the game and work his way up into a better position to make a difference, from the inside. And that started with earning a bit more respect, and a bit more power, around the Mews. He turned off the flow of water, groped for his towel on the toilet seat, and gave himself a summary drying, letting the air do the rest far better than his towel ever could, while he brushed his teeth and shaved.

It is notoriously hard to think anything much over the noise and the invasive taste of tooth brushing. But afterwards, as Liam ran the sharp metal of his razor across his face in carefully learnt movements, the resolve took a clear form in his mind. A plan of action.

First thing, when he got to the Mews today, he'd march straight in to see the Editor and tell him enough was enough. The man couldn't have his cake and eat it too. If he wanted Liam to be managing the production team, then he'd have to give him the official status to go along with it.

Executive Producer would do just fine, he added in silence, with a determined swipe of the razor. It had a nice ring to it, and it meant Liam would be in a much better position to protect his contestants, and make sure the truth of their lives didn't get manipulated and sacrificed for whatever reason, however noble the Editor could make it sound.

As he got dressed, he also mused there might even be a pay rise in it for him, if he played his cards right. That wasn't the point, of course, but it wouldn't take much for him to finally reach the sort of income where he could afford a proper house, farther away from all this urban mess. Something with some proper parking, more light, and a few trees or something. Maybe even something with access rights to the superconductor highway, straight into work!

He made his way out the door and off to find his car, twitched his fingers through the virtual commands that would have something hot and mostly edible waiting for him at the local drive-thru, and set off on his way through the suburban sprawl to the Mews.

A deep thrill[I] buzzed at the back of his brain as he prepared himself for the confrontation with the Editor. And damned if, despite his better judgment, he wasn't looking forward to it.

[I] From the Old English, "to pierce, penetrate." Presumably with emotion, but I'm sure Freud would have a thing or two to say on the subject.

21

"Let me get this absolutely clear," said Ed the Editor, leaning forward across his imposing desk and steepling his hands. "The reason you just barged in here is to demand a promotion to Executive Producer on the show. Does that sum it up?"

Liam felt a rush of blood redden his cheeks and fought to stay calm. There was so much riding on him making his point firmly and clearly. "Absolutely. And I'm going to have to be firm here, Ed. It's vital, and I won't take no for—"

"Fine. It's a great idea," interrupted the Editor, leaning back into his padded leather chair with the sort of smile usually reserved for particularly smug crocodiles.

"—an answer, and I... Wait, say that again?"

"I said fine. You've been doing great work so far, and you're right. It's high time we recognised that and gave you some more responsibilities around here." The Editor paused, flicking a hand through his AR interface and opening up a new tab. "Even though 'Executive' might be a step too far. Supervising Producer, that's the ticket, at least for starters. Shall I send the recommendation to Corporate straight away?"

Liam blinked, feeling lost at sea. He'd been prepared for a fight, and this complete capitulation made him feel like there was something he was missing. "Yes, that'd be fantastic. But you're definitely sure you agree with my promotion?"

"Absolutely," replied the Editor, treating Liam to that reptilian grin again. "Why wouldn't I agree?"

"Well, no reason really, I suppose." Liam had to stop himself before he started arguing in favour of the Editor fighting him on this, even though it seemed like the man had just given away a huge chunk of his power base at the show, without the slightest resistance.

"In fact," carried on the Editor, filling in Liam's silence, "this suits me to a 'T.' The show benefits from having stronger, direct management of the nitty-gritty of daily production woes, and I benefit because I get to leave that to you and focus more on the big picture decisions, and interfacing with Corporate. Everyone wins!"

Liam had enough experience with the Editor to be wary of his "everyone wins," which coming from his mouth usually meant "everyone who matters"—to wit, Ed, and Ed alone. It all felt too good to be true, but that alone wasn't a good enough reason to pass up the opportunity.

"'Everyone wins' sounds good to me," he said, trying to match the Editor's unnerving grin.

"That's my man," replied the Editor. "Let me sort it out with Corporate while you go announce the good news to your team. And don't forget, I'm always right here if you need any advice managing your new responsibilities. Make sure you close the door on your way out," he added, dismissing Liam with a wave of the hand.

Liam's first new responsibility was less glamourous than he'd been picturing: there was a gap in the contestant monitoring schedule, and he was the only one available to fill in, so he ended up having to spend his first morning as Supervising Producer monitoring Spike Bighorn's feed.

At least he managed to get Barry to scrounge up an ancient

physical screen for him so he wouldn't have to watch it direct in his AR display. He wasn't sure how he would have coped with direct visual immersion into the ins and outs—such as they were—of a professional android fornicator. This way, he could keep some form of distance and control, which was a good thing, because the man was unquestionably in full swing.

Liam was, at best, an amateur when it came to pornography, but it certainly seemed like the Erobots were putting Spike through his paces. From the first-person perspective, the orgy of limbs and erogenous masses took on a bizarre grace, like an acrobatic ballet routine. As Spike gave and received in kind from his various partners of either nominal sex, his own fleshy and well practiced moans meshed with the recorded voices around him, so that one was indistinguishable from the other, at least to Liam's inexpert ears.

It was such an alien experience, to view this intense pornographic orgy, scripted to within an inch of its non-life and executed with mechanical perfection, from within the eyes of the only human being in front of the podcams. From between a pair of spread android-gynous legs, there was a glimpse of what were presumably other human beings, as they milled about their various off-screen production activities. But instead of being reassuring, the presence of other people simply added to the bizarreness of this robotic orgy, experienced from the inside and performed in grunting silence. Liam felt like he should be getting aroused, almost on a moral level, but something just wasn't working for him—a blessing, undoubtedly, since he was, as he just remembered, still in the workplace.

The weirdness of the whole experience reached its summit when one of the electric jezebels took a shot of synthetic semen along an exposed joint, creating a short-circuit that sent her leg twitching like an epileptic tap dancer. The director called for a halt from her seat behind the main podcam console, and the mass of writhing plastic flesh crystallised into so many individual statues, each frozen position more ridiculous and more grotesque than the next.

The malfunctioning madam was removed, and Spike eventually disengaged enough limbs and orifices to pull himself out of the frozen orgy. With one last glance back, he headed over to his own little corner and towelled himself down—with a towel bearing a massive advertisement for the production company, Galatea Entertainment, Liam noted with a smirk.

In fact, having noticed one advertisement, he became aware of all of the other product placement logos located throughout the set, strategically placed on various bits of skimpy clothing doing absolutely nothing to cover the 'actors,' reflected in mirrors and on bed covers... Even Spike's own less-than-genuine Native American bead bracelets were embroidered in a pattern which, from his angle, was clearly a stylised rendition of the well known "chemical hazard" logo of the world's most popular and expensive sugar/caffeine/opioid power drink: RedCorp's very own Sinner-G.

Well, Spike's employers certainly hadn't taken very long to figure out that having one of their porn stars broadcasting live 24/7 was a great way to generate new advertisement revenue, with product placement touching—how many people exactly? Liam pulled up the viewership data for Spike's live feed. Yikes, over ten million concurrent viewers? At 10 o'clock in the morning. Of course, that was just in his time zone and meaningless for a large part of humanity. Nonetheless, there must be a lot of boys and girls in Europe and Africa whose idea of light, late-morning entertainment was a heavy helping of android sex, with a side dish of product placement.

Liam slid his hand off the editing panic button that would freeze the feed and reached over for his celluloid cup of sugar-free caffeine water. With viewership figures like that, Spike must be doing something right and wouldn't be needing editing any time soon.

22

After what passed in the modern corporate world for "lunch," and
consisted in the cold objective light of noon of little more than a hunk
of coarse bread—presented as "raw" but really just cheap—smeared
with a nutrient paste it was best not to inquire into too closely, Liam
was back behind his AR monitoring interface, with his finger on the
big red editing freeze button as instructed by the Editor. He hoped
that, whatever the Editor was doing with Corporate, he'd be able to
respond within the thirty-second editing delay period they had built
into the live feeds, because Liam certainly didn't want to have to be
the one to call the shots and be responsible for doctoring the feed,
should the need arise.

Luckily, his afternoon assignment was a breeze: good ol'
broomstick-behind Brad Leigh, out on his Germ Bouncer rounds
and taking his job far too seriously. The public seemed to love the
man for some reason, though Liam was damned if he could figure
out why.

It was hardly high entertainment, watching from inside Brad's
eyes as he sat in the seating area of what he insisted on referring to
as his "patrol car," checking and double-checking his gear, from the
various syringes, nanotrackers and random pointy things in his
medical kit to his operational gear, which included short and long-
range tasers, straightjackets, and an actual combat-grade smartrifle.

Liam had no idea how anyone could have thought it was a good idea to let a cowboy like Brad loose onto the streets with a weapon that was certified to pump out 20 individual headshots a second. That being said, he had to admit it gave him a peculiar thrill to see the smartrifle's targeting protocols load into Brad's AR display as he picked up the weapon and gave it an unneeded polish—more like a caress, really.

The live feed jostled as Brad's car arrived at the location of his latest unwitting target, which looked like a pleasant enough suburban residential unit, hardly a hotbed of disease and contagion. With crisp, practiced movements, Brad grabbed his gear, swung out of the car, and leapt into action. As soon as he started pounding on the door, his well oiled routine started running into trouble, in the form of an obstreperous door security AI.

"Greetings, Mr. Esposito. Please state the nature of your business with Ms. Perez, and refrain from knocking quite so violently on my door frame."

Even from within Brad's eyes, it was evident that he was getting agitated. Bits of spittle darted against the door as he spoke. "Goddamnit it, my name isn't Esposito, it's Brad Leigh, Disease Monitoring and Prevention Corps number 259—"

"Sorry, Bradley who?" interrupted the AI, somehow managing to sound smug at the fact.

"Not Bradley, you useless pile of zeroes and ones! First name Brad, last name Leigh, check my official ID tag already."

The AI actually made a point of letting out a pensive "hmm" as it pinged his ID and cross-referenced it.

"I'm sorry, but my facial recognition program lists your identity as Mr. Sam Esposito, Mr. Esposito. I can't corroborate this ID."

Liam let out a sigh of thanks that his editing instructions did not concern swear words or other expletives, which were given free rein and even encouraged in the show, because Brad, at the end of his wits, which were probably not very long to start with, let loose a torrent of vulgarity that may well have scorched the paint from the door.

Not that this would have mattered in the least.

"Fuck it, this qualifies as wilful obstruction." Reaching into his belt holster, Brad pulled out a pad of what looked like used chewing gum and stuck it to where the door hinges would be.

"Mr. Esposito, please refrain from vandalising private property or I will have t—"

Neither Brad, Liam, or the other viewers ever found out what extremes the door AI would possibly threaten, as the nanite paste rearranged the door hinges' constituent molecules into an explosive gas, which detonated—knocking the door flat into the corridor inside with a minimum of effort and a maximum of dramatic effect.

Brad strode over the fallen door, stopping to pick up the now inert nanite paste and pop it back into his pouch, with a little pat. The tasteful interior décor was difficult to appreciate, not just because it was covered in bits which were until recently part of the front door, but also because Brad didn't spare it a second glance as he followed the arrow in his AR display. Navigating him through a mini-map based on up-to-date planning records for the building, the arrow soon took him to the bedroom where the DNA tags in the bedding had flagged a woman with a potential outbreak of Andes hantavirus.

Brad drew his short range taser and swung the bedroom door open. He scanned the room, but the rumpled bed was empty and the single window was closed. A whimper came from beyond the closed en-suite bathroom door, and Brad made his way over to it, pulling Liam and hundreds of thousands of viewers along with him.

"Agent Brad Leigh, Disease Monitoring and Prevention Corps number 2599401-51, ma'am," he recited to the closed door. "Under articles 5 through 11 septies of the World Health Convention, and article 8 of the UK Disease Prevention Act, 2048, I am entitled to your obedience and cooperation in the prevention of a public health risk which has been diagnosed within your system."

"¿Uy, que quiere? ¿Que hace en mi habitación? ¡No me lastimes!"

"Damnit, it never rains but it pours, doesn't it?" muttered Brad to himself, as if forgetting that that included viewers all around the world. A flick of the eye switched a "Universal Translator" toggle at the bottom of his AR display to "on." and he spoke again.

"Can you speak English, ma'am, or do you have a translator app?"

Either she didn't understand him or chose to remain quiet. Brad's translator app helpfully provided a phonetic guide to saying the exact same thing in more or less understandable Spanish, at the same time his tactical analysis routine finished its structural report on the door, identifying the handle as belonging to a mechanism without a lock.

The choice must have been an easy one for Brad, since he simply shoved the door open, sending the short, terrified lady inside careening against a sink cabinet. Showing as little care for her feelings in the matter as he had for her property, Brad raised his taser and shot the home's owner with both prongs.

"I really don't have time for this shit," muttered Brad as he waited for the disease vector to stop convulsing, before walking over to stab her in the neck with a dose of viral antigen-administering nanites. "Assholes thinking they can travel all around the world and bring their filth with them. No respect for other people, that's what their problem is."

He printed out a paper copy of the bill for services rendered and left it by the sink. As he made his way back out through the breached door to his waiting vehicle, and the next vector on his triage list, he whistled with the satisfaction of a job well done.

23

Peoples' reactions to his new status as a major podfeed host were an interesting experience for Liam, and one which, if pressed, he would have to confess he rather enjoyed.

He was used to the odd, or sometimes even, stare of recognition from his years as the Channel 2 weatherman, but that had been little more than a passing annoyance that came along with the job. This was entirely different. It came with more perks, for starters, and sometimes even for entire meals, including the wine.

He got invited to parties, and not just the work ones you get sent an invitation to from some mailing list and where not a single one of the strangers there makes the least effort at pretending to be interested in your existence. No, these were proper parties, which he received proper invitations for. The secretaries knew who he was when he called up to confirm, the valets addressed him by name when he pulled up in his new sedan, and the waitresses remembered what he had ordered the first time for the well deserved subsequent rounds. Although, to be fair, it was true that all three were more often than not the same outsourced person.

These parties weren't all fun and feasting, mind you. As the various AR recreations of retro video games and pieces of abstract artwork attested, they were usually held by some corporate bigwig or another. A fellow swimmer of the entertainment shallows of the big commercial pond, or sometimes from a completely different area with some obscure tie-in which Liam only realised upon watching the daily business news feed sometime later, after a major deal or merger had taken place.

It was always strongly intimated in private that attending these events was an integral part of his new function, and Liam soon realised that this was because he was a conversation piece. People flocked around "celebrities" in the same way various insects can't help having unfortunate encounters with the indiscriminate bug zapper. This aura he now seemed to radiate for some unfathomable reason was the ideal stimulant, it seemed, for the instant electronic knotting of indissoluble contractual bliss, as such things go.

For he soon came to admit to himself, despite his reservations, that this was indeed his new status: he was a celebrity. Host and Supervising Producer of his own show. Oh, he had no illusions as to how deep that celebrity went, and was all too aware of the fact that speaking of "celebrities" as a whole was like grouping sand and mountain ranges together under the "hard bits" category. It was nonetheless clear that he shared, even in the smallest degree, in that basking golden glow which tinges how the world at large perceives the famous. It was mediocre, but by the gods of entertainment, it was his, and he was enjoying it more than he cared to admit to anyone other than himself.

In fact, he soon learned from his nightly virtual and physical shoulder-rubbings with the affluent that it was the "done thing" to mock celebrity and deny, at every possible occasion and whatever the company, how much this phenomenon was a profoundly enjoyable one. After sticking to a strict policy of cautious listening, he had quickly caught on and, in order to avoid standing out and displaying openly how wrong this all seemed to him, he joined in, in carefully average measures. Having given it some thought, he decided this behaviour must be an attempt by the rich and the famous at curtailing jealousy and making themselves seem more in touch with the common

Man, more "human." He mocked them in private, but as far as he was concerned, they could do whatever they felt like.

He could hardly complain, but the parties were definitely cutting into what meagre sleep time his demanding work schedule left him. He was sure that in the old days a feed like his wouldn't have been run with a production team of only five people, but such was the result of the constant push for maximum productivity and minimum costs. The live feed monitoring alone forced him to put in hours which defied all labour laws. It was wreaking hell on his health and, he had no fear of recognising it, on his frame of mind.

It was what he had signed on for, and in all fairness he had been prepared for it. If only the work had been living up to expectations, it wouldn't have been so bad; but his resolve—to play the game while acting responsibly with regard to the effects of what they were doing— had been most sorely tried, right off the bat. It was the editing that did him in and forced him to take action.

"Sir," he eventually worked up the courage to say, barging into the Editor's office as politely as possible, "I would like to speak with you about the segments for this week's show."

The man didn't even bother to look away from his live feed screenings on the wall-vidscreen. He simply waved vaguely at a chair, presumably inviting Liam to sit down and continue, and not even registering Liam's refusal of the offer, which Liam found far more infuriating than anything the man could ever have said.

"Ed," he resumed after a calming breath. This most certainly caught the man's attention, and Liam had to repress a smirk before continuing. "This is important. I've been talking with the team, and we aren't comfortable with some of the editing choices in the segment rushes for the Sunday feature show." This was stretching the truth a little, since when he had briefly mentioned the issue to them, they had contented themselves with a vague nod while backing away, but it was for a good cause. The Editor turned to look at him, the silence hanging over them like a solid gold yet fully operational replica of Damocles's famous sword, displayed at the end of a very thin piece of string. Liam swallowed.

"I know we've talked about this before," he said, with a slight wheeze, "and last time was one thing, but in these segments it's almost as if we are intentionally playing the contestants one off each other."

The Editor rested his chin on his crossed hands and blinked, which Liam took to be a request for him to continue. "Well, that's a bit too close for comfort to actually manipulating the outcome, isn't it? I know that's what everyone expects, but it doesn't mean we actually have to do it."

"Argyle," broke in the Editor, like a brick through a display window, "we are here to entertain. What this means is that it is our function to 'hold things together.'" He clasped his hands in demonstration. In another circumstance, he might have been in fervent prayer. "This very literally implies a hands-on approach. The feeders demand that we intervene so that what we show them is what they want to see, something in which they will be able to take an interest. The contestants expect no less of us, that we make their lives interesting enough to create a bond between the feeders and themselves. This is what they signed on for. We would be lax in our essential function of mediation if we did not translate the raw material into a finished product, in a language all feeders will respond to. This requires us, and here is I think the central point behind your unease, to appeal to the base categories, the archetypes, which the viewers unwittingly identify with and expect. Oh, our contestants have their individual traits and their eccentricities, and therein lies their charm, but at the end of the day, they will inevitably fall into the feeders' preconceived categories of people and personalities. We are simply making this as easy as possible for everyone involved, because it is one of the keys to a successful feed."

He paused, as if watching Liam's thoughts race through the maze of this monologue, the kind which people tend to skip reading when they encounter them in a play script, or perhaps a novel, and rightfully so. Just as Liam was emerging and about to answer, Ed cut him off.

"Now, I fully understand your position, and it is justified. It is too late to modify the segments for this Sunday, but what I can offer you is that from here on in, you and your colleagues will be systematically included in their assembly, and will thus be able to contribute to keeping them as close to nature as possible. What do you say?"

Liam realised this was final, regardless of anything he might add. He nodded and made to leave of his own accord, before his dismissal compounded the pervading feeling that he was a schoolboy again, preached to and scolded by the teacher. Ed caught him in a verbal lasso before he could make good his tactical retreat.

"Ah yes. Argyle? One last thing. I have been discussing things with Corporate, and we think it is high time that you had a clearer leadership role in our little team here. From here on in, we'd like you to take a firmer hand in directing the collective efforts, and this matter is as good a starting point as any. I'll make certain they'll put out a memo to that effect tomorrow. Good day to you," he finished, addressing his live feed screen once again.

24

From there on in, it had only gotten worse. The hours, the little white lies, the big red ones... he had to not only take part in them himself, but he also had to enforce and justify them to Barry, Lee, and Carpentiere. He was their Supervising Producer after all, and the only one around to make any decisions—and take any blame when something went wrong—since the Editor hardly ever showed up at the Mews anymore, working nearly full-time from Corporate HQ downtown.

Sometimes, in his darkest hours, Liam saw himself as at least as monstrous a being as a Finn Oldman, if not worse. After all, he knew better. It was impossible not to take a personal interest, both in the contestants and how they'd be affected by their media-mongering machinations, as well as, more poignantly, in his co-workers.

Carpentiere's little girl had been sick on Tuesday night, and it was by all accounts rather bad. He was pretty choked up about it, but from what Liam had managed to gather, on Wednesday morning the child had been rushed to the hospital and was still there under intensive care. Carpentiere didn't seem to want to face going into the details, and Liam certainly had no intention of forcing them out of him. He tried to do what he could to let him off work early, but deadlines were deadlines, and every man, woman and, indeed, child had to be ready to make a few sacrifices.

Then there had been that business with Lee, later that same afternoon, obviously, as if the basic work wasn't more than enough to deal with as it was. He had the sneaking suspicion they were intentionally trying to make his life hell. Would they gain anything from breaking him? In any case, Lee had managed to mess things up for him with Corporate, already. He had received an irate-sounding ring from Corporate late that afternoon, just as he was about to call it a day.[i] They were after the expense slips from the previous week's contestant audition forays into the wild world at large.[ii] and didn't sound particularly happy about it. After a mental moment's jig and reel, Liam mustered enough sense to remember he had charged Lee with the task of managing the archaic yellow, cyan, and fuchsia stencil-copy slips they had to fill in for each and every expense. He assured the man that he'd sort it out post haste, and went to seek the answers. He did not overly enjoy them once they were found, and he had the sneaking suspicion that the people at Corporate would be even less partial.

"Hey, I sent them like you told me to," went her response, as she paused in her sequencing of the live feed coverage, "but it turns out that the ones you had given me were the wrong sheets. I had a word with them, and apparently they change the colour-coding every week, for security reasons. And you know that fuel we, and by 'we' I mean you, put into the van? They're saying we should have used Petronext, not Totaloil, since they belong to a rival corp. They didn't seem particularly fussed about the fact that Petronext doesn't have a station for miles in that part of the city, and are refusing the reimburse it. Sorry."

She had little else to tell him, so he decided to take it to the Editor.

"You can hardly expect Corporate to pay for fuel bought from a rival petrol chain, now can you?" Ed seemed profoundly amused, which irritated Liam even further, after the half-an-hour rigamarole

---

[i] The day itself is hardly ever bothered about what people choose to call it.

[ii] Not to mention wide, as a result of years of evolutive adaptation to the fat and energy-enriched fodder of global society.

with secretaries at Corporate until someone could track the Editor down for him. "And as for this whole expenses business… well, it's unfortunate that you took the wrong week's slips, is all I can say." Ed conveniently forgot to mention that the forms had been in the Editor's own office, and Liam had only taken them following the man's not overly precise instructions. "Of course, it was technically Lee's mistake, but she was acting on your orders, and it was your role to supervise her. You are the Supervising Producer now, after all."

Liam clenched his jaw and held back an outburst. He hated the words "Supervising Producer" more and more each day.

"You don't just delegate things and forget about them, you know," carried on the Editor, patronising as ever. "There's a bit more to it than that. Why, any idiot could be in an executive position, otherwise." Ed chuckled, but Liam failed to see either humour or reason to humour the Editor, and so stayed respectfully, if reproachfully, silent.

"Well, the best I can do is put in a word for you at Corporate. I think you'll probably still end up having to foot the gas bill, but I'm certain I can convince them to be lenient regarding the slips, this one time." His picture in the comms window gratified Liam with a little smirking grin that was undoubtedly supposed to look comforting and understanding, but merely managed to make Liam feel like snails had suddenly started crawling all over his skin.

"In the future, do keep a closer eye on your subordinates, Argyle. Surveillance is the biggest part of a hierarchical position, after all. We can't have you going around shirking your responsibilities, now can we?" he concluded with the sort of paternalist smirk you'd love to smack.

"Responsibilities," Liam said to Mary, who was unlucky enough to have been dusting in Liam's little office when he entered, and thus became fair game for him to vent at in private, as he sat in the swivel chair behind his desk. "How dare the Editor, of all people, preach to us about shirking responsibilities? I mean, if a hierarchy just means having multiple people doing and re-doing the same work, how is anything ever supposed to get done?"

"Right you are, sir," replied Mary, leaning against her cleaning trolley with her sprayer and cloth still in hand. "Speaking of which, I suppose I should get back to—"

"But don't get me wrong," carried on Liam, cutting Mary off mid-escape attempt. "I'm a big believer in the Corporations. Always have been. I grew up idolising the men and woman who gave life to them."

Mary sighed, stowed her gear away in the trolley, and stood at attention. "Is that so, sir?"

"Please, no 'sir' here. It's Liam, remember?"

"Right you are, Liam," replied Mary, a corner of her mouth twitching with a little half-grin. "And why do you think you've always thought so highly of our employers, then?"

Liam opened his mouth to answer the question, then closed it again when the words failed to come.

It was odd, come to think of it. He was over forty years old, and he'd never once stopped to wonder why he considered corporations to be naturally above individual people. Wiser. Stronger. More efficient. Less prone to irrational emotions. He hadn't questioned it when studying political philosophy or ethics in University, and he hadn't once blamed the corporate structure itself for any of his dissatisfaction with his career and work life. Not before *Grass is Greener* came along, that is.

But, so help him Adam Smith, he was questioning it now. Could his blind faith in the superiority of the organisation over the individual just be something programmed into him? Because what he'd just experienced today was the complete opposite of efficiency or moral strength. It was cowardice and irresponsibility rubber-stamped and enforced through corporate hierarchy.

Had there ever been any critical thought about modern corporate structure at school?

"Sir? I mean, Liam?" prompted Mary, a worried look on her face.

Liam gave himself a little shake. "Yes, sorry. I was just thinking about what our schools teach children about the Corporate Council, and all the good big organisations have done for the world. It's only the truth, at the end of the day. That's history in a nutshell. Social and technological progress goes hand in hand with the history of Corporations and organised labour."

Mary treated Liam to a tired, sceptical look. "Sounds nice and simple."

"It really is," replied Liam, drawing deep on his memories from school, and wondering why he was so eager to impress the cleaning staff. "The Maurya Empire and the Roman Empire were built on the backbones of legal Corporate entities. And the fabled Roman legions were run much more like businesses than the old national armies. The great early Corporations, like the venturing explorer-businessman, Venice, and the East India Company opened up the world."

"I guess I never thought about it that way," said Mary, nodding in resignation.

"The list goes on. The printing press. The Encyclopaedia and Enlightenment. The transition from the small, individual workshop to mass production chains. Consumer goods. Affordable comfort for all. The Space Race, followed by private Corporations carrying on in space where the old nation-states left off."

Mary nodded again, edging her trolley toward the door. "It all certainly sounds very good and proper when you put it like that. Like destiny, that sort of thing."

Liam's cheeks flushed with pleasure. "Well, I won't deny progress has been… bumpy, at times. But yes, stronger and stronger organisation has unquestionably made life better and better for the individual people being organised."

"Speaking of organisation," Mary tried once again, taking advantage of a lull in Liam's thoughts, "unless you need anything else here, I have a leaky sink to fix in the bathroom, before someone slips and I need to rush them to the hospital."

"What?" Liam blinked and looked up in surprise. "Oh, yes. By all means. Don't let me detain you."

Mary made good her escape before Liam could engage her in another rambling conversation. But Liam's thoughts were turned inward, and more troubled than he cared to admit.

So what if his nagging doubt were founded? Did it matter if his view of history and the world were just the product of a biased Corporate-funded education system? Did it make it any less true?

He didn't know the answers. The questions alone were enough to make his head hurt. Nothing a stiff drink or four wouldn't cure, but it had been a long day, and he figured that was probably enough introspection for now.

There was one thing he was certain about, though. He'd be taking care of those damn expense invoices himself from here on in.

25

Liam surveyed his open drinks cupboard. Maybe he should be watching the drink. He knew that was the rehab training talking, but the thought remained just as strong. He probably had been overdoing it a little of late, he admitted to his inner confessor. In fact, it had almost been like old times again.

If only they hadn't had to cancel the Wine and Warfare tonight. He wouldn't feel so damnably guilty about the idea of having a drink if they were all together, and he really needed to blow off some steam.

The IMs off of Hank and Kyla, saying they both had other things planned tonight, were still hanging just at the edge of his peripheral AR vision, where he'd shoved them with an angry flick. He had also received a Com call from Steve saying he was "real tired" from work this week and didn't think he could make it, so they'd decided to just cancel it for this week.

It's funny. Steve had seemed more preoccupied than anything else on screen, but then again, it was often hard to tell with such matters. Still, Liam really would have preferred to have them over: he thought he could use both the wine and the gaming release. Solo play just wasn't the same, so he decided to fall back on some more reading. He had forgotten just how many interesting books he had loaded onto his tablet back in his philosophy days at University. Like everyone else, he had only read a small fraction of them at the time, only excerpts really, and only as imposed by the coursework.

Resolutely shutting off his AR display for the first time in weeks, he scanned the tablet's impressive index. The first to leap out at him and tug at something deep within the onion-layers of his thoughts and self was Erasmus of Rotterdam's *Praise of Folly*. He thought he would placate this urge by simply skimming the medieval work, but found it to be a surprisingly engaging read. He only stopped when tectonic-class stomach rumblings made him realize it was now past 9:30 p.m. and he had been reading the thing, out of time, for hours. He put the tablet down as if it had short-circuited and scalded him, but only long enough to knock up a hot bowl of soup with barley and pre-cooked and chopped veg. He couldn't help but start to read it again, while trying not to splash soup everywhere—an evil he judged necessary.

Resolutely removing his AR reading glasses, as he knew he'd be tempted to flick the AR back on every five minutes to look up a definition or a name in the online encyclopaedia, he finished the tome some hours later. Sleep crept up his spine on hobnailed boots, yet only served as a sensory backdrop as he got caught by the web of cross-references in the footnotes and railroaded into flight about one hundred kilometres above the surface of Friedrich Nietzsche's *Twilight of the Idols*.

He went through something disturbingly close to what he imagined an out-of-body experience to feel like, and the tiredness certainly did not help in this respect. A strange cocktail of emotions, equal parts terror and elation, mixed with ample ice and put through the blender, ran through his consciousness as it sped over Nietzsche's marble-carven precepts and admonitions, taking in both individual features and panorama.

At geological lengths, he managed to pull himself free of the gravity well of Nietzsche's mind workings, and rose to glance at the clock. He could not remember ever being up quite this late and yet not having a single empty alcohol vessel strewn about his person. As this flashed through some isolated level of his consciousness, most of it merely clamoured that a visit to the loo was of the utmost urgency. Never one to repress such bodily diktat, he climbed the stairs and headed to the facilities—but not without a pause to grab his tablet beforehand.

Temporarily freeing the mind from the constant weight of having to control the centrifugal urges of the urinary tracts and the bowels is always a greatly pleasurable thing. Properly harnessed, it can also be very conductive to strength and clarity of thought. This was a large part of why Liam had always enjoyed reading on the can, as it were, and one at least as important as the objective fact that there had been very little else to do with that inescapable part of the day since the demise of handheld gaming.

He was one of those old school gamers who refused to recognise fuzzy AR timewasters as actual games, and only activated his AR during toilet time when it was absolutely necessary, or if he had forgotten to bring his reading tablet. In the present case, he used his moment of clarity to make a conscious choice as to what he was going to read on his way to bed, perchance to sleep: Thomas More's *Utopia*.

He rose, stumbled into his room and out of his clothes, then pulled the covers from the foot of the bed. Never having thought of himself as anything other than a bachelor, even during those brief stints of relative sexual abundance, he had never had to make the effort to understand the obsession with "making" beds. Unless someone was coming over for a visit and had some remote chance of entering the bedroom, for some strange reason, he really did not see the point. He certainly didn't mind an unmade bed, as you were only going to mess it up again that very night, in just about any case.

Only then, comfortably snuggled deep within the slightly ripe comfort of his bed covers (they were a bit overdue for a wash, he noted in passing), did he return to the tablet. Utopia, he sneered in disdain, making the same self-satisfied mistake easy thinkers have made since the book was written, which is to assume[i] a book written about a self-definedly impossible ideal is necessarily as sarcastic as they. Tossing all forward-thinking together in the same boat that will never float, such a one stops at the first built-in impression and scoffs at the supposed inherent fallacy of that placeless utopia, by definition unattainable. In this, they utterly fail to see the point oncoming with all the concreteness of a falling tower block: a utopia may be, by definition, unattainable; this does not reduce in the least the very real merit, and even necessity, of pursuing it.

Silently mocking the generations of fools who fought and died for one utopia or another, Liam slid deeper into the mattress, and into sleep.

Mind-flashes against the black screen of his eyelids. A mask, but then, it is a person. Same thing. Female. She looks vaguely familiar. She starts moving.

He still does not recognize her, but he knows she is Mary, the agency worker. Isn't that odd? They speak; the words register only as movement in that somehow blurred face. She moves past other persons. He follows.

The people change. The ground stretches and drops away, but somehow his feet are still on it, and he himself does not move. Blood pounds through his world at an alarming pace as he pulls and pushes, fighting to free himself from the mounting torture. His heart feels like it must explode—

—he gasped, not sure whether the scream had only been in the nightmare or if he also screamed out loud. His vocal cords made a mucus-covered "glug" sound deep in his throat, and he was suddenly

---

[i] See supra, only very much more so.

aware of the chill of cooling sweat making the bed sheets cling to him. A pant. He would change them in the morning.

The people are milling about him. They seem interested. Perhaps merely curious.

The ground! It is still falling away! He arches into the tugging void as he struggles against the stretching. He will break! He cries out for help. Wakeupwakeupwak—

—rgh! Definitely out loud that time. He glanced over at the clock: 2:30 a.m. Not good.

He dragged himself up, stumbled to the bathroom, and turned on the lights. The searing blindness helped him focus. He poured himself a glass of water from the tap and sat to drink it on the toilet, feeling a little pang of guilt, as he often did, at betraying that supposedly quintessential trademark of manhood which is peeing standing up. He had to get some sleep in; there was still a lot of work to do to get Sunday's feed ready. Popping his AR glasses back on for a quick check of his inbox, he reminded himself there was no reason for him not to sleep, after all. He couldn't even remember what was bothering him anymore. As he eventually made his careful way, blinded once again, back through the darkness to his body-warmed bed, he reflected that it would be nice to have an actual weekend every now and then. Or even just a free Saturday.

He supposed it was part of the job description. "Nothing for it…" his fading consciousness was vaguely surprised to find himself actually mumbling.

The Moon. It waxes huge and full in the night. Fascinating.
It grows bigger. Fear me, it seems to say. It grows bigger still.

Surely it must hit the Earth! The collision never happens, ever-imminent. Liam cowers under the oppressive moon-glare. He gives a mental shriek.

Again? He decided to force his eyes open and turned over to look at the clock. His eyes focused upon the time: an hour and a half until the alarm was supposed to go off. He slid over and fumbled with it a bit, giving himself an extra fifteen minutes, as much margin as he could allow himself. His mind felt like it had been stuck full of needles by an apprentice acupuncturist. He drifted.

The alarm screeched, and he silenced it without conscious thought. Had he slept? He had no idea. Too late for it now, in any case. There was half a bag of coffee left downstairs, he recalled, as he shambled over to his wardrobe. Should just about do it.

26

I must be allergic to this stuff, at least a little bit, he reckoned, as Mary set about him with the orange gunk. *It can't just be that I don't like it.* Couldn't the computers just edit the make-up in without him actually having to wear the stuff? They did that all the time, right? Surely it would look better than this mess.

This was the first real weekly feed, with the contestants all live on the set and jumping through the hoops they had set for them, he reminded himself with an internal sigh. He was looking forward to it like his first enema.[i]

Mary must have sensed his tension because she was quick to say, "That's enough for now. How about we give that some time to settle in while I go and fetch you a nice cup of tea from the trolley." Or at least something to that effect. He wasn't really paying attention but nodded anyway, and probably mumbled his thanks when she came back with the hot plastic cup. These outsourcing people did have their advantages, he reflected, as various adverts, alerts, and spam messages popped into his AR view, all demanding their usual share of his divided attention.

They finished make-up ahead of schedule for a change, so he went and stood to the side, watching the final preparations for the

---

[i] "Throwing in," though techniques may have evolved somewhat since Proto Indo-European times.

set and feed equipment. The contestants were standing by the water cooler, performing the delicate balancing act of avoiding his, each other's, and anyone else's eye, while still endeavouring not to look nervous. AR displays, even when not necessarily turned on, were a great excuse for the socially awkward or uncomfortable.

He was somewhat pleased to see that this included both Brad Leigh and Suicide Jill, but was put off to see Finn Oldman brazenly stop Mary as she pushed the trolley past their knot, managing to con a tiny bowl of snacks from her. Did he know what people thought about him? It's all fun and games until someone loses an eye. In his AR display, the numbers on the big clock shifted into the dreaded conjunction. Time to get his game face on.

He stepped forward onto the set Mary had installed in the Mews central warehouse area. Long gone were the surgery props and the fake medical team. This was to be their permanent Sunday feature set-up, and it was a spartan affair: a few uncomfortable-looking chairs, a podium for Liam to pose behind every now and then, and a great many stage lights, all set on a blue chroma key backdrop.

Nothing else was needed. Everything else about the show, from the scenery to the props to the free-floating AR windows showing the various pre-prepared footage sequences, would be rendered in real time by Barry's cave of machinery and displayed in all its AR glory in the product going out to the viewers. This was common practice, but their show had the added spice of allowing the viewers an easy and equally real-time glimpse behind the curtain, since they could still have each candidate's internal live feed going while watching the weekly feature broadcast in another window.

The set was bathed in a glare which seemed to have little other purpose than to block out the rest of the world. A funny thought really, since, in fact, its goal was the exact opposite. He smiled and nodded to the contestants as they filed past to their seats, like schoolchildren fresh off the playground at recess. Somehow, he felt much more in control this week, and his mind wasn't quite so torn this time around. Sure, he still had just as many misgivings about how they had spent the whole week doctoring the live feed footage to make it as interesting as possible, but he was much more grounded. It felt pretty good. Then, the red light lit above the podcams and all thoughts were crowded out by the rehearsed lines and stress-fuelled smiles of showmanship.

The initial sequences had always been easy, and things were even more so now that the cameras spent more time on the different candidates than on him during the middle bits where he had to introduce the next sequences. Everyone got their thirty seconds of fame as the show focused on the selected highlights from their week's activities, ranging from Brad's door-busting antics to Finn Oldman getting a commendation for his health claim rejection record. Liam flew through the sequences on gold-winged boots, every word, every stance oozing assurance and charisma. He was on a roll.[i]

Then came the new bit, the sequence they'd dubbed "Crossfire" despite Liam's vocal dislike of the name. The Editor had scolded him. "Don't change a recipe that works, and in the business, you'll be hard pressed to find anything more tried and true than the Crossfire. It's a classic." So they'd set up these chairs on little revolving plates, and sure enough, the contestants were soon swivelling from their well ordered initial lines to face each other in a crude and somehow angular circle. Set spotlights flared with rainbow edges in their eyes. Each contestant's implanted lenses had the feeders skipping from head to head, skin to skin, catching every glance and every nervous reaction to the new setting.

He took position at his little podium to the side. It was going to be a massacre. His mouth went on of its own accord, and he soon found himself having to run to catch up with it.

"Tonight, we will be opening up the voting for the first elimination

---

[i] Less like butter, more like Branston pickle.

round. To help you, our feeders, make your choice, we decided to ask our contestants to say a few words about what they think of each other. Here's what they had to say."

Ugh, why didn't I screen this before they showed it? Inner Liam groaned as he watched the first clip's victim, poor Azar, work her way through a venomous tirade against Juliette. She may only have met her in person for the first time last week, and even then only briefly, yet that seemed to have been enough to form a profound dislike.

"I just know about these things. I see someone and I know if they're up to no good," said a very confident Azar in the clip. Her current self was looking somewhat less sure of herself in her seat there, directly under the glare of the other contestants' combined first-person viewership, but she seemed resolute. "I mean, it's a privilege to get to participate in a show like this," continued the clip-Azar, "and we're lucky to be getting nice, new implants like these ones. Moaning about it is just plain rude, and very revealing about true character, in my books."

The display paused, just long enough for the contestants to start stirring and for tensions to escalate, before playing the next clip.

"I don't know about you, but I've had it up to here," growled the unmistakable tones of Suicide Jill, as she gestured to someplace above her ample frontage, "with suck-ups and phoneys like that Azar, let alone Spike Toaster-Porking Bighorn. People aren't stupid; they know that we're chosen by RedCorp and that the Corporation controls everything that happens here. They don't also want to have to watch us kiss their asses as well. Or just pretend that everything is hunky-dory, like Usnavi. I mean, personally, I like the kid, but he needs to wake up. I don't care how many people are looking out of your eyes— they can't open them for you."

The sound of Finn Oldman cackling brought Liam back out of his AR overlay and back into present focus. He was sitting back in his chair, laughing at the nastier quips in the sequences, goading the other contestants on, and clearly enjoying the whole proceedings as much as a cat in the aftermath of an industrial accident at a feather pillow factory. He was in such good spirits that he wasn't phased in the least when, in the next sequence, Professor Fourka called him "a conniving little twit with all of the humanity of a broken anvil," Liam noted.

The free-floating window kept on Augmenting reality with reckless abandon.

"Seriously," boomed the voice of Brad Leigh, "I don't see how anyone could possibly have it as bad as I do. My daily grind has me fighting on the front lines to defend the world against dangerous diseases, for crying out loud. The rest of them are just whiners. I think it's pretty clear that I should win the show." The set broke into[i] pandemonium, the contestants rising to their feet, spit flying as, enraged, every one of them defended their claim to shame.

A downward glance told Liam that the main feed had abandoned all pretences and was now focusing solely on the upcoming melee, switching between the various first-person perspectives and ceiling-mounted aerial views.

Finn Oldman was grasping the back of his chair all too innocently, he noted with alarm. While the chairs were designed to be riveted to the floor for safety, it struck Liam as curious that no one had seen it fit to actually do so. He snorted. *I'm even being sarcastic with myself now. Dangerous, that.* It looked like he was going to have to step in, since he could no longer see any excuses that would allow him to avoid doing so.

A discreet twitch of his left middle finger activated his pre-set alert function, which would turn on an equally modest red light somewhere in Barry and the Editor's displays, letting them know that he was about to improvise and they would need to adapt on the fly.

"And now," he said, feeling like a ringmaster sent in to lead negotiations after a mutiny in the lion cages, "the time has come to

---

[i] With a heavy crowbar

see who *you*—" he was really getting into the swing of it now— "the feeders, think deserves to stay in the fight."

An eerie calm fell over the contestants, who suddenly understood what World War I soldiers must have experienced when the other side came out of their trenches and said the local equivalent of: "Hey, it's Christmas, so let's let the machine guns cool down for a while, have a drink, and kick a ball around, what?" Surprise, a new focus, and a common fear combined to make the drawn lines of battle nothing more than that, if only for a fleeting moment: drawings.

"It is now time to vote, and find out where," Liam paused for effect, feeling so on top of his game he must be able to spot his new house from up here, "the Grass is Greener. Voting is now open."

He risked a quick glance at his AR overlay to confirm that the control room had kept up with him and the voting interface had kicked in, replacing the live feed with blaring commercials. He knew the handy tactile voting box would sit in the corner of all of the show's feeds for the next week, giving plenty of time and incentive to boost the ratings as much as possible. So occupied, Liam did not see the diminutive figure approach him until it was too late.

"Hey!" protested Spike, squidging him in the ribs with a massive finger. Liam refused to consider where said finger might recently have been. "Where do you come off, calling to vote like that? My sequence didn't even get played. That's bias, that is!"

"Oh shut it," said Juliette, wading in. "You have nothing to complain about, unlike some of us who didn't get a chance to see if some others were ready to own up to their slander—to my face!" she spat, her tone rising toward the end as she glanced at Azar, who was putting on, albeit involuntarily, a rather good impression of a terrified coat stand.

Oldman brought up the rear, actually hopping in his attempts to get somebody's attention, to the tune of "Not yet! Not yet! I haven't had time to explain how bad our dental plan is yet."

At that, everyone seemed to break into cacophony, amidst which

Oldman, as the resident expert in the cost, and therefore value, of a good knock upside the head, decided to give his chair a swing into the amassed lot of them, for good measure.

As luck dictated, he managed to miss connecting with any of the competition and sent the furniture-cum-bludgeon on its way, sure and true, straight into Liam's temple.[i] As the cheap engineered alloy of the chair struggled to occupy the same space as the carbon, water, calcium, and some-other-bits locally referred to as Liam's skull, all he registered was a blur like a sudden flight of startled birds, and a sharp percussion. Cool movies with intricate first-person perspectives of shell-shocked soldiers and car accident victims had set him up for a major let-down, as the last thing he thought before nothingness engulfed him like a blue screen was, inanely, *What was that?*

---

[i] Leaving Liam, not for the first time, without a god to pray to.

27

Beeping.

Sounds like a heart rate monitor. Am I in hospital? Oh, dogs, I'm in hospital, and I'm pretty messed up by the sounds of it, if I'm saying dogs instead of gods. Am I alright? What's wrong with me? Why can't I see? Am I blind? Am I paralyzed? Might I die? What happened? Wait, my sight is clearing up. Oh...

The statutory condom distributor was blinking its little red light at him to show, even without the AR notice, it was empty and in need of a refill. Somehow, he'd never noticed it made a sound before. Now that he could put it into context, it wasn't so much a beeping as a buzzing, and seemed strangely over amplified. Such a loud sound certainly couldn't come from a mere flashing light. In any case, even the shittiest hospital wouldn't have taken things quite this far. He was clearly in the bathroom.

"He's coming around," a voice bellowed, as his ears perceptibly tightened in adjustment to the everyday assaults of the realm of consciousness. Far beyond its routine spin, the world seemed to have a wholly new rotation to it. A few seconds of frenzied data selection and analysis tentatively led his brain to identify the voice as belonging to Barry.

The man's face loomed above him, as full and orange as a harvest supermoon, and a decidedly unwelcome "helping hand" forced his muscles out of their state of contented, if somewhat bewildered, paralysis and into grudging movement.

Liam groaned, not at any pain, but in protest at being forced to return to an upright position that he found about as desirable right now as open-chest surgery by an intern freshly out of anaesthetics and using a blunt spoon. His head throbbed violently at this convoluted thought and gave his second, deeper groan a much sounder basis.

"Glad you came around," said the moon face, "the Editor was afraid we would end up having to call in Health Services, and you know how much they charge you[i]..."

This fraternal call to union through shared lamentations, usually echoed unfalteringly by anyone who has ever needed a stitch or ten, went eerily unanswered, as Liam struggled with reality, the way an eighty year old obligingly tries to grope the prostitute a well intentioned but profoundly misguided friend has provided him for his birthday: while keeping a careful distance, and with the profound impression of having been cheated out of something that had always taken for granted and should by now be, by all rights, second nature, just like riding a bike.

Barry stuttered, and tried to fill the unexpected void. "So... err... just so you know, we had to wrap up the feed without you, after the accident."

Which bit was the accident precisely? pondered something within Liam. *That things got out of hand, or that he was the one who got hit?* He supposed that, in the literal sense of the term, being hit in the head with a chair is, in the long run, just as much of an accident as everything else.

"Luckily, it's mostly automatic after the voting's started. Everyone was very subdued after we carried you out. That Oldman guy was very apologetic, and then we cut straight to commercials. Now we're

---

[i] They were famous for taking the expression "an arm and a leg" to greater lengths than ever before.

back on just the first-person live feeds. The clip from Oldman's point of view when he swings the chair already has more hits than anything else in the show so far, so congratulations are in order, I suppose."

Indeed, thought Liam, although the question remained as to what, or whose, order that was.

"So... erm..." Barry faltered, out of words and in decidedly uncharted territory. "Can I get you anything?"

The impulse to answer "a bottle of gin" rose to about chest-level before he could fight it back. "No," he said. He leaned over the sink to take a sip of water, then spat a bit out. Pink gunk swirled down into the drain. He must have bitten his cheek or tongue somewhere along the line. Nothing to be done for it now, so he postponed checking which it was and filed it for later examination. "Thanks, but I'm fine."

Barry needed no more excuse than that to escape. "Right then, if you're certain. I'll be off then. See you tomorrow, Liam," he added with a big grin about as credible as a missionary the day after the Judgment Day of your choice, and sidled out.

Liam stood staring at the stranger in the mirror and listened to the creaks, thuds, and muffled vocal sounds of the Mews winding down to its troubled automated sleep. His AR glasses lay, reverently placed, by the side of the sink bowl. Nanopixel filaments made a tiny, desperate bid for freedom from the jagged edge of the shattered right lens. The bathroom seemed to have been touched with a subtle yet nonetheless effective ward against intruders; a silent stigma, but no less real than that used in times of pestilence.

Urh. Liam surfaced, shaking himself both physically and mentally. *If I'm well enough to have that kind of thoughts, then I'm well enough to get on home.*

Leaving his broken glasses where they lay, he stumbled into movement and made for the door. If he could get past how strange everything looked without the AR trappings, then he'd probably be able to focus enough to remember where home was.

28

Liam convinced himself that he deserved this as he listened to the ice tinkle against his fresh whiskey glass, and grinned. The new job had its perks[i]. One of them was having enough funds available to be able, when putting his shopping order through, to go for the expensive stuff at the top end of the price list without any more qualms than were strictly necessary. He made his way over to his armchair with only the slightest stumble and melted into its nanomolecular-moulded padding. The bottle went on the usual table at his side, its height just right to make picking up and dropping the bottle effortless.

He took his first gulp. *It's a funny old world.* All this brain-power, all this effort, all these machines at work to make something like the GiG possible. All that attention and energy spent by people around the world following the stories, getting the latest info, preparing to place their vote. He took a slightly deeper drink than he had expected, and sloshed his lip and the tip of his nose. *It's not as if their vote matters*, he added, wiping himself dry with his sleeve.

And when you come to think of it, with all these people follow-ing and voting for rubbish like this stuff, what might actual politics have to learn? The means are obviously there. Be it through AR glasses, lenses, and implants or even through old physical devices,

---

[i] Diminutive of "perquisite" or, in Latin, that which is "thoroughly sought after." Perks aren't some sort of side benefit; they are the main event.

people can access any info and participate in any debate, anywhere, with every bit of convenience and ease. Sure, the political process isn't like a reality TV show. But security shouldn't be an issue: the new generation models have much tighter security than any manual process in history ever had. Consumers wouldn't have it any other way, not with everything from banking details to porn internet histories at constant risk. He sipped, and refilled.

Our tech obsessions should be giving us actual info, on important things, and not be wasted on this trash! Liam was damn sure that if people could vote in an AR window, you'd get a fuckload more than the usual one-in-five people actually bothering to vote. *What's stopping it? Is it a lack of will?* It was so easy for society to believe that individuals just don't care and couldn't be bothered to take an interest even if it were handed to them on a silver plate.

I'd certainly take an interest, if I knew my vote would actually matter, and I really don't think I'm all that unique in that respect. I'm certainly no better than anyone else. How could anyone not take an interest when given a chance to have their say and help decide the matters that affect their lives directly?

Then again, would people be able to get as passionate about politics as they are about drivel like RealPod?

And then there's the fact that I would be out of a job if something like that ever happened. Hmm.

He pulled himself up and out of his slump, forcing his charcoal-smoke eyes to focus, through the pleasant ethanol blur, on the time display at the bottom of his new, state-of-the-art nanopixel retina implant display. The ones that came with the bone conducting sound implants. It was laughable that he had stuck to his old AR glasses for so long.

One a.m. already? No time to sit here remaking the world, I need to get to bed if I want to get any proper sleep in. Early start on next week's show in the morning, after all.

29

The Editor's oversized, wall-mounted physical screen displayed a face. A male face. The sort of face that is constantly wearing a pained expression, the same way a silver screen vampire wears its false teeth. The face belonged to Ali Fourka, and the Editor was currently staring it down with a look that would have made any passing small rodent or other animal of prey run for cover in a pawful of milliseconds.

The first synthetic voter polls had revealed that, after last week's feature show, Fourka was by far and large the favoured choice for elimination this week. Liam would have thought that maybe that bastard Oldman's over-eagerness with the chair would have counted for something, but knowing this business it had probably made people like him all the better, if anything.

The Editor had called a general meeting that very morning to present the fact of Fourka's elimination and to discuss how to make it as entertaining as possible for everyone involved.

"We should include the scenes where he was badmouthing Oldman, directly followed by those where he was cowering behind Jill during the melee," he said, visibly repressing a sigh, but with a look of longing he could not hide. "Any other ideas?" he quickly added, covering for himself.

"Err[1]..." said Barry, "I have a chum, err, colleague, who does the networking in the Publishing department. Maybe we could see with the bigwigs there about some sort of cross-promotion. You know, we put their magazines and such in the feed, they put some of our content in their magazines. If we hurry, we could get some stuff about Fourka out before Sunday. You know, coverage of the melee last week, some juicy rumours, that sort of thing. It could really build up some interest and excitement."

"Yes," said Lee, not one to be outdone. "And we could also start organising the post-elimination for him as well: the talk feeds, the live events, the merchandising, all of that business. With the popularity of the show, eliminated contestants are going to become household names for a while, and Fourka certainly needs to do his part to promote the feed in exchange."

"I like it. That's the kind of thinking I want to see. You two get right on that, and I want results before we leave tonight. Anything else?"

Silence. While this was indeed an excellent opportunity to show initiative, competence, and worthiness for promotion, that realization that it also entailed an unexpected amount of very real and immediate extra work left all tongues temporarily in the possession of proverbial cats. Tangible downsides did much to curb any potential enthusiasm at abstract advancement opportunities.

Regardless, Liam still ended up having to work late nights all week in order to prepare the best possible elimination for Professor Fourka. There was something particularly perverse about preparing the fallout of a vote that was supposed to be still underway, while at the same time keeping an eye on the various live feeds. At least the fancy new top-of-the-line AR implants the Corp bought him to replace his broken glasses made multitasking while keeping up with his share of the feed monitoring duties that much easier.

---

[1] To "Err" is human, but to persevere in saying "Err" is worthy of the hottest damnations of hell, as the saying should go.

Professor Fourka seemed to be pretty much resigned to his fate as he went about what academic duties Birkbeck hadn't taken away from him yet and preached to the sparse assembly of largely uninterested management students, as per his habit. Something about modern societies becoming "reality intolerant." Business as usual, there.

Suicide Jill's live feed was probably, to the Editor's delight, where things were moving and happening in the days following the weekly feature. True to Emile Durkheim's studies, Monday proved to be a particularly busy time for her, especially what with the days getting shorter.

Liam had been the one on monitoring duty, comfortably set in his new car on the way to work, when Jill had been called in for the most gruesome job they had captured on her live feed to date.

"Ugh, Hackney again," she said with a snort when the orders came through on her AR display. Her clean-up van made an automatic and undramatic left turn to take her there. "Why am I not surprised." Jill had quickly decided to provide running commentary of her own life for her viewers—she was the only contestant who seemed to be treating the show with proper competitive spirit, and the viewers loved her for it.

"I swear, if I have to see that pile of old rubbish they call the Hackney Road Conservation Area one more time, I'm going to take architectural justice into my own hands and knock the whole lot down, just see if I don't!"

She took a swig from her thermos, then paused as more data on the job scrolled into view.

"Hold the big white phone," she said in apparent surprise. "This one might be worth your while after all. I know that looks like a load of paper pusher gobbledeegook to you lot, but what it means is that we've got a double suicide on our hands. Probably a lover's pact, we get those every now and then. I blame Shakespeare, myself."

Jill was on a roll, with the London urban clutter serving as backdrop for her latest rant. "Bloody romantic idiots, what do they think they're trying to prove, anyway? They're lucky enough to find someone who doesn't just want to screw them, but actually likes them and wants to stay with them afterward. Do they even stop to think how many people out there would love to be in their shoes? No, they're too good for the rest of the world all of a sudden, best to end it there while the ending is good and leave it to the Post-Tops to clean up the mess."

The van pulled to a stop, and Jill clambered out with a sigh to unload her cleaning gear. "Bloody typical," was all she had to add on the subject. Lifting the machinery and coils of vacuum tubes and pulling a rubber cleaning jumpsuit over her street clothes stole her breath and rendered her silent, for a rare change.

She grunted her way into the depressingly average tenement building and up the filthy stairs. The yellow arrow guiding her was the only bit of colour she could see, and a blessing, as focusing on it allowed both her and the viewers to avoid having to look too closely at the surroundings and their evident multipurpose as urinal.

The door to the mess-makers' little single room lay half-open. By the looks of it, whoever had found the bodies hadn't bothered to close the door or secure the site behind them—there were bits of glistening tubing, which Liam refused to think of as intestines, hung neatly over the doorknob. The door had clearly lain undisturbed since the event. Anyone who might have been interested in robbing it knew damn well, from personal experience, that anyone living in a place like this would have nothing worth stealing.

Even after five years of experience and hardening, Suicide Jill couldn't suppress a little quiver of fear at what she was about to discover when she pushed the apartment door open. She resumed her running commentary, probably because anything was better than the silence.

"I've tried to ignore it, you know. To make each new corpse into a thing, just another impersonal job." She edged the door open with her toe and stood in the open doorway, steeling herself. "But, you know what? Try as I might, there's always some part of me that just can't forget the people that these messes were, not so long ago. Women, men, and enbies—like you and me."

Jill made a show of taking one last deep breath before stepping into the dark room, and Liam wondered how much of Jill's speech was honest introspection and how much was just a speech, for the sole purpose of the show. If nothing else, it was good showmanship, since it gave the viewers more time to tune in as fans got the word out via social media that something was about to happen on Jill's live feed. The viewing figures in the corner of Liam's display were probably the only thing around here that couldn't lie: it seemed to be working.

"Here we go, guys."

Jill's lenses auto-adjusted as soon as she entered the dark room, adding a surreal, night-vision tinge to the blood and guts that coated the room.

"I know you can see this, but you're really missing out on the smell, guys." Jill paused just long enough for effect, before delivering the punch line, with an apologetic shrug. "It's just offal."

Liam, just like viewers everywhere, was too engrossed in the scene they were seeing through Jill's eyes to care too much about the horrible pun. Primitive instincts yelled that the still-oozing, red masses littering the room belonged inside a person, not sprayed across the walls and cheap furniture like some sort of retro charnel house décor.

"Well," said Jill, once the silence had become unbearable, "I'm pretty sure the bits around here would add up to roughly two whole human beings, but it would be one hell of a puzzler to fit them back together..."

Responding to the combined horror and morbid fascination of millions of viewers, she took one tentative step forward into the room, then another. Navigating her way around the biggest chunks in her path, four steps were all it took to get her from the door to the rough centre of what was still, under all of the gore, a functional bedroom/kitchen/living room combination affair. With mounting horror for all involved, she bent down and took a closer look at a discoloured lump in the middle of the room.

"Is that—"

The bubbly mass twitched below her, and Jill leapt back, nearly slipping on a tube of some sort in her haste, and bolted back out of the open door.

"Oh, fuck this. Fuck everything about this. I'm calling it in."

Liam wondered if all the other viewers were feeling as grossed out and confused as he was, as Jill brought up her telephone interface and cycled through her contacts list with angry flicks of the eye. Eventually, she stopped the list and chose one of the names, a certain "Kader," with a virtual stab.

Whoever Kader was, he answered the call with the sort of grumble you get from someone who had been doing something infinitely more interesting in AR when disturbed, and was eager to get back to it.

"Kader, you fuck, this job is no goddamn suicide pact. I've got the residue from a nanopaint bomb still twitching in the middle of the room. Bring up the file and get the code on this one switched over to what it is, which is a fucking double murder. This is not our business, get the rent-a-cops in."

Vulgarity seemed to have done its work to get Kader's full attention.

"Now hold your horses there, Jill. Let me bring up the file. Right. Yeah, no can do, Jill. Secufax has already been on site. They were the first called, and their agent flagged it as suicide before we were even called in. They wouldn't like it if we try to send it back to them now."

"They can go fuck themselves, Kader. Their 'agent' never even opened the door. He probably just pocketed the bribe from the building's superintendent to keep everything hush-hush and walked off for an early lunch." Jill's audio seethed over the feed, and Liam could only imagine her expression. "In the meantime, the only people who have been here are myself and the killer, just before they lobbed in a plastic bottle full of shrapnel and wallpaper nanites set to populate without limits. There isn't enough left of them to be sure, but judging from the amount of gore and the names on the door here, I'd wager that 'Lucy' and 'Amanda' were two consenting adults who didn't ask to be blown to smithereens by some repressed bigot with a can of nanopaint. Now will you please change the flag on this one so I can get the fuck out of this stench and go take a long shower?"

Kader made one of those annoying teeth-sucking noises, which sounded all the worse for coming disembodied through an AR call connection.

"Yeeeeah. But seriously though. What makes you so sure it isn't a suicide pact after all? They could have just wanted to show how deep their love was with a grand gesture."

Jill was silent for a few terrifying seconds, and Liam could just make out her clenched fist at the bottom of the feed's view.

"Kader," she said, in tones as calm and patient as the grave. "I'll use my fist to show you how deep your asshole is if you fuck me over on this one. People don't usually stop to make souvenirs after committing agonising suicide all over the walls. Here, someone decided to leave a lovely selection of entrails draped over the doorknob for whoever would have to deal with this mess, and that isn't going to be me!"

"Jill, calm down, alright? Look, it's not our job to make a fuss about this. What's done is done. Just turn on your Funfilter and get to work with the machines, okay? It'll be done before you know it."

Jill sounded subdued, almost tired, as she answered. "Man, you know I hate using those filters. They make me feel weak."

"Jill, they're so popular for a reason. There are times when you have to deal with something you don't want to have to look at. When you've got an AR filter that will turn it all into flowers or ice cream or whatever else does it for you, then you'd be stupid not to use it, right? You buckle down and take care of it now, and I'll put you down for an hour's overtime due to stress. How does that sound?"

Jill sighed. "Sure, man, I suppose so. But you owe me one, you hear?"

"That's the spirit. Rock on, Jill." Kader's voice cut out without wasting a second, as he rushed back to whatever AR timewaster he kept himself entertained with between calls.

"Right," Jill said out loud to herself, as if remembering the millions of viewers who had followed that exchange. "Fuck me."

She flicked open her main app menu and loaded up a program called "Funfilter - Fun for all ages, from 2 to 102."

Liam remembered when Funfilter had just been a silly add-on to video messaging services, letting you look like an idiot with huge anime eyes or rainbows puking out of your mouth. It hadn't taken long before the geniuses behind Funfilter realised the real money lay in real-time filters which could remove and replace anything disagreeable from view. With disclaimers in place to cover the inevitable tripping-over-invisible-objects-and-down-stairs incidents, it was one of the biggest successes of the early AR boom. These days, Funfilter came loaded by default into all AR operating systems, and the owners were off living in some corporate paradise on Mars or something. Lucky bastards.

Jill busied herself getting her equipment ready while the filters kicked in. By the time she had the portable incinerator unit warmed up and strapped to her back, the bits of guts still swinging from the doorknob had been replaced by colourful festive garlands, bringing back many happy childhood memories for Liam. Even the door itself looked like a better, more trustworthy sort of door, and Liam was pretty sure the hallway had not been in such a good state of repair a minute earlier.

With her multi-purpose cleaning hose at ready, Jill walked back into the room. No hesitation marked her steps this time, and sure enough, everything in any way disagreeable within the room had disappeared. It now looked as if some unruly children had decided to have a food fight in their otherwise well appointed nursery.

In resigned silence, she set about cleaning up the smears of what appeared to be chocolate pudding, the trails of spilled spaghetti—no meatballs—and the chunky bits of cake and hard candy that the irresponsible children seemed to have scattered all over the place. A couple of particularly large pieces of fresh fruit were too big for the multi-purpose hose, even on its widest setting, so Jill had to pick them up and feed them by hand into the incinerator unit. She did her duty without any visible qualms, other than perhaps a little shudder, which may just have been a glitch in the broadcast.

Soon, the children's nursery was back to its gleaming, cheerful self. Even the stubborn toffee stain in the centre of the room had come up eventually. Jill exited, closing the door gently behind her, then peeled off her chocolate- and fruit juice-smeared jumpsuit and gloves, which she tossed into the incinerator as well.

With a twitch of her eye, she moved to turn off the Funfilter, which the program only accepted to do after multiple confirmations that this was what she really wanted to do and disclaimers regarding anything unpleasant she might see once the filters were off.

What passed locally for reality came back into focus, bit by bit, as the filtering dropped out. The corridor was just as dark as before, the paint just as peeling, and the closed door was once again a shabby, ramshackle affair. The only difference was that everything seemed a bit hazy, as if there were some moisture on the lenses in Jill's eyes—but surely, that was simply another glitch in the filtering program.

With the fun and games over, the viewer count started dropping, as feeders around the world moved on in search of greener, more entertaining pastures.

30

Usnavi Musibay's excitement was contagious. Liam was so proud of getting him onto the feed. If there were one saving grace about the whole sordid business of the show, it would be this one, that he had helped, at his level, to make the world aware of the plight of people like Usnavi, be they handicapped like him, displaced, or just plain down-and-out. The world would do something about it, would want to help, once they knew, once they had shared his reality. How couldn't they? The boy was just so damn likeable.

Today was a big day for Usnavi. He was due to start a new medical trial, and the Corporation behind it—a branch of SyneDeal, the freeloaders—were pulling out all the bells and whistles to turn it into a publicity event, given the show and its live viewers.

Usnavi was more than happy to abandon his usual routine, which from his explanation consisted mainly of unmarked commercial buildings and service doors, and took great pleasure in the VIP lab tour he was now getting, taking Liam and all of the other viewers along for the ride. They were even telling him a bit about what they were putting into his body, for once.

"We're all very excited about our new line of ninja viruses, Mr. Musibay," said the SyneDeal PR doctor with the white medical coat and the friendly AR nametag labelling him as "Doctor Flatt." He ushered Usnavi over to the middle of the room where an AR display had been set up, showing an entertaining but confusing combination of molecules and DNA helixes, rotating freely in the air. "Our proprietary ninja virus techniques are the way of the future, Mr. Musibay."

Liam guessed that Usnavi had been called 'Mr. Musibay' more times today than in the rest of his life put together.

"Bacteriophage viruses have been around forever, of course, and human beings have used them since before we were human. Our noses are full of them, for example, housing them and relying on them to feed upon harmful bacteria in the air we breathe." Liam decided he would take the doctor's word for it, and avoid visualising that too clearly.

"We've been using bacteriophages widely for decades now," carried on the presumably good doctor, "ever since bacteria strains resistant to the old antibiotics became prevalent. Of course, the medical body should have foreseen that this was only postponing the problem and that the worldwide use and abuse of bacteriophages would lead to the evolution of bacteriophage-resistant disease strains, in turn. It's basic natural selection."

Usnavi spoke up at this, possibly to show that he hadn't fallen asleep. "Does that mean we can never have a lasting treatment for germs? One they won't grow resistant to?"

"Excellent question, young man," answered the doctor, pleased as a dog with two tails, and just as surprised. "That's precisely where our ninja viruses step in. Through an alliance of bio- and nano-engineering, we've been able to create viruses that are armed and ready to deal with just about any kind of harmful bacterium."

The doctor paused, allowing the AR display to illustrate his point. As they watched, animated virus strings—equipped with humorous little virtual black masks and katanas—twisted, flexed, and penetrated crimson red bacteria globules with reckless abandon. When the cluster of bacteria had been entirely destroyed, the doctor carried on.

"Natural bacteriophages have evolved to destroy just one kind of bacterium, which is why you have to take so many different kinds of bacteriophages to be properly protected. Instead, our new ninja viruses will be able to feed off any bacteria they are programmed to, neutralising the development of any natural resistances by 'reacting' to them, if you'll excuse my use of the term, and adapting their methods of attack in real time."

"But what about the good germs. Bacteria, that is. Those are a thing, aren't they? Good bacteria, that your body needs to stay healthy?" Usnavi sounded pretty eager to show he was clever and attentive.

"Yes..." The doctor seemed less pleased with this question than the previous. "You are correct, of course. It is precisely because of this need to balance the power of our new ninja viruses that we are now moving into human user evaluations." The doctor smiled at this, his PR face coming back to the fore. "Imagine, young man. Thanks to your work with us today, billions of people around the world will soon be completely protected from all sorts of diseases. Aren't you a lucky one!"

"Oh, yes, sir!" replied Usnavi, his grin reflected in the polished chrome of the lab counters. "So, these will be cheaper than the current phage treatments, then, right? So that billions of people can get some? It's just that most of the people where I live can't afford to get the current phage treatments, the ones that don't hardly work anymore anyway. But I suppose it'll be cheaper with just one kind of ninja super-phage, right?"

The doctor coughed and adjusted his collar, which had suddenly grown tight somehow, before answering. "I'm sure they'll work something out, yes. Can't really say, that isn't my area, of course. However, if we're done here, perhaps you'd like to see what we've set up for your first dose of the new ninja virus?"

He ushered Usnavi out of the lab and on to the next stage of the scripted publicity tour, taking Liam and the live feed viewers along for the ride.

31

Liam couldn't get past the question: what was he doing here, still at the Mews, at this time of night, and on a Saturday of all things? He knew all too well that taking a long walk off a short pier would be a better use of his time than asking to actually be paid for all this extra time he was putting in. Everywhere else, the hour was nominatively happy, and he sure would have been happy to be able to partake.[i]

At least the late night on Friday hadn't made him miss out on Wine and Warfare. He hadn't heard from the gang, so he assumed they were still mostly laid up, tired, and so on. Or maybe everyone was stuck working to all hours like he was, he sighed, as a flick of the finger minimised the AR Solitaire game he'd been half-assedly messing with and he got back to the actual work.

Right, so he was supposed to open this sequence here, insert that here, and here, and here... He had had all of an hour's "training" in doing this, watching over Carpentiere's shoulder as the man caught up on some urgent sequencing one day during the lunch break, and now he'd been turned over to the uncaring arms of the tutorial software.

It really wasn't his cup of tea. He had been trained in the realm of thought, in the humanities. He had always thought of computers

---

[i] An example of what is known as a back-formation, from "to part-take," which is to say, to take part.

as a tool, something to be used as a medium in the professional field and as a means to his entertainment ends in the private. Instead, with his expensive new retinal implants wirelessly tethered to the sequencing unit before him, long after he should have been in the comfort of his home and liquor cabinet, the relationship had somehow reversed. The computer was using him, forcing him to jump through its procedural loops as it fed him inane and mind-numbing instructions (click, click... click).

The software was most definitely the master tonight, although perhaps the correct term would be mistress. Indeed, he shared a strange pang of sympathy for the Frenchman who, given the task of officially naming these strange new computing machines so very long ago, had for some time hesitated between the masculine "Ordinateur" and the feminine "Ordinatrice."

And anyway, what good have these things ever done for us?

The involuntary Monty Python reference was not lost on Liam. He had, after all, received a classical education. And what's more, it was fitting. Was not the modern computer empire rivalled only by the Roman Imperium of old? The Red was everywhere. Not only in the economy and in growth figures, but also in the minds and hearts of billions. It was even in their very cells, every second of every day, energy pulses carrying all and any sort of information through the very matter of their being, any potential health consequences down the line be damned.

Still, there was no doubt that being able to perform just about any menial task with AR software guiding your every move, step by step, was progress, of a sort. The Red was the great equaliser, the great unifier. Without its cultural bonding, the true modern international community of values and references would have remained a pipedream. *A utopia*, Liam realised with a mental snort.

Having somehow finished the work while he pursued this runaway train of thoughts, he shut down the offending machine with a vengeful stab of a hardwired physical button. No gentle AR

prompt to please shut down whenever is convenient for you tonight!
It took its time and made him wait as it shut down several applications,
but in the end, whirred off into uneasy rest. *That's one less mind for
the Red, you bastards!* Liam quickly scolded himself for his silliness at
the thought.

Well, that's done, came Liam's mantra as he blinked his retinal
clock into focus. He couldn't stop from admiring how intuitive this
new tech was, and how much crisper it all looked than he expected.
Form was one thing, content was another.

*Right. Factoring in an hour either way to get back home, and even if I
forgot about eating and showering and somehow went straight to sleep, I'm
looking at, what, two-and-a-half hours? Two-and-three-quarters, tops? Ugh.*

Equal parts of resignation and disgust washing over him like
second-hand bathwater, Liam hauled out the crappy emergency
futon from the bottom drawer of the office supplies storage and
spread it out on the ground. The room being what it was, this gave
him the disturbing sensation of having to sleep at the foot of the
computer terminal. However, his body would have none of this
squeamishness, and so he crumbled to the feeble mattress, barely
taking time to remove his clothes and summarily sling them over the
back of the various office chairs. Before he remembered to set an
alarm someplace, he was fast asleep.

A vague sense of confusion, of lack of control: what is this
thumping? What is this rushing? What is this feeling of spreading, of
spinning, of rolling so very thin?

"Ah!" said a choked voice. It echoed so perfectly with something
inside him that he slipped directly from sleep to a certain degree of
wakefulness, without an instant of that in-between part he had
always taken such luxury in maintaining for as long as possible.

"Yes," he said in a surprisingly normal voice, as if caught mid-conversation, "I'll be right out. Thank you." He rose to shut the door in one viscous movement.

What a deep sleep. He couldn't even remember falling asleep, or anything else between then and now. Well, there was maybe something… a vague impression but nothing you could actually call a dream. A mostly peaceful night for a change, now there was something he hadn't had in a while.

It was only then that a slight draught shook him and helped him realise two things: first, that the voice he had just risen to answer was Mary's, and second, that he was naked.

32

It was some five minutes later that the door opened again to allow passage for Liam Argyle, whose resolutely composed, and even defiant, posture contrasted directly with his ragged hair, crumpled clothes, and bleary, sleep-encrusted eyes. He strode across the main hallway of the studio, trying to broadcast an unabashedness[i] that he desperately wished he could feel.

However, the empty warehouse slept uncaring, its AR tags still dim in their power-saving night mode, unaware that by nightfall it would again be transformed into a temple of voyeurism and decadence for feeders the world across and back again. In the meantime, Liam squinted into the gloom as he made his way to the bathroom, trying to avoid the embarrassment of running into Mary.

Luckily, she was, as always, the first one at the Mews, in order to get things cleaned up and do the computer maintenance. Unluckily, as Liam now discovered to his regret as he pushed open the door, the first function also included cleaning the men's bathroom.

"Ah," said Liam, echoing the woman's own exclamation in a similar situation a mere few minutes earlier. "Err, don't let me stop you, and, umm, sorry if I, err, scared you earlier." He coughed. "I'll

---

[i] Being "abashed" means being so embarrassed or upset that you lose control and simply leave your mouth hanging wide open. Give it a try yourself: "A-baaaaaah-shed." Yes, word origins are often that simple.

just be taking a shower then." Hoping to leave it at that, he started sidling around the cleaning trolley.

"Oh, no, Mr. Argyle." As soon as Mary had gotten over the surprise of the Liam-shaped monster barging in on her usually peaceful morning routine, she had somehow managed to completely block his way to the little shower at the back of the bathroom. "It's me as should be apologizing, barging in on you like that."

"That's perfectly alright, I assure you. Umm, I'll just..." Surely ending the conversation would let him get past her and her trolley and into the shower—if you could call it that, without any extra jets or sonic or anything. A wooden bucket with a hole in it would have had the same qualifications.

"No, no, I wouldn't hear of it. You just stay right there and let me make it up to you." She rummaged about in some arcane[i] drawer of her over-laden trolley and pulled out a little pre-pasted toothbrush in a tube and a hotel-sized[ii] bottle of something that was probably shampoo.

"Here, you take these and do what you need to do." She paused, considering[iii] him a bit. "Oh yes, you'll be wanting these as well, I'm sure." She fished out a disposable razor and a mini-bottle of foam. "And here's a towel."

"Right, err, thank you. Always know where your towel is, right?"

She gratified him with a chuckle. "I'll leave you to it then. Come find me when you're done and I'll fix you up something hot from the trolley." She swung said offending object through the bathroom door and out into the pervading non-gloom of the main hall. With a thud, the closing door restored both Liam's privacy and a good part of his shattered dignity.

---

[i] Hidden, and thus, etymologically, "well-guarded."

[ii] As in, "of the size of those commonly found in hotels," not as in. "of the size of commonly found hotels." I can see where that might be confusing.

[iii] To observe the stars.

Well, a shower would do me a world of good. He looked down at the miscellaneous instruments in his hands with much the same degree of innocence and confusion which his first ancestor to have discovered fire must have experienced while staring at the bright, inviting, yet surprisingly painful colours dancing on the stick.

By the time his self-awareness had recovered sufficiently to stop and analyse where his apprehension was coming from, he had already lurched over to the shower and entered the searing and mind-blanking heat of a decent wash. Vague recollections of classic myths of purification through water and of long-established religious ablution rituals started trickling through his thoughts.

Then, his new implants interfaced with the tags in the shower cubicle seamlessly, setting the water temperature to precisely match his preset preferences and automatically offering him a selection of shower-time AR games, local or multiplayer, and podfeeds to choose from. From that point on, there were no more thoughts, other than a pause every now and again to remind himself that there were definite benefits here, when everything was said and done.

33

It was a much cleaner, civilised, self-controlled, and therefore docile[1] man who emerged from the steam-filled washroom. He gave Mary a cordial greeting as he spotted her taking out the bins.

"Better?" She grunted the words as politely as she could manage from behind the stacked rubbish.

"Aye, very much better. Don't know what I would have done without you." He paused, the long-atrophied roots of chivalry, solidarity, and basic decency nagging at him as he watched her wrestle with the door. "Um, perhaps I could give you a hand there?"

The scene froze as abruptly as the nostrils of a scientist emerging from a heated plane into the depths of polar winter. It was a good handful of moments later that she replied, "Yes, that would be nice," in a curiously deadpan tone which nonetheless set the scene back into movement again, the dance of the planets resuming its regularly scheduled course.

Liam went over to help her get through the door (well, he held it for her), and then heave the bins into the dumpster out back (one, to her four), before heading back in to help himself to a nice warm bun and hash browns off the breakfast trolley Mary had knocked up, his just reward for a job well done. Panting slightly, she joined him a few minutes later, just as he was finishing off his first helping and

---

[1] Literally, "easily taught."

pondering the merits of a second. The hash dealt out, the bangers thoroughly banged, and the brown water supposed to pass for coffee poured and served, there was nothing else for it but to start up a conversation[i].

She opened the hostilities with, "So, long night, I take it?" between a forkful of banger and a bite of a bun.

"Yes," he managed to say after tactfully wedging his food in cheeks and under his tongue. "I've been at it all week. So much work goes into the preparation of these live feeds, it's unbelievable."

Mary poured herself a cup of tea. "Aye, tell me about it. I'm the one who is going to have to cart out all the props from the store and get it all set up for tonight."

"Ah, yes." Liam's cheeks reddened with each heartbeat. "So, um, how is that going for you, anyway?"

"It should be ready for tonight," Mary said with an expression of utmost serenity, as she stabbed her banger. "That's if we don't get any major hardware failures, or any spills that need cleaning up. I'll already be plenty busy as it is."

"Well, I just hope it goes better than last week," Liam said with a wince, not particularly listening to what Mary had to say anymore.

"I'm sure it'll be fine, Mr. Argyle. After last week, they'll do everything to make sure things don't get out of hand, don't you worry. Just took us all by surprise last week, it did. Now we know what to look out for." Her hand came to rest on his shoulder and gave him a good firm pat. He looked up from his plate, into a face lit up with a smile like a scimitar catching the light of the midday desert sun.

"You know, we don't get to talk like this anywhere near enough," he said. Against all expectations, he was smiling as well. "It's always go, go, go. We never get to take the time for a good sit down and an honest chat. We really should do this more often."

"Right you are, Mr. Argyle," was her only response.

---

[i] "Conversation" literally means "the act of living with," just as "versus" originally means "to change with."

34

Where had the day gone? For one long, glorious, drawn-out moment it had seemed like he would be able to lean back and oversee the final preparations for tonight's live feed forever, that the time itself would never arrive, like some temporal turtle that the arrow could never quite hit. The people had buzzed around like busy little drones all day long. Just looking at them had made him comfortably drowsy and numb.

And now, here he was, his face full of gunk, dressed up like the buffoon[i] that he, not to cut too fine a point, essentially was, and walking toward the set with a shambling pace that would have made even the most dejected of death row inmates, on their last legs, as it were, proud.

His step picked up a good deal more spring as he observed[ii] his contestants[iii] all sitting there, revealing different degrees of the same expression, both tame and wary. The fact that, by now, last week's chair-related antics had been entirely forgotten by the feeders had not been lost on any of them, nor had the immediate consequence:

---

[i] "Someone who puffs out his cheeks" (Try saying it and pay attention to how your cheeks move on the "buff" part)

[ii] "Watched and kept safe"

[iii] "Those who call to witness"

this week was very much up for grabs, and any of them could be getting the proverbial axe.

He slid with astonishing ease from being Liam Argyle to being approximately one-point-seven-five billion Liam Argyles on screens and overlays the world over. It was all so easy now; there was nothing out of the ordinary, other than a profound sense of inner balance and a slight floating feeling which for some reason reminded him of the bouncy castles of his childhood.

There was no stress, not like the other times. It was truly so very easy, it was child's play. There was nothing to do, other than say the right words at the right time. Everything else was designed to just follow its own course without any input or responsibility on his part... Not unlike the weather used to, come to think of it. It was all so very lovely. He could even come to enjoy it, in time, like one might grow to enjoy a scalding hot bath, or even the reportedly fiery lakes of Hell.

The AR set was perfect, his contestants all played their parts admirably, there were no technical problems whatsoever, and the sequences summarising the highlights from the weekly live feeds fired off with military precision.

Other than double-checking that the chairs had been securely bolted to the floor this time around, he didn't have a care in the world—in either of them, in fact, the real one or the Augmented one. The contestants were going through their usual posturing and in-fighting, but Liam didn't let it get to him or break his rhythm.

He was resolved that even the Crossfire segment wouldn't get to him this time. Jill was up to bat, again. Sprawling in the seat of her works van as the urban smartgrid handled the actual driving, she ranted and cursed and swore and roared. She went on about politics, about how politicians were all such limp-dicks that they, the people, had to vote in clowns to do their work for them now. She went on about the economy, about how the real joke was that, for all their posturing about fighting corruption, the clowns didn't have any more of a clue about how things should work than the other bastards used to. She went on about the other vehicles on the road. She even went on about having to go on about everything. But first and foremost, she went on about the feed: its creators, its contestants, and, especially, its viewers.

People tended to enjoy that sort of abuse, especially when it came from a source so safely remote, and one whose existence could be turned on and off at will. In that respect, Suicide Jill had more than a smattering of the divine about her.

And, indeed, it seemed to be going down particularly well with the feeders. The first results from the composite feeder testing showed that, thanks in a large part to Jill, the show was maxing out attention levels from all socio-eco-demographics. The advertising brain time was ripe for the selling.

On cue, Jill's rant gently faded to deep blue—clinically proven to hold feeder's attention up to thirty-five percent better than the traditional black—to be violently replaced by a blaring announcement for Alimart, "Meals delivered piping hot to your door, three times a day, seven days a week. Please enquire about our special bachelor rates." Any poor, hungry soul who happened to touch the vidscreen at this point, or simply twitch their eye the wrong way if watching through AR relay, would be caught in the commercial web and would most probably not emerge before having contractually obliged themselves to a lifelong supply of reconstituted hash vaguely resembling traditional meals.

The advertisements then lapsed into a series of indistinguishable pushes for over-the-counter mood-altering drugs. Predictably, each promised more complete relief from reality than both the previous and the next, despite the well known fact that they were all owned, at the end of the myriad corporate labyrinths, by Khemtech Industries and were essentially the same synthetic oblivion in different coloured packaging. Liam's body seemed to be taking all of this in with its usual gaping idiocy, so much so that he nearly missed the next segment he needed to introduce during the break between advertisements.

"And now," boomed Liam's voice through implants, glasses, and podscreens around the world, "we've come to the moment we've all been waiting for. I know I certainly have."

He turned to grin at the contestants, before returning to the main podcam. "We're making history here tonight, folks. That's not an exagger-ation. For the first time, people from all around the world have been called upon to vote, together, in a single event. And boy, have you answered the call. Over the past week, no less than two-point-two billion individual women, men, and enbies have signed up and cast their vote, and the last votes are still coming in, since voting doesn't close until I say so, in a minute or two. But really though: more than two billion people."

Liam paused, nodding in a caricature of thought as he let the figure sink in a bit, for emphasis.

"That's damn impressive, folks. Whatever the outcome of the votes, we've done something incredible here, all together. It's almost as if people were just waiting for the possibility to come together and vote at a worldwide level."

A little alert flashed on Liam's AR display, warning him to get back onto the prepared script, and he gave himself a little shake.

"Well, there you have it, folks. You've followed the lives of our contestants for two whole weeks now, you've cast your votes over the past week, and it all boils down to now, the moment of truth."

Liam took a step back to stand amidst the contestants, while still facing the main podcam. Once he had reached his mark on the floor, he opened his arms wide.

"I'm going to ask our technical friends in the back to close off voting now. Don't worry if you haven't had a chance to vote yet, because we'll be opening up the next week of voting the very second that the results are tallied and we announce who you, the people, have decided to eliminate this week."

Liam made a show of raising a finger for silence as he looked away, as if listening to somebody speaking to him, presumably a god of some variety.

"The results are just coming in now, ladies and gentlemen, and—oh, deary me, it's a doozy. Juliette," Liam said, pausing for effect, "you've dodged a bullet there today, since you came in second with thirty-two percent of the elimination vote, in front of Spike with twenty-one percent—sorry, big guy. But with thirty-eight percent, it's clear: Ali Fourka, the people have decided. You're out."

Professor Fourka's live feed appeared in a floating window for all to see, but only for a moment. Liam thought it was a bit over-dramatic, but the image of his live feed fading to black before shutting down altogether was certainly an effective one.

Liam went over to the man and put a consoling arm around his shoulders. "Hey, look at it this way. People have decided you have the best life out of all of our contestants. That's a compliment, really, isn't it?"

Professor Fourka nodded. He did not seem fazed by the news of his elimination in the least—most likely since it was not actually news for anyone in the know. He simply asked if he could say a few words before exiting, a wish Liam was more than happy to grant him.

"As I take my leave of this program, I would like to deliver a word of warning. To the viewers, first and foremost: be wary. What you are being presented with as 'reality' programming is anything but. It is a product of entertainment. You all know this, of course, since you participate in it and in the illusion of reality it creates, and this is not really a danger in itself. The danger is when you forget it is just entertainment, however grounded in reality it may be, because at that point the illusion becomes the new reality. It shapes your view and expectations of the world, and it reduces your possibilities of acting upon the real world even further.

"To the producers, corporate backers, and the host of this show, a word of warning as well: such deliberate shaping of society's worldview is a double-edged sword. Since it defines the perception of reality, 'reality' entertainment is inevitably political in nature, in that it affects and reflects the life of the City, especially in the modern global City, with its various regional neighbourhoods and national blocks. Be wary of this inevitable political effect. Neglected or mismanaged, it can do us all great harm, and yourselves the first. Need I remind anyone how the first generation of reality show 'celebrities' came to invade the political sphere, heralding the final victory of celebrity over policy, transforming political parties into cults of personality, and leading directly to the abdication of decision-making to the Corporations?"

On that chilling note, Professor Fourka took a little half-bow and exited the stage. The Editor decided this was a good time for an energy-pumping jingle and a commercial break, which Liam welcomed like the first cool evening breeze on a scorching summer's day. He popped off the AR set for a quick hit of caffeine water, and stopped as he passed the Editor on his way back to the set for the wrap-up and transfer back over to the live feeds.

"Hey, Ed. Listen. I was wondering... do you think we should cancel the talk feeds and promotion week for Pr—I mean, for Ali Fourka? After that little speech tonight, I don't know if it's in our interests to give him even more of an audience." Liam was both disappointed and proud that he had managed to say "our interests" without even a quiver in his voice.

"Liam, my boy. Well done out there tonight, first of all. As for Ali Fourka, I wouldn't dream of cancelling his scheduled promotion run. Trust me, the interviewers we've lined up won't give a hoot about his political science claptrap. They'll pepper him with questions about Spike's big horn and the size of Jill's cleavage, which is what their audience wants to hear about." Ed waved an arm, for emphasis, as he spoke. "He'll have his final lap around the racecourse, and after the next Sunday feature, your friend Finn Oldman will become the new eliminated flavour of the week, sending Fourka back into ridiculed silence in his closet office at Birkbeck, where he will be the University authorities' problem, and not mine."

The Editor inflicted another one of those hated smiles upon Liam and gave him a gentle yet definite shove back onto the set, leaving him little-to-no time to process what he had just been told about the result of a vote that hadn't even opened yet.

"The commercials are nearly done, believe it or not, so get back out there. When you're done, come see me in my office so we can talk this over some more, and prepare for Oldman's elimination next week. Ta!"

35

It is amazing, Liam mused, how human beings are geared toward routine, which always settles in, even in the most extraordinary of circumstances.

Three weeks in, and Liam already thought of himself as an old hand at this live feed monitoring business. It was easy, really. He had long since given up worrying about having to intervene in a feed. It was clear the Editor and the higher-ups were happy to let the contestants go about their lives and put on any antics they felt like. It seemed that, as far as the feed was concerned, everything goes, including potentially disturbing events, like Jill's clean-up session last week—or even Professor Fourka's subversive classes and speeches.

Not only was it easy, but Liam had to admit he was growing more and more fascinated with these live feeds. At first, he hadn't wanted to touch the things with a laser pointer, and yet now, he caught himself popping into the live feeds to check up on his contestants, even outside of work hours when he was back home—including in bed and on the toilet, which he didn't find as disturbing as it perhaps should have been.

So it was with pleasure that he logged in to the live feed server that Tuesday, only to have any possibility of pleasure dashed as he saw that he was assigned to monitoring Finn Oldman today.

Liam's instinctive hatred of the man had only gotten deeper over the course of the show—and would have even without the chair incident, he was prompt to reassure himself. Oldman was human scum. There was no other way of putting it. A product of modern corporate world-society, certainly, in the same way that scum is the product of the stagnant waters of its pond. But scum, nonetheless. The man didn't have a moral bone in his body. And yet, he seemed to be taking to the show like a fish in water—or perhaps that should be an eel or something, thought Liam, before reminding himself there was such a thing as taking a metaphor too far.

Today, Oldman seemed to be playing hooky from work at the Health Services, which was a blessing in itself, since Liam didn't think he could have taken another day of watching Oldman violate medical confidentiality on an industrial basis and receive commendations for how efficient he was at declining treatment coverage.

Instead, he was strutting through an upscale commercial district, probably one of those new corporate complexes in Runnymede. But instead of stopping to look at the products on display in the shop windows, his attention seemed to be focused exclusively on the ladies walking around or sitting at café tables. Liam wasn't certain what Oldman was doing, but he had the feeling he wouldn't like it and his hand slipped back into its old position next to the big red live feed interruption button.

As he watched, the man scanned an indoor café terrace and locked eyes upon an attractive, copper-haired executive type sitting by herself, sipping a coffee and messing with something or another in her AR display.

Bold as a brass monkey with polar fleece undies, Oldman marched over to her table and sat straight down. She jumped and sputtered, but he made sure to speak up before she had a chance to start protesting.

"Smile, my dear."

From the sound of his voice, he was clearly doing likewise. "You are being broadcast live to every *Grass is Greener* viewer around the world."

By the look on the poor lady's face, she knew what *The Grass is Greener* was, and those magic words raced through her brain to collide with her mounting indignation at the man's behaviour, leaving her shocked and speechless in the aftermath, which Oldman took as an invitation to carry on.

"That's right, I'm Finn Oldman, one of the contestants in *The Grass is Greener*. I'm sure you've heard of our little program, with our twenty-four-hour live feed implants." He raised a hand to tap his temple, looking his target up and down in the process. "It opens all sort of possibilities, taking part in a big show like this one, you know. It won't last forever, of course, but even afterward, there are plenty of opportunities for... self-improvement, once you've become so well known. And I'd really like someone to share those opportunities with."

A look of horror crossed the silent woman's face as Finn finally delivered his prepared pick-up line.

"So, what do you say? Do you have celebrity in you? And if not, would you like some?"

The woman blurted out something inarticulate, and ran away so fast she knocked over her chair. Rising, Oldman went to pick it up.

"Ah, well, I guess she didn't have it in her after all. No worries, there are plenty more where that came from." Oldman swaggered on to another part of the shopping complex, leaving Liam with mounting horror at the realisation that the man was right, there most certainly were women out there who would be attracted to him simply due to the meagre sort of celebrity he had achieved through the show. Heck, after today's stunt, he would probably be getting propositions before the end of the day.

At least they had avoided the full-out sexual aggression scenario Liam had dreaded for a moment there, he consoled himself, taking his hand off the big red button once again.

36

Thursday brought another difficult live feed, but for entirely different reasons.

Azar Acquah had called in sick at work—a first according to the records the show had obtained—and was now dragging herself on foot all the way across town to the no-premium emergency walk-in clinic. It was pitiful to watch the woman, who was clearly in even worse shape than usual, haul herself through the filthy sidewalks of "Greater London," an expression which was growing more and more oxymoronic by the day.

Safely ensconced in the efficient and uncaring self-driving transport system, private vehicle owners and public transport users alike zoomed past, just as uncaring as their computer-regulated vehicles. In an age where getting worker A to worksite B as fast as possible was the only metric by which the transport system was judged, the rare pedestrians who were too poor to purchase a public transport pass—or get a job where one is provided for them—were at best an embarrassment, and usually regarded as a nuisance, a throwback to the time all those decades ago when the city was defined as a throng of people in the streets, as opposed to the efficient, faceless mechanical hive the current generation had grown up with.

Being a pedestrian in 2072 was an extreme sport. The urban smartgrid left little to no provision for walkers. There was no such thing as a crosswalk. Every kilometre or so, each major road would have the mandatory underground walkway that allowed pedestrians to cross to the other side—if they could find a path through the refuse, homeless people, and piles of human effluvia which were a hallmark of these tunnels, which doubled as impromptu homeless shelters since all public support had been withdrawn and the subway system had been "cleaned up" and militarised with corporate security forces.

Trying to cross the street itself was a high-risk proposition. Since the rules stated pedestrians weren't supposed to ever be on the street itself, smart cars were not programmed to register them, or stop if detected, any more than they would stop, and hold up the entire system, for a stray cat or dog. This was the main reason why cars no longer had front or rear windows: so passengers had an excuse to ignore any bumps they may feel during the ride, since they had no way of checking anyway.

Aged beyond her years, Azar was in no shape for any sort of death-defying street dash. They all watched as she slalomed her way down streets and through noxious tunnels, looking worse and worse with every step. Liam was concerned at her video angle, bent over like a top-heavy willow. She must really be feeling like crap, he thought—while repressing the guilty thought that at least the viewers, and himself, were spared having to look too closely at the dismal city surroundings, which not even a mother could love.

Like an outboard motor boat running out of fuel, the woman sputtered, shuddered, coughed, and then, inevitably, keeled over. As Liam watched in horror, her angle tipped even further and, her legs turning to unwieldy jelly, she slumped sideways against the blistered dome of a broadcast Pod—identical around the world, State-implemented as per World Court rulings, and found anywhere there was electricity. Azar wasn't moving, and didn't seem to have much to say—hardly riveting entertainment.

The thought reminded Liam of why he was watching in the first place, and he reflexively mashed the big red button, freezing the live upstream and alerting the Editor for immediate action, since the thirty-second live feed delay immediately started ticking away into nothing, taking with it any possibility of managing the situation without interrupting the feed.

The Editor's voice instantly rose out of the air next to him, without Liam having even had to accept the call. The background sounds were muffled, but it sounded like he was at some sort of gathering. A meeting, perhaps?

"Argyle, what happened?" His voice snapped like a bullwhip, setting Liam's every nerve on edge.

"Ah! Sir, it's Azar Acquah, sir."

"Yes, I can see that. What did she do?"

"She was having health issues, and now she's collapsed on her way to the medical clinic. Should we send a medical team, sir?"

The Editor let out an audible sigh, before resuming, all traces of tension gone from his voice. "I see. Just a moment, please, Liam."

Liam waited, and was surprised to see the live feed timer resume, without any input from him. The display in the corner of his admin feed told him there were only just over ten seconds left on the delay clock, but even as he watched, imperceptible micro-staggers of the feed started building it back up again, a few milliseconds at a time.

Azar still lay unmoving, eyes half shut and one gnarled black hand spread against the bottom of the Pod unit's gunmetal dome, when the Editor cleared his throat to announce his return to Liam.

"There we go, Liam. No harm done, "

Liam couldn't hold back the retort. "No harm done? Ed, she could be seriously hurt. She could be dying! We have a responsibility to do something."

"Now, now," scolded the Editor, his condescending voice feeding directly into Liam's skull through the small miracles of bone conduction and making a great impression of what he imagined the voice of a god might sound like. "There's no need to go around bandying words like 'responsibility.' Our sole responsibility is to do our jobs and make a great show, for the whole world to see."

"I'm not certain looking out through the eyes of an unconscious woman makes for a great show, Ed."

The Editor actually chuckled at this, making Liam feel sick. "I beg to differ. What you're looking at right now is precisely what we've been looking for all along on *The Grass is Greener*. Real life! Honest, chilling, riveting, and pure. Look at the viewer ratings, Liam. They don't lie. Word about this is spreading like wildfire. No show has ever let you look out live through a dying woman's eyes before."

"Dying? Ed, we can't just let her die!" Liam felt on the verge of tears, and was glad he didn't have live broadcast lenses fitted into his own eyes.

"Figure of speech, dear boy! Just a figure of speech. I'm certain Ms. Acquah will be perfectly all right."

Fate, ever a bastard, chose that very moment to prove the Editor right, as the view wobbled and Azar was turned over. She blinked and shook her head a little, then focused on the figure before her, a man in a cheap business suit, learning over her with an expression of concern.

"Ma'am, are you alright? Can I get you anything?" Some jaded part of Liam thought the question sounded a bit too mechanical, too rehearsed. Had the man actually been checking her to see if she were dead before lifting any valuables? Liam scolded himself, this time, as Azar came to her senses.

"No, thank you. No. I just had a bit of a dizzy spell, that's all. I was on my way to the walk-in clinic," she added, apologetic for some reason, as if she had offended the man somehow by falling unconscious on the sidewalk between his office and his bus stop.

"The one over in East Enfield? You were going to walk all that way?"

As she wobbled to her knees, Azar let out a choked cough, one she had clearly tried to hold back. "I couldn't seem to find my bus pass, so I didn't really have any choice."

The man didn't seem fooled and cut her off. "Let me help you, Ma'am." Azar must have looked as if, in what pride she still had, she were about to reject the offer, because he insisted. "Please."

Liam felt a wave a relief as Azar nodded and the man he helped her back to her feet.

"The bus stop isn't far," said the man, his tone reassuring. "That's where I was going anyway, and I'd be happy to buy you a pass to Enfield, and a return as well, if you'd accept it."

"That would be lovely. Really lovely," answered Azar, walking as best she could to keep up with him. "I can't thank you enough."

The fuzzy feeling percolating through Liam's mind was so unfamiliar that he almost didn't recognise it as renewed faith in humanity—at first, he thought it might be a stroke. Of course, the Editor soon broke the spell.

"Ha! A good Samaritan! What did I tell you, my boy? Real life, red in tooth and claw! That's how we make a good show, by Alan Sugar's ghost!" At this, the Editor actually cackled. "Let this serve as a lesson to you, Argyle. The red button is for real emergencies only! Like when a contestant is threatening to break the rules or attempt to sever the little window on life that we're offering the world. Not when someone falls over. Watch out for the feed itself, Liam, and let Nature sort out the rest. Are we clear?"

"As a dead man's agenda, sir."

The Editor was visibly thrown by the sudden morbid turn of Liam's thoughts, but seemed pleased enough. "Right. As long as we're clear. See you at the Mews tomorrow."

Gods, Liam needed a drink.

37

Back home, the tinkle of ice at the top of his second glass of gin whispered to Liam that he would probably enjoy a good, escapist fantasy read. Maybe something like Tolkien.

Liam didn't have the heart to start a re-read of *Lord of the Rings*, and he had never been able to read *The Hobbit*—the Dwarves' tasselled hats from the beginning of the book clashed too violently with the rough imagery forced upon him by the classic, action-packed films he had watched in his youth.

He just couldn't face fantasy anymore, not the kind of classic fantasy Tolkien, C. S. Lewis, or Ursula LeGuin would have been able to offer. Some mindless fantasy movie or game was another thing entirely. He could watch generic black and white characters smash swords into each other all day long, and if it had gratuitous sex and/or dragons, then all the better. But what he was still honest enough to call proper fantasy, the stuff that created a coherent other world and held it up as a mirror to our own, he hadn't been able to stomach for a while now. Real life was hard enough to deal with as it was, without trying to muster the energy to care about another reality entirely.

What he needed was an illusion world he could lose himself in, without having to think about it—and even more importantly, without having to feel or care about it.

How did everyone else manage it? Oh, right.

He poured himself a third drink and, for the first time in his adult life, did what he had always prided himself in not doing, what he had thought defined him as different from everybody else—he shut down his reading app and loaded up the mass-produced video entertainment network. Afraid he might second guess himself or lose his nerve, he stabbed at the series in the "Fantasy" category that had the highest viewer count and settled down into his moulded chair.

When, an hour later, he realised his bottle was empty and it was probably time to get to bed anyway, all he could remember of what he had watched was a blur of swords, the clank of armour, and splashes of blood.

Everything seemed to be accelerating around Liam, as if the Earth had gained rotational speed, in defiance of all natural law, and everything was somehow moving all the faster and more frenetically for it.

Another week down, another weekly elimination feature. The show seemed to pretty much run itself nowadays, like a hamster in its wheel. Liam refused to dwell too long on the comparison.

This was the best show yet, and not only because of the growing viewing figures. Though the voting wasn't finished yet, it was no secret that tonight would see the exit of Finn Oldman, which pleased Liam to no end. Oldman was quite the pain in the neck. Liam still had twinges from the chair incident, and he was itching for revenge. He didn't think the Editor would let him get actual revenge on the man—although perhaps he would have, had Liam asked, come to think of it. It would have made for an entertaining show. Shoot, too late to ask now, in any case.

Liam would have to settle for the satisfaction of seeing Oldman booted from the show and back into the Health Service office anonymity where he belonged.

Sure as broken New Year's resolutions, the votes came in resoundingly in favour of eliminating Oldman, with Juliette Binns and Spike Bighorn pulling up the rear—as it were—but with barely half the votes.

Liam considered whether he should be feeling guilty at taking so much pleasure in the man's elimination, but he told his conscience to stuff it, especially when he saw how Oldman was taking the news.

Far from being hurt or depressed, Oldman seemed to be treating his elimination like some reward, basking in being the centre of attention. Before Liam's astonished eyes, he even did a couple of victory laps around the set, before racing over to embrace what could only be his new partner—a bleached blonde woman with a chest so full of silicone it could have grouted an entire kitchen, with enough left over for a half bath. Who had let this woman into the Mews in the first place?

Oldman swung both her and her grouting—which seemed to have a mind of its own—around, and together they gave the cameras a cliché movie kiss. The weedy man grinned at the public at large.

"Sorry to leave you just when things are getting good," he said, "but a gentleman doesn't kiss and tell, or even broadcast. Argyle, be a pal and tell your people to shut off these lenses of mine now, there's a good fellow. Lynne and I have some catching up to do, if you know what I mean."

Liam sincerely wished he didn't, because then he wouldn't have to scrub away the mental image of that walking shit Finn Oldman and the stupidly grinning pile of chemicals next to him in the act, such as it may be. That a man like Oldman could have used his show, used Liam himself, to increase his social status and his reproductive desirability made Liam want to grab an axe and bust open the bottom of the gene pool, starting with Finn Oldman.

It was therefore with a sigh of relief that he finally saw the back of the man and announced that voting was once again reset and renewed, until next week's feature show.

After a hasty exit from the set, Liam sat in the bar-equipped comfort of his new car and tried to convince himself that, with a major pain in his backside gone, things could only get better from here on in. He very nearly succeeded, as well.

38

Surely there must be a law somewhere against shit hitting the fan before eight a.m. on a Monday, right?

He wasn't even supposed to be monitoring Juliette Binns today in the first place. His roster had him with Usnavi Musibay, a cakewalk and the perfect thing after a rough Sunday evening show and an even rougher Sunday-to-Monday morning trying to drink the memory of it into submission.

But then Usnavi, bless his soul, had to go and catch a fever or something, leaving him bedridden and dry heaving, his stomach contents long gone. Liam had tried to argue to Ed that there was plenty of merit in sticking with Usnavi, that there was important social commentary in the unwanted side effects of the so-called "ninja virus" and, especially, that there was no need to reassign Liam to another feed. Ed had replied in no uncertain terms that social commentary could go take a flying leap and would happen whether Liam was monitoring or not, and so now he was stuck watching Juliette Binns in her bathroom, trying to make herself look human again, after a long night shift.

Even in his foul mood, Liam had to sympathise. Being called out for a series of night-time emergency AR repair interventions, especially just after the stress of a big weekly elimination show, really sucked a big one.

And so Liam sat, watching Juliette look at herself in her bathroom mirror and go about her morning rituals. Riveting stuff.

Still in a huff, he walked over to the caffeine water distributor and concentrated on pouring himself a cup without spilling it everywhere. It took all of fifteen seconds, but it was long enough for Juliette to leave the mirror, make her way over to her affordable apartment's excuse for a toilet cubicle, and stop.

Liam sipped at his cup and watched as Juliette stared at the toilet, as if indecisive about something. *Come on, girl,* he thought. *You've either got to go, or you don't.*

But Liam was as misguided as he was uncharitable. Juliette seemed to steel herself up for something, and, just as she strode forward, the screen in Liam's AR display went black.

In a world with a more dramatic turn of mind, this would have been the perfect opportunity for Liam to perform the traditional "spit take." But this wasn't, and so he didn't, contenting himself with another befuddled sip of his energy drink while he waited for what he assumed was just some small technical glitch to sort itself out, as such things usually did in his experience.

And yet, even to Liam's untrained lenses, this seemed odd. Juliette's AR interface was clearly still working and broadcasting, since he could see her display, with its start menu, time, shop, and program tabs.

Furthermore, he could still hear the watery sounds and muffled bangs from next door, which were the fitting soundtrack of any cheap apartment bathroom. Everything was still on and working. Whatever had happened, it was only affecting the visual feed. Almost as if—

The feed interruption alert flashed in his view, bathing his whole display in a lurid red. He looked over to the button, which remained resolutely un(im)pressed. A remote activation?

The Editor's voice pounced upon his consciousness again, as uninvited as a cougar at a stag party.

"Argyle!" boomed his voice, out of thin air. "Where are you? Why didn't you interrupt the Binns feed?"

"I—I was just looking into the malfunction, sir, and—"

"A malfunction, is it, Argyle? A human malfunction, then. Our Ms. Binns thinks she can break her contract and keep her eyes shut when she wants a bit of privacy. A bit of alone time. After signing on for *The Grass is Greener*! The cheek!"

Liam wondered, for a moment, whether he was referring to anatomy or attitude, but wisely decided not to raise the question at the present time. "I see," he lied instead. "The clock is ticking, Ed, and we'll soon be out of feed delay buffer. What can we do?"

Liam's question was meant to be rhetorical, but the Editor clearly took it as a challenge. "You're right, time is wasting. I'll show you what we do," he seemed to threaten.

As he finished the sentence, a bright red system error message flashed against the eyelid darkness of Juliette Binns's feed. However, as Juliette was qualified to tell, this was no classic registry error or nagging alert to restart the system. This message had teeth.

"User JBINNS: You are in breach of contract with THE GRASS IS GREENER, Section 5.4.9 entitled 'WILLFUL RESISTENCE.' You will cease breach of contract within TEN seconds or punitive action will be implemented as per Section 14.2.11 subclause 3 entitled 'ESCALATING ELECTRIC SHOCKS.' This is your only warning."

Scary stuff, thought Liam, but a pretty clever trick nonetheless. Hadn't he read about an early sociology experiment that went something like that?

The seconds passed, and Juliette seemed to be calling the Editor's bluff. Her eyes seemed even more tightly shut than before, if anything.

"Well, Ed, it doesn't seem to have worked. Nice try though. What do we do next, go see her or something?"

"What you do next," intoned the Editor, with heavy emphasis on the *you*, "is march straight back to your post and flip open the pad with the feed interruption button."

Liam was there faster than you can say "Pavlovian," and sure enough, the dramatic big red button was actually a big red flap, covering a simple touch pad bearing the label "Electrics."

"Wait... You mean that we can actually do that?" asked Liam, with equal measures of revulsion and curiosity.

"Argyle, do you know how easy it is to administer pain when you've got high-powered equipment implants inside one of the most vulnerable parts of the human body? Well, you will do. We're nearly out of buffer, Argyle. Press the button."

Liam fought with a veritable menagerie of conflicting impulses inside him and tried to stall while he worked it all out.

"This button, right here?"

"Now, Argyle!" The Editor's voice ran out of his implants, through his bones, and straight down his nerves to his fingers, seeming to bypass his brain altogether. He pressed the button.

On Juliette's feed in a corner of his display, the effect was instantaneous. The feed seemed to twitch along with the electric convulsions of her eyes, and the little scream of literal shock Juliette let out confirmed that the button did indeed work. Her eyes flung open, and as they did so, the system message faded away—though for some reason, overexposure perhaps, the word "ESCALATING" stayed around a good couple of seconds after the rest had disappeared.

"Boom!" yelled the Editor into Liam's cartilage, yet again. "And the feed resumes, with a whole three seconds to spare on the buffer clock." He cackled. "At this rate, you'll be running this whole show soon, Argyle, and I'll be keeping in touch from Corporate Paradise Mars!"

Oh, gods, thought Liam. *An upwardly-mobile corporate beast.*

"The main thing," continued the Editor, oblivious to Liam's horror, "is to keep a constant watch on her and, especially, make sure the feeders don't find out about Ms. Binns's little act of rebellion."

The Editor paused, pensive.

"For now, at least," he added, and Liam shuddered as he imagined the kind of grin which was undoubtedly splayed across the Editor's features at that very second.

"In any case, don't worry about it, Liam," he carried on. "Juliette is the given favourite for elimination in this week's early polls anyway, so you won't have to keep up your solemn vigil for too long."

39

Misery loves company, and when company isn't readily available, it will often settle for the next best thing, which is, of course, either reality television or pornography. Spike Bighorn qualified as both—which wasn't as rare as it probably should have been.

As such, Liam probably shouldn't have been surprised to run into a new problem to handle on his first break from a week of solid Juliette-monitoring. The weekly elimination feature couldn't come fast enough.

To his augmented eye, it seemed like Spike was going through the regular motions—mainly different forms of thrusting and bucking as he penetrated and was penetrated in turn by his various mechanical Erobot co-stars. It was certainly more entertaining than watching Juliette's terrified toiletries, or Usnavi, who had spent most of the week bedridden, with his immune system going haywire.

Still, super-realistic execution or not, the sexual act soon acquired a boredom all its own, especially when performed with such cold engineering, with the artificial stop and go of professional cinematic production, and without any of the musical and post-production trappings[i] that were such a large part of what made the final pornographic product so titillating.

There was very little risk of any *Grass is Greener* rule-breaking

---

[i] "Ornamental cloth for a horse." No, really.

here, especially from Spike, who was as comfortable in the limelight as a bug in a whorehouse rug. Liam's attention was therefore partial at best when a scream, mingling human pain with mechanical distress, rang over the feed and through his head.

Spike's field of view was tilted at a strange angle, as if he were bent backwards, and to the side. Whatever was torturing the man, it seemed to involve his nether regions, and Liam was thankful, for once, that the feed's field of view was limited in scope.

"Cut!" came the bellow from the lady running the show, and who would probably have insisted on being called director. The screw-bots froze in positions each more ridiculous than the next, leaving Spike impaled and helpless on a mechanical schlong.

The bright advertisements covering Spike's android partners took on a macabre tone as Liam watched the man struggle and yell out in pain, trying to extricate himself from the—somewhat ironic—spike he was stuck upon, to no avail[1]. While this was unfortunate for Spike, there was clearly no rule-breaking going on here, and so Liam decided to pass the time in speculation about what had gone wrong. Surely this wasn't just another rip or tear, however unspeakable. A seasoned professional like Spike Bighorn could soon have gritted his teeth and pulled it off—or out, as the case were—as he had many's a time before.

This must be something altogether worse, which left two options. Either it wasn't just a rip or tear but an actual snag on something vitally important within Spike's own inner mechanics, which was terrifying and would probably be an issue for the feed, or else some sort of muscular problem was stopping Spike from making a rear-guard retreat.

The director seemed to have come to the same conclusions.

"Oh, alright then," Liam heard her mutter, before she bellowed "Cut!" again, this time gesturing at a set technician who eventually caught on and scampered off-camera and returned, after a few bangs,

---

[1] "To have worth"

clangs, and choice swear words, with a hand-held rotary saw. He moved into position behind Spike, making Liam nervous even though he was a continent and an ocean away.

"Don't worry, now," said the man, sounding nearly as nervous as Liam felt. "This won't hurt a bit," he added in tones suggesting he was mostly trying to reassure himself, and failing miserably.

"Just make it quick," Spike muttered through gritted teeth, and soon the whine of the power saw sent chills down the spines of everyone involved.

The whine changed to the shriek of tortured alloys and the feed's view started shaking and shuddering, presumably along with Spike. It was a strange experience. Hopefully, it was just the impact of the saw cutting through the offending mecha-member, but the saw could also just as well be slicing through the base of Spike's spine at that very moment, and neither Liam nor any of the other viewers would have any idea, unless some screaming started.

It served as a cold reminder that, however intimate, however immersed in the skull of the contestants he might feel, it remained just a gimmick. It was limited, nothing more than a glorified parlour trick. Would technology ever be able to fully immerse one person in another's experience of the world? Maybe these new synaptic interfaces the tradeshows kept harping on about, but even then— wouldn't that just be a better camera, letting you feel, smell, and taste, instead of just see and hear, but without giving the slightest real inkling of what it was to be the person in the recording, with their own experiences, outlook on life, and beliefs? He didn't know, and wasn't sure he ever would—but at least it made a good distraction from the terrifying saw-noise, which sounded like it was right behind him, and which, at long last, cut out.

The same agency worker was clearly on both technical support and medical duty, since he put away the smoking saw and reached for a first aid kit. Still wracked with pain, Spike managed to turn a bit and watched as the improvised medic withdrew a scary-looking set of clamps from the kit and took position by Spike's afflicted bottom.

"There's just this bit that stayed inside to get rid of," the techie said, apologetic. "One last blow for the team, right?"

Spike started to reply, probably to tell him just where he could stick his blow for the team, but was interrupted by further spasms of pain when the techie shoved in the clamps and found a good position, before ripping out the larger-than-life compu-cock end. Liam offered a silent wince of male sympathy, both for Spike and the mutilated manbot.

Spike fell into a writhing heap onto the floor, and the medic placed the excessively hard-ware into a secure toolkit before pulling out two nanite syringes, one labelled as painkillers and the other for medical diagnostics.

The first killed all of Spike's pain receptors, bringing a halt to the shudders of the feed and the motion sickness it undoubtedly induced in viewers all around the world. As the techie applied the diagnostic nanites to Spike's bottom and waited for the results to come in over his AR display, Spike was able to piece back together the understandably scattered threads of his mental cloth.

"You know," he said, with a croak in his voice entirely unlike anything Hollywood has taught the world a frog is supposed to sound like, "this is probably where, in one of the more story-driven classic pornos, I would be cracking a joke about how I usually like to be on first name basis before we start using the clamps."

He pulled himself up into a sitting position and turned to face the techie, who had a far-off look as he scanned the medical diagnostics coming in.

"Of course, these days, there's no such thing as first name basis anymore. Or rather, everyone's first name is public property, on display in the AR profile along with everything else. So, I suppose you could say everyone is on first name basis now, in a way. But I'm not certain it actually means anything anymore..."

Spike shook himself. "Listen to me ramble. You must have given me some good stuff there, doc. So, tell me... Greg. What's the damage?"

While agency placement training covered basic first aid technician basics, along with cleaning, catering, electrical maintenance, software debugging, and all of the other myriad tasks expected of the modern outsourced wage slave on his or her zero-hour, zero-job security contract, bedside manner had, sadly, not been considered a necessary skill.

"Whoa," said the young man, who in another, kinder lifetime would have probably been known as Greg the Surfer Guy. "I've never seen reading like this before. Is Tetanus even still a thing? Man, I've got to look this one up."

Spike rose in careful steps, like a ziggurat, and stood waiting in palpable dread for the medical encyclopaedia's verdict. The studio warehouse was strangely silent all of a sudden, as everyone other than Spike, Greg, and the Erobots had long since found an excuse to disappear, proving once again that the risk of legal responsibility for a cock-up—literally, in this case—is far more effective at clearing any given area than a mere bomb threat or fire alarm. This psycho-sociological breakthrough had revolutionised the security industry over the past ten years, with all previous sirens and alarms, which only made people waste time standing around debating whether this was just a drill or something, now being replaced by stern voices demanding to know who had knocked a hole in the window. Even in windowless office spaces, evacuation response times were at an all-time low.

"Well," said Greg the Agency Dogsbody, finally making his way through the medical articles thrust at him by the diagnostics system. "The good news is that it's curable. That's about it for the good news. As for the rest, I've never seen an infection spread this far before it gets picked up by a DNA sensor. Come on, man, I'll help walk you to a medicar."

Greg moved over to offer Spike an arm on their way out of the building, which he shook off with a small wave of the hand.

"It's all over your muscles," carried on Greg, making conversation as they made their slow, aching way toward the door. "No wonder you were in such pain. It's a surprise you could move at all. For the infection to take root that deeply, it can't have been introduced at skin-level. You'd have to get it from something penetrating really dee—"

Spike was completely oblivious, shuffling along as best he could, with the memory of muscle cramps hiding behind the painkilling nanite haze like a teenage Facebook conversation—never quite erased. Liam, however, was very curious as to why the Agency guy had stopped mid-sentence, or, more accurately, he was very curious if his suspicions on the matter were right—which they were.

Greg let out a nervous chuckle as they reached the main doors. "So, it seems like we won't need to call a medicar in after all. Corporate tells me it's sent its own medical staffers to pick you up. I guess it's your lucky day."

The doors opened, letting in a trio of interchangeable men with smiles straight out of a dental nano-reconstruction advert and white coats labelling them as doctors, whatever their actual qualifications may have been—this was still Hollywood, after all.

"Mister Bighorn, and not a moment too soon. Look at how tired he looks, David," said the first in line, grabbing Spike by the arm.

"Right you are, Josh," replied the second in line, in tones so identical the men might as well have been joined at the larynx. "Casebook overexertion if I've ever seen it. Let's get him hooked up to some solution." He took Spike's other arm, and together they combined physical force and power of authority to usher him out of the building and into the bracing urban smog.

"Right then," Greg called out from somewhere behind Spike. "Hope you get better. I'm going for a caff."

The door shut behind them and cut off any other comments.

Soon, plunked into a seat of moulded white nano-gel, with the best liquid oblivion medical science had to offer pumping through his impressive veins, Spike was so far beyond caring he could probably see it coming back around in front of him again.

Liam, however, had pointed questions, and he knew just who to point them at.

40

"Did I do something wrong?" demanded Liam, barging into the Editor's office with as much anger as he could muster.

The bastard never even bothered to look away from his desk display. "Argyle, just the chap, do take a seat. I'll be with you in a moment."

Liam resolved to make a point and remain standing, but his heart wasn't really in it anymore. Anyway, he couldn't even tell whether the Editor was aware of his small act of defiance and just pretending to ignore it, or if he was really so engrossed in whatever interface he was in that he really had no idea. Liam's resolve soon melted in the face of social awkwardness, and he decided to cut his losses and sit down as he'd been asked.

Coincidence or not, the Editor immediately surfaced out of whatever augmented system he had been obsessed with, and smile at Liam. "There we go, sorry for all of that. Now, you were saying?"

Liam tried to recover some of his anger, but suspected the best he could manage now was to blush, or perhaps look like he had a bad attack of wind. He ploughed on regardless. "I was asking whether I had done something wrong, not interrupting the Bighorn feed when he had his muscle spasm attack. That was your order to send in the medical team, right?"

Liam had been prepared for a shouting match, for accusations, for lies. The Editor's easy-going laughter disarmed him completely. "Liam, dear boy, you performed exactly as expected, and as needed. Have no fear. Have you seen last week's ratings? As far as I am concerned, you can do no wrong."

He smiled again, before adding, almost as an afterthought, "Of course, you are correct, as well. I called in the local office's medical response team to do a bit of damage control, but that was through no fault of yours. This called for something a bit subtler than the big red feed interruption button."

Ed the Editor waved his fingers in a passing imitation of Sir Alec Guinness's classic bout of Force-enhanced civil disobedience, and a medical display popped into Liam's AR display. Pulsing in real-time, it showed what Liam just about recognised as a spinal column and back muscles, lit up like a corporate Holiday Tree which wouldn't dream about excluding a single cash-bearing consumer over something as petty as religion. Reading the legend, Liam noted that the seething red blotches covering the display were sites of bacterial infection.

"Liam Argyle, this is Clostridium tetani. Clostridium, this is Liam Argyle." The Editor couldn't help but laugh at his own little joke. "I can't blame you if you don't recognise it, Liam. The poor thing has seen better days. You can't get within two meters of a rusty nail anymore without your safety interface blaring at you, and monitor nanos will detect and treat any Tetanus infection long before it actually has an effect."

The Editor went very serious and fixed Liam with a concrete gaze.

"Do you know where the name 'Clostridium' comes from, Argyle? Let me tell you. It comes directly from the ancient Greek term for the threads of fate, the spindle from which all of our lives are woven." He paused, presumably to let his big flourish sink in.

As he waited for the Editor to continue and get to the point, if there were one, Liam realised he really needed to go to the bathroom.

"That is what we are looking at here, Liam, and sadly, Clostridium has lived up to its name and sealed poor Spike Bighorn's fate, at least as far as the feed is concerned."

Liam perked up at this. More manipulation of the feed. At least he was on familiar ground again. "Spike? But he's so popular," he said, surprised at how tired his own voice sounded. "Anyway, I thought Juliette Binns was up for elimination this week."

"A mere reprieve, certainly," replied the Editor. "Intelligence is adaptation to changing circumstances, Argyle, and in this matter, our course is clear. A Tetanus infection like this one will take weeks, maybe months, to clear up, and we can't let the feeders realise Mr. Bighorn could only have gotten such a bad case from a poorly maintained Erobot phallus."

The Editor sighed and made another wave through the air, almost reluctantly. A shiny, animated, and surprisingly-graphic advert for what could only be an Erobot appeared beside the live medical display. Liam was surprised, then slightly embarrassed, at recognising the Erobot in question from some of Spike's pornos. It was an exact replica.

"This is classified material, Argyle, and you weren't to know, but a RedCorp subsidiary owns these little beauties and has a major public launch campaign planned for next quarter. Now that Erobots are accepted as the norm in pornography, it is time to take it to the next level and give the discerning consumer the chance to make the most of that yearly bonus and purchase his or her own perfect copy of a favourite porn star, fresh and ready for use, straight out of the box. Plug and play, if you will.

"Of course, we cannot have rumours—however true they may be—spreading about catching Tetanus or a whole slew of new and exotic STDs from a penetrating robo-cock, now can we?"

Liam sat in silence, before realising that the Editor actually seemed to be waiting for an answer.

"Err—I should think not," he eventually stammered.

"Good man, I knew you would understand," said the Editor with a nod. "So I'll be counting on you to downplay the whole Juliette Binns 'thing' during the weekly show and highlight instead how Spike Bighorn has been living it up all week in privileged Corporate comfort. Almost as if he had already won his ticket to Paradise Mars!"

Liam wasn't certain, but was that a bit of froth he had seen at the corner of the Editor's mouth there, for a second? The man was quick to wipe his mouth with his fingers, disguising it as a pensive pose, before carrying on.

"Yes, we will make certain that you have plenty of material to use. Just a simple pulled muscle and general tiredness, and Mr. Spike Bighorn thinks he can lord it over everyone else. We'll have the public hating him in no time. They're all rather jealous of him in the first place, anyway, for some bizarre reason."

"I blame the parents, myself, sir," Liam replied. He felt like he needed to contribute something, and that usually worked in his experience with people who sounded like they had gone mad.

"Indeed," said Ed the Editor, eyeing Liam like an organ grinder who has just been handed a tax return by his monkey. "Well, see to it then, Argyle, and keep the Binns situation under control as well, will you? Increase the shock power a bit further, if you have to. Ms. Lee tells me that has been working well for her."

41

Over three billion viewers. A three with nine zeroes behind it. How could a single one of them be fooled by the skin-thin façade of happiness coated over the faces of his tortured and disturbed contestants, as they sat lined up in front of the Augmented global firing squad for yet another weekly feature? If all three billion viewers were fooled by this, they might as well all be zeroes.

At least Usnavi had made it out of his sickbed and over to the studio for the weekly feature. The Editor had told them all how vital it was—by contrast, it put the final nail in the virtual coffin of Spike Bighorn. There was poor Usnavi, everyone's little brother, soldiering on, while Mr. Bigshot Spike was, in all appearances and official soundbites, too tired out from screwing for a living and too whacked-out on designer drugs in a RedCorp medical haven to even bother showing up.

It was almost as if he thought he had already won the whole show or something. As if he were already living the corporate dream in the effortless bliss and chemical comforts that Paradise Mars held for the elite of the elite. And, of course, for the one least fortunate soul in all the rest of the world, courtesy of *The Grass is Greener*.

That was the Editor's favourite spin on Spike's colorectal misfortune, and Liam had to admit it seemed to be working. Envy and jealousy were powerful motivators.

Sitting next to ailing Usnavi, Juliette Binns somehow looked the worst off of the lot. Her eyes were Sarlacc pits, and her haunted gaze seemed to follow you around the room, like some cheesy Halloween rip-off of the Mona Lisa. Liam had to keep repeating to himself that it was all necessary, and for her own good really. She had agreed to let the show do whatever was necessary to protect itself when signing on to the show, after all, and it was only temporary—she would be eliminated soon enough. Liam was grateful she was at least keeping up appearances and chattering on, more so than usual, if anything. Her anxiety was obvious, however, and Liam winced a little every time she jumped in her seat, at the slightest noise or provocation.

Further down the line, Brad sat at smug attention, lord of all he surveyed—at least in his own mind. Jill lounged in her seat, which was impressive in itself, since these clinical, corporate chairs were designed specifically to be as uncomfortable and relaxation-proof as possible. The faint smile on her lips seemed to tell the world that she knew what was really going on here, and Liam wondered how much of that was still true, at this point, and how much was just posturing.

Sandwiched between the two of them, Azar Acquah managed to offer a brave face to the viewers, but she looked nearly as worse for wear as Juliette. She had recovered well after her day off, along with a few days of cheap and moderately effective antibiotics prescribed by the walk-in clinic on the off-chance her inflection wasn't entirely resistant. Luckily, she had won that particular evolutionary lottery and had been back at work the very next day, prodding away at the appliances, furnishings, and closet contents of the rich in order to make them "dumber" than their costs and aesthetics already made them.

Liam was worried about her, though. He had been monitoring her, on his own time over the past couple of days, and she had none of the energy she used to put into her work, her bearing, her life as a whole. In everyone's eyes, and in the show's endless marketing and spin-off commentary feeds, she was still the embodiment of bravery and positivity in adversity, especially since the previous week's "Good Samaritan" incident. But up close, Liam just didn't feel it anymore, or at least not as strongly. Her general happiness with her lot in life, which had always been so infectious, now felt faded, distant—like the signals from a deep space probe, speaking slower and slower until it loses the sun's energy altogether.

Liam was vaguely aware of going through the motions of his prepared speech regarding the unfortunate elimination of everyone's favourite porn star, and how sad it was that he couldn't make it to be with them all in person. Mostly, however, he couldn't stop looking over to the contestants. The expected reactions played over their faces like notes from a well-tuned piano—neither Juliette's poorly-concealed horror at not having been eliminated this week nor Jill's blatant contempt for the whole process were any kind of surprise, and that wasn't what kept snagging Liam's attention.

No, it was the physical image of the five people before him that kept him glancing back again and again, almost as if he needed to keep checking that he had seen it right the previous time. Just five of them, lined up in front of the world. Was this really all that was left? Five lives, supposedly the worst the world had to offer. Five contestants remaining, and what had he done for them, for any of them, since the beginning of the show?

The show came to a close, and the voiceless crowd from around the world cheered Liam on, the roar deafening inside his brainpan. Liam was grateful Mary hadn't found the bottle of Sipsmith V.J.O.P. gin he had stashed behind the bathroom garbage bin—or, if she had, had left it there out of pity for Liam. Neat gin was basically just a martini without the fancy glass, right? *Right*, he reassured himself, as he took another swig from the already half-empty bottle.

42

"Good news, Liam," petite Norma Lee somehow managed to boom into his ear, waking him up from the little eye-rest he was having in front of his display at some ungodly hour the next morning.

She had the good tact to pretend not to notice, and carried on. "Looks like we won't need to keep increasing the shock power on poor Juliette Binns. Not that I minded it all that much, truth be told, but it's probably a good thing. I don't think I could have increased the settings that much more without risking some sort of visible damage."

Liam tried to shake the alcohol out of his thought processes, and just about managed to keep up with what his nominal co-worker was saying.

"I asked the Ed if we were going to need to bring Binns in for an 'upgrade' on her implant power cells, and he told me to stop the contractual discipline measures altogether." She let out a dramatic and entirely fake sigh. "All of a sudden, keeping her within the show's rules just isn't important anymore. I don't know. Makes me wonder why the hell I've been putting in so many overtime hours over the past week that the calluses on my shock-button finger have started growing their own calluses."

Liam's sodden brain was too busy considering what the hell

"hungover[i]" was supposed to mean, anyway—hung over what, exactly?—to apply basic self-preservation filters, and, in a rare moment of honesty, Liam spoke the first thought that came to mind. "That's horrible."

Norma's self-preservation filters, on the contrary, were fully armed and operational, and she shrugged, dismissing the whole question as she stomped back out of Liam's personal space. "Eh, it's nothing a good manicure session won't sort out. Nice of you to say, though. I just wanted to let you know because I saw you're on duty with Juliette this afternoon. Toodles!"

Liam's rational mind knew his door was just a bit of cheap particle board—a.k.a. "engineered solids" because it sounds more expensive—but his senses told his rational mind to take a leap off any convenient salient point as the door slammed shut with portcullis force behind Norma Lee.

Understandably, Liam didn't feel quite up to another etymological punching bag session with the Editor, so he decided to employ the tried-and-true better part of professional valour, also known as email.

From: Argyle, Liam <agent44269@entertainment.redmail.com>
Sent: 18-04-72 9:43 AM
To: agent2766@entertainment.redmail.com
Subject: J Binns measures

Hi Ed,

Norma has just been in to tell me we're ending the behaviour measures regarding Juliette Binns? Is this correct? What happened?

Best regards,
Liam

---

[i] "A thing left over from before," first recorded usage in 1894. It only took eight years for it to become almost exclusively reserved for, well, hangovers.

Liam was keen to keep things on a friendly tone, using the Editor's proper name to show how at ease he was with the whole thing. However, a savvier swimmer of bureaucratic waters would have known that putting anything in an email, with a written trace, can and often is interpreted as an attempt to build a case of some sort: a declaration of war.

From: agent2766@entertainment.redmail.com
Sent: 18-04-72 9:51 AM
To: Argyle, Liam <agent44269@entertainment.redmail.com>
Subject: Your enquiry

Dear Agent 44269,

There seems to be some confusion, as I have no idea what you are referring to. In my editorial capacity for 'The Grass is Greener,' I may not be privy to all choices made by the production team and yourself in the management of each individual contestant, which I am of course not involved with directly. I trust that you will inform me of any actions your team and yourself may have taken if these have any bearing on my editorial work.

Regarding Ms. Binns, I have received reports today, coming from various entertainment news feeds and 'fan' sites, that she seems to be unsatisfied with the privacy intrusions inherent in her participation in the show. In the absence of any possibility of withdrawing from the show, she seems to have used her professional skills to obtain raw internal footage of alleged instances of behavioural conditioning through electrical shocks, which she then sent on for public broadcast.

Are these the measures you are referring to? If so, you were perhaps in your legal rights with regards to Ms. Binns' contract to enforce her obligations toward the show. However, the moral side of things must also be carefully weighed in such situations. Of course, I know nothing of these matters, and it may all merely be hearsay.

In any case, I must insist, for the good of the show and its image, that any such measures, should they have ever existed, cease immediately. It is, perhaps, best to let the public judge the merits or flaws of any grievances Ms. Binns may have. That is, after all, the whole purpose of 'The Grass is Greener,' is it not?

Please do not hesitate to share any relevant information with me, I am more than happy to provide any assistance I can in this matter.

Kind regards,
Agent 2766

The Editor's response, put together with astounding speed, dinged as it arrived and hung in Augmented glory before Liam's eyes long after he had finished reading it. He sat stunned, as the lives he was supposed to be monitoring flitted by, uncontrolled, in his Augmented sight. It wasn't so much the stab in the back from the Editor—he had never trusted the little man half as far as he knew he could throw him, and often wished he could. His shock was more profound, like that of a man who hears the creak of thin ice beneath his feet, but who didn't even know he was on ice in the first place. Let alone what toothsome monsters lay waiting in the depths. His position was suddenly threatened, and up until then, he had had no idea it could be threatened.

He was still sitting stunned when the Editor opened his door, with the well-fed air he always had after a lunch time spent schmoozing up other corporate bigwigs in some Michelin-starred crab bucket downtown. The gods know it wasn't what passed for food in those places that could satisfy a man; it must be something in the air, letting them feed off the social status which fell like marine snow, in a constant flow of filth.

Luckily, it was very hard to tell the difference between a Liam hard at work monitoring AR feeds and a Liam merely sitting in his chair, gazing off into nothingness and realising how tenuous his position in life truly was. Since the Editor clearly cared very little either way, he carried on regardless.

"Argyle, hard at work as ever, I see," he said, in the same tones one might use to comment upon how wet the rain is today, or how dismally the local sports team of choice was performing. "I just wanted to make certain there were no hard feelings about those messages earlier. I have to respect a man who tries to stand up for himself, but there have to be boundaries, you know."

The Editor was grinning at him, one toady to another from across the corporate lily pond, and yet all Liam could see was the fresh gravy stain on the man's lapel, still moist and shimmering as it soaked into the ostensibly expensive nano-engineered threads.

"Well, that's all behind us now, anyway," said the Editor, a bit unsettled at the lack of any response for him to edit into his own narrative. "There's no harm done, in any case. It's not like your team did anything wrong, of course. We just couldn't keep up the pretence, not after Binns managed to smuggle those raw videos out."

The Editor chuckled, startling Liam out of his stupor and making him chuckle as well, out of sheer nervousness. The Editor needed no further encouragement to label Liam as "one of us" and speak to him accordingly.

"And why would we bother with sanctions, when the public will do the work for us? Have you seen the latest feed from Entertainment Hourly?"

Liam tested out a noncommittal smile, which seemed to work well enough. "As you say, Ed, I've been hard at work."

"Oh, you have to see this, it's absolutely delicious." At a flick of the editor's fingers, the feed popped into Liam's Augmented view. The worrying, predatory look on the Editor's face was hidden behind a free-floating window showing the public's reaction to the Binns video leaks, with running commentary. Literal running commentary, that is, with an almost supernaturally fit entertainment "news" person of indeterminate gender sprinting through a crowded subway station with a giant Augmented sign over their head inviting one and all to share their opinions with the world regarding *The Grass is Greener*. Just a sentence or two, before the reporter bolted off to the next "person in the street" who flagged in their AR display that they wanted their fifteen seconds of fame as well. There were many takers, and there were no half-measures in their opinions—the show didn't give them time to have any opinion more complex than black or white, anyway.

"What is Juliette complaining about, anyway? Privacy? Who can afford privacy these days, anyway?" asked a salaryman in a run-down business suit.

The camera-person bobbed away and ran over to the next opinion-monger, a girl who didn't look old enough to vote, with a baby strapped to her chest and a hazy look in her eyes. "It's bad, of course, that she's suffering so much from being in the show. But it's also, I don't know, a bit fun to watch. You know what I mean?"

This feed wasn't the sort that sat around answering rhetorical questions, and so zipped off to a group of stooped women, sitting around a tiny café-style table, in full-body burqas. They laughed as the feed arrived, egging one another on to speak.

"You get what you ask for sometimes, you know," chittered the voice under the snazzy violet-coloured number on the left. "She should not have joined the show if she did not want to be there."

"It is very entertaining though. She has the most inventive ways of showing how much she hates being on the show," added one of her friends, from under a more drab, grey-brown coloured veil.

"Don't be so mean!" said one of their friends, her laughter turning the reprimand into a joke. "It's not her fault! She needs something to make herself look worse off than the others, after all! She was nearly eliminated last week!"

The show's view left this cluster behind it, their laughter fading away as it moved on in search of fresh victims. The Editor clearly felt that his point had been made, since he shut the window in Liam's display with another half-flick of his hand. Sure enough, the look on the man's face was still the kind that would send a shark rushing back to its resting place, having just remembered it left the cuttlefish boiling.

"Impressive," said Liam, using another of his noncommittal favourites, which seemed to always be interpreted to mean whatever the other person wanted to hear. He had yet to be proven wrong a single time.

"Isn't it just?" replied the Editor, confirming Liam's theory. "It couldn't have been better if we had actually had the budget to hire actors again."

Liam wondered at the use of the term "again," but decided to keep his mouth shut.

"Far from being negative for the show, the Binns leaks have turned into a decent publicity stunt! Amateurish, of course, but free publicity is free publicity. It might even carry us through to the season finale, without any of the traditional middle-of-the-season sag in the ratings."

"Even when Juliette—Binns, that is—is eliminated from the show?" Liam asked, before he could stop himself.

The Editor nailed Liam with a shrewd[i] look, along with an ostensibly pensive "hmmm" before answering him.

"Yes, you've hit the only potential issue, of course. With new popularity levels like this, we may have to review our elimination schedule. We simply can't give up an opportunity like this. We'll just have to keep our Ms. Binns around a little bit longer and find some reason to cut someone else this week. Azar Acquah, I suppose."

The Editor walked over to Liam's chair and clapped him on the back. The touch made Liam's skin crawl like one of those 3D-printed insectoid machines. He still managed to smile and nod, somehow.

---

[i] "Evil, malignant"

"Oh, one other thing," added the Editor, as he made his way out of the glorified closet which served as Liam's office. "My friend at Corporate said they'd be sending some sort of personnel memo out today to all unit coordinators, which includes yourself for the team here, of course. I'm sure you can handle it, along with finding some dirt to use on Acquah, right? Great," he replied to himself, careful not to leave Liam any time to sort out the jumble of questions competing for attention in his cortex. "I'll get out of your hair and leave you to it then. Can't wait to hear what you've come up with at the editorial meeting tomorrow morning!"

The door shut, and Liam turned back to his interface. He toyed with the feed list, opened windows, then closed them all again. He closed his eyes, but still the AR interface from his fancy new lenses floated against the back of his eyelids.

It was funny, surfaced the thought. He had already grown so used to them that he had forgotten how strange it was to never be able to disconnect, not even with your eyes shut.

All such thoughts were soon chased away, however, by the flood of conflicting emotions and general bewilderment which broke through his poor attempts at ignoring them.

What the hell had just happened?

43

A large part of the answer came some thirty minutes later, just before the statutory mid-afternoon caffeine water and bathroom break, in the form of a pointed and disembodied "ding" from Liam's inbox.

He welcomed the excuse to stop digging through Azar Acquah's personality file and live feed analytics, looking for something he could say at the meeting the following morning to avoid looking like a total idiot. But there was nothing there. Other than her health issues, Azar was a model contestant; she loved the show, and loved the Corporation even more for giving her the opportunity to take part in it. And yet, he had to find some excuse for kicking her off the show and make it seem as if it were the viewers' decision.

Surely, any email that could give him a valid excuse to take his mind off Azar, and what they were about to do to her, was a good thing, he reasoned. He then read the email and realised the limits of such self-serving logic, which has nothing to do with reason.

From: noreply@corp.redmail.com
Sent: 18-04-72 2:47 PM

To: Unit Coordinator List
Subject: Budget Drive

Dear Unit Coordinator,

Please be advised that, in application of quarterly budget drive objectives, your unit's allocated downsize quota is:

1.1 FULL-TIME EQUIVALENTS

Report of reduction quotas being met must be received by:

25TH APRIL

Coordinators are reminded that, as per statutory contract conditions, failure to meet all or part of personnel reduction quotas will be compensated automatically, first onto the coordinator's position and, if necessary, across the rest of the unit.

Regards,
Corporate

Liam's mind reeled like an old celluloid war movie. They hadn't even bothered to pretend it was anything other than an automatically generated email, with the deadly little digits piped in directly from some algorithm's table.

They wanted him to downsize, or get fired himself, as the message made certain to remind him at the end. How the hell did you fire four-tenths of a person, anyway? The message neglected to specify how much each member or organ could be counted as. Maybe they had another table for that sort of thing? It sounded like the sort of thing the Editor would save in his browser window's favourites.

Liam shook himself, then grumbled in silence at the roughness of the shaking. There was no need to panic, he tried to convince himself.

It was like this at the end of every budgetary year;[1] he had been through all of this many times before. Of course, that had been on the receiving end, the non-consenting victim side of things. He had never thought he would one day be on the side of the heartless bastards he used to mock and curse, a ritual he joined in along with everyone else.

Still—he could be a bastard, too, if he had to, he supposed. The important thing was that this was expected, normal. It would have happened regardless, whether he was unit coordinator or not, so it didn't really have anything to do with him, when you thought about. It wasn't actually him firing anybody, and he was in it just as much as Lee and Carpentiere. Even more so, since he was the designated goat for this particular sacrifice, unless they could agree something.

Surely the others would understand how much his genitals were in a vice grip on this one, and would help him find a solution. He'd just call them into a meeting, and they'd sort it out amongst themselves, like responsible adults. Yeah. There was nothing to worry about; he would have this all sorted out in no time.

After a nice still drink or two, he added, grabbing his coat. If they wanted him to take the responsibility for something like this, they would just have to accept him knocking off for once at three p.m.

Whoever "they" are, added a small voice, but Liam was already on the way to his car, on the way to hearth and cup, and was beyond caring.

---

[1] The budgetary year is unequalled by any other measure of time ever established by humankind, in that it is not concerned so much with the passing moments of one's life as with passing movements in and out of one's wallet.

44

Was he right to feel guilty about Acquah? The show had done pretty damn well by her, when you got right down to it. Through the GiG, they had taken a penniless, tumour-addled recluse and turned her into, well... into a household name, for one thing. Even if the rest hadn't really changed for her, that still had to count for something, right? That was one change for the better, at least. Liam kept telling himself that as he finished editing the footage from Acquah's feed this week, to showcase just how fast her health was falling to pieces and justify her elimination on a sympathy basis.

The Editor had loved the idea, and now he had two hours left to get the sequences finished if they wanted to get them out in time for the big entertainment commentary feeds to do their job and spin his sorry excuse into a credible reason for Azar Acquah's elimination from the show on Sunday.

Was Acquah really that hard done-by, then? What about them: Liam, Lee, Carpentiere, and even poor Mary? They were the ones who had to take a massive pay cut, across the board, just to avoid anyone being fired and to keep the show running. It was him, Liam, who had had to spend all week listening to Carpentiere moan about his daughter's medical bills, let alone Lee going on and on about her other career prospects and threatening to leave the show if she had any share in the pay cuts.

He had convinced them, in the end, that the pay cut would be only temporary, that they could fight to get it re-established next year. He certainly hoped so, in any case. Even under threat of random sacking, Lee and Carpentiere only accepted the cuts after he agreed to take a thirty-five percent loss himself, versus only twenty-five percent for the other three. Still, traditional game theory had prevailed, and both of them had accepted to lose the twenty-five percent rather than risk a random chance of being fired altogether. Out of principle, Liam had made a point of including Mary in the discussions as well, even though she really didn't have any say in the matter as an outsourced Agency worker. They'd just replace her overnight if there were any problem—and anyway, it wasn't as if she were in danger of being fired. The show physically could not carry on without an Agency worker to do all the menial work.

Just in case Corporate decided to pull the same stunt next year, maybe he should look at getting an intern or something in, someone who could take the fall next time around.

Christ, was that how Corporate management thought? All the time?

For once, the regularly scheduled Sunday torture session came as a welcome distraction.

45

Seconds after Liam had made the announcement, Mary had already scuttled off with Azar's vacant seat, unnoticed by any of the billions of the Sunday elimination show viewers. The thought of the ever-shrinking row of contestant chairs depressed Liam so much that he pushed it back into his mind's vestigial secondary hard drive, focusing instead on the worn-down woman he was holding around the shoulders. It was a good thing he was focusing on her, too—she felt so light beneath his arm, he could have knocked her off the set with one involuntary twitch[1].

Up until now, what with a busy week of fame and business opportunities to look forward to, the eliminated contestants had all taken it well, or at least with good grace—other than Spike Bighorn, obviously, who had only found out about it when brought out of his designer medical coma three days after his elimination. But even in the usual, stress-blackened state of consciousness that he relied on to get him through the weekly feature shows, he couldn't avoid noticing just how miserable Azar looked. It was so at odds with her usual steadfast happiness, even in the face of adversity.

Liam couldn't very well comment upon it to her, not at the key moment in show, with every single viewer watching their every move. Instead, he gave her an extra little squeeze to make sure he had her

---

[1] "To pull apart with a quick jerk," *i.e.*, most Twitch streamers.

attention, then hit her with the full force of his fakest, most over-the-top show business grin. She got the message, and put up enough of an excuse for a smile for him to be able to carry on with the show.

"Now, Azar, I'm sure I speak for all of us here at *The Grass is Greener*, as well as all the viewers out there around the world, when I say how much we've enjoyed having you here on the show with us. Can I get a big round of applause for Azar Acquah, everybody?"

Liam paused, smiling and nodding, as if thanking the non-existent studio audience for their equally absent applause. And yet, he knew there was always that one person, in any given group, who would clap like a trained seal at the slightest hint from a show host. Raised to the scale of his world-spanning viewership, Liam was confident he had just caused enough clapping to counter-act at least two faerie-realm genocidal wars—perhaps three. He played it "by the tutorial," as the kids say, leaving the standard five seconds before resuming.

"Thank you, thank you. Everyone wishes you all the best, Azar, and with the stresses of the show gone, I'm sure you'll be feeling better and back to your old self in no time. I guess that just leaves one question everyone will want to know the answer to: what comes next for Azar Acquah?"

She cringed a little at his question, almost as if she wished he hadn't asked her to speak. Liam first thought she was having some sort of panic attack and only recognised her silence for what it was, the struggle to hold back something you've been trying not to say, at the same time as she lost that struggle and blurted out what she had been trying not to say.

"What about the lenses, Liam—Mr. Argyle, sorry?" Even under the liberal smear of orange goop on her cheeks, the beginnings of a blush were poking through, and her voice was a touch lower than usual. "Do you really have to turn them off, like you did the others?" She latched onto Liam's shoulder like a mussel to a sea scum-covered rock.

He had never really thought about it before. Did they really have to decommission the lens implants when a contestant was eliminated? He didn't really see it as a big deal himself; lenses were cheaper than clean water these days—but he could see how someone like Azar could want to hang onto high-end lenses like these, since she couldn't afford the cost of a daydream about buying a set on her normal income. They had taken her old lenses out at the start of the show, and given her medical history, he could see how she could be touchy on the subject.

He put on his most compassionate face to calm her down.

"Azar, I understand why you're upset, but there's no need to worry. Everything's going to be fine."

Azar carried on, clearly not listening to him—Liam hoped the viewers couldn't see that as well, it certainly wouldn't do his ratings any good.

"It's just that I wasn't expecting to be eliminated tonight. Not with being sick, you know. Why eliminate me and not Juliette, who isn't half as bad off and is begging for it?"

"Now, now, Azar," cut in Liam, speaking over the end of her sentence in an attempt to drown it out, "let's not go second guessing why the votes went the way they did, shall we? The people have spoken, after all." Liam chuckled, out of sheer nerves; but luckily, Azar didn't seem aware of having muttered a dangerous truth, and carried on speaking mostly to herself, as she tried to hold back tears of desperation.

"I don't understand. It can't be me tonight. I didn't bring any new lenses. I don't have any to bring. I—" she said, before stopping with a choke, as if the words were clogging her throat in their rush to escape from her inner turmoil. "I need the lenses, Liam. I've always had them. I can't just not have any. I'd rather go blind before going around without my lenses. Much rather go blind, in fact; you could just get one of those cameras fitted, the ones they wire directly into your optic nerves."

Liam smiled and nodded, terrified at this train wreck of a departure from the usual post-elimination preening he expected from the candidates. Behind him, he could sense Brad and Jill stirring in impatience at how long Azar was taking; Usnavi was too good-natured to comment, and Juliette was too vacant-stared to notice. At some point some, someone would probably start making faces at the virtual crowd, mocking her. Liam was slightly ashamed at himself as he realised that he really wished they would, if only to distract and entertain the viewers a bit while he sorted this mess out.

Azar, in the meantime, seemed emboldened by her own profession of faith in the advancement of technology. She mustered enough courage to try to barter with Liam.

"I don't suppose that, under the circumstances, they could just leave the implants on for me? Just this once? Of course, you can cut the live feed now that I'm out of the show, I don't need that, but can't you just leave the lenses online? At least for a bit?" Her tone was more full of wheedles than a starter Pokémon player's line-up.

Before she had even finished the first sentence, Barry's voice barged into his consciousness, in all its high-fidelity, bone-conducted glory. Liam felt like he should have resented Barry's voice barging in on him without warning, or giving him the chance to accept or refuse the call, but that was only a tattered remnant of his principles talking—and not very loud, at that.

"That's a great big negatory from a technical point of view, my friend," Barry's voice grated inside Liam's skull. "These new implants are designed exclusively to support our live feed. We can't leave them on after the broadcast has been shut down, and we certainly can't leave the broadcast on. We don't have the budget to give her anything else, and her old ones are in the biohazard landfill where they belong. You'll have to find some other solution here."

Liam blinked to show he understood, then turned to Azar, without missing a beat at the end of her final question.

"You know what, Azar?" he said, fake grin spreading from ear to unbecoming ear. "You've been such a good sport since the beginning of the show, I think we can do even better than that. Unfortunately, it's not technically possible to leave the show's lenses on, and we will need them back, but I will personally take you to buy a set of top-of-the-line, perfectly safe lenses as soon as we're done with the show. What do you say?"

A look of indecision was still plastered across Azar's face, but Liam basked in the worldwide cheer he imagined at his magnanimous announcement. It felt good. After all, he'd signed up for this to help people, hadn't he? It seemed like a lifetime ago, and a lot had happened in a few weeks, but that was still his purpose, right? To help make the world a better place, however small the gesture?

"I guess so," said Azar, making Liam jump back to focus. A brief rush of terror pulsed through his veins at the idea that Azar might have heard and answered his private questioning. "Yes, that would be lovely, Liam. Thank you!"

Azar gave him a nominal hug around the waist—he had been squeezed harder by rutting poodles. He checked to make sure his grin wasn't slipping, then returned Azar's hug with exaggerated care, before disengaging and leading her over to the lens retrieval booth so he could wrap up the show. Liam counted his blessings; after all of that, Azar was mostly unresisting.

46

Liam somehow managed to drag the words "See you next week" out into the full ten-minute outro sequence required by the advertisers, then spent half an hour being cleared of the hated orange nano-goop under Mary's tender care. He was finally feeling human again as he emerged and started hunting down Azar. He soon found her staring, rapt, at the clear plastic of the caffeine water dispenser as it bubbled and kept its contents fresh. She shifted out of her aquatic reverie as he approached and broke the silence.

"It's strange, Liam. Without lenses, without menus and advertisements overlaid over everything, you notice things that you would never have noticed otherwise. Simple things, but beautiful in their own way."

A look of fear crossed her face, and Liam felt a pang of sympathy.

"Don't get me wrong," she rushed to add, with a slight stammer. "I need those new lenses like anything. I can't tell you how grateful I am for your help, Liam."

He felt a bit uneasy at how comfortable she seemed to be with using his first name now, and not "Mr. Argyle," but decided not to hold it against her.

"Don't you worry, Azar. We'll have you sorted out in no time. Shall we?"

Feeling like a knight errant, he guided Azar out of the glorified warehouse doors of the Mews and tried not to gag as they were assailed by the unfiltered airborne stew of pollutants and human effluvia which passed for "air" as soon as you left the climate-controlled security of a proper building. His nose shivered visibly as it prepared for the onslaught, and they both soldiered on into the night.

In a society where everything you could want—and a large amount that you probably didn't—was available for delivery at the inadvertent flick of an eye, it came as a revelation to Liam that going to physically buy something could involve inconvenience, and even effort. Lenses needed to be tailored to the individual eye, as measured when ordered. It was a quick and easy process, but one which presented a problem when you didn't have a personal AR network link to order lenses online from, because you didn't have lenses in the first place and needed to buy some.

Hence, the single type of physical shop that had flourished in the largely virtual economy of the 2070s was the corner lens repair shop, where underpaid and possibly illegal workers would fire up the biometric booth and get you back into the Augmented world faster than it took you to browse through their selection of impulse-buy sugar-enriched snack foods and drinks.

That was the theory, of course, but after ten minutes of wandering out randomly, Azar trailing behind him like a very confused duckling as they both waited for his map app to locate a shop for them, he had to conclude there was no market for lens shops in the middle of corporate warehouses and parking lots. They would have to move further downtown, which, to Liam's great reluctance, meant he would have to give her a ride in his new car.

Liam was surprised at how strongly his instincts rebelled at the idea. Why did it matter if he gave her a ride? Wasn't he putting the time and effort in to help her, anyway? What difference did it make?

Both Azar and he were silent as they marched through the frigid night air toward the nearest parking lot and his waiting car. It was only as he signalled for the door to open, and watched as Azar slid into the seating compartment first, as gallantry commanded, that he figured it out. His car was his private space, a luxury provided to him by his newfound corporate status, and to some degree an extension of his self. Letting Azar into it meant a fundamental change in their relationship, one that he wasn't sure he wanted. After monitoring and managing—even in internal monologue, he stopped just short of saying "manipulating"—their lives for months now, he didn't know if he was ready to deal with any of his contestants other than as a host. With Azar eliminated, and now sitting there in his car across from him, they were just two people, almost equals.

Liam told the car to find the nearest lens shop for them, and it set off on its own merry way. Since Liam was still brooding, Azar was forced to make conversation.

"I wasn't expecting it to feel so odd, being dropped from the show and not having so many strangers staring out of my own eyes anymore. It feels... liberating, in a way, I suppose. I've often thought that all of these lenses and cameras everywhere forces everyone to be... I don't know. Well behaved? A bit false, maybe? Politically correct, that's what I mean, I guess." She chuckled at herself a little, clearly nervous in a situation as unnatural for her as it was for Liam. "I'm not boring you, am I, Liam? You need to tell me if I am. I have no way of knowing otherwise."

Liam forced himself to deliver a half-hearted "No, of course not. I've often wondered the same myself. Please, carry on." Apparently, half a heart was enough to keep the conservational haemoglobin flowing, as Azar launched into the rest of her musings and left Liam, much to his relief, to his own.

"Well, I suppose it all comes from how anyone you come across nowadays could be recording or even broadcasting your every move. And even more importantly, anyone could be watching—including people you know, and who know you. Work people, friends, family, whatever. You never know who could be watching at any time, so you have to always be on best behaviour, sort of by default. In public at least, that is.

"That should be a good thing, I suppose, but I don't know if it's possible to always be on best behaviour. Maybe that's why everyone is expected to be so miserable and selfish in private. Just to balance things out, that sort of thing."

Liam caught his brooding thoughts and focused on Azar for the first time since they'd entered the car. Was she having a go at him, with her reference to selfishness? No, he decided, she was legitimately pouring her thoughts out to him. With embarrassment creeping up his cheeks like a colony of red slime mould cells migrating to a richer food source, he spouted out the first reply which came to mind, just to show he was listening.

"You may be right, you know. That would explain a lot. With individualism repressed and pushed out of the public sphere, you would get all sorts of twisted versions of it in private. Unhealthy perversions of natural individual instincts."

Liam stopped as he realised that Azar was looking at him with tears in her eyes. Not the intended effect.

Without thinking, he reached across the cabin and put a reassuring hand on Azar's brittle-feeling arm, which again seemed to backfire, as his guest burst into full, gasping sobs. She had never done anything like this over her whole period on the show. Not once. Liam would have known.

"I'm sorry," she managed to say between splutters, eventually. "It's so silly of me."

"No, it isn't," replied Liam, mostly because he felt that was what you were supposed to say in this sort of situation. "It's good. It's natural to cry. Let it all out, then tell me all about it as soon as you're ready."

She sobbed a little more at this, before pulling herself together with a series of controlled breaths. She looked so frail. Liam wouldn't have thought she had that much water in her whole body.

She mopped at her eyes with a corner of her coat, making Liam feel ashamed again, this time at not having tissues at hand in his car for unplanned guests who might spontaneously burst into crying.

"I'm sorry, " she said again, as if it were some sort of punctuation mark you had to use at the start of every sentence. "It's just that... I don't know. All that talk about lenses and repressed individuality..." She looked at him, looking for something in his eyes which she clearly didn't find. "I've always had a bit of a blind faith in technology as a force for good, you know? Especially lenses, bringing new worlds to everyone, and bringing people together. I didn't have much of a choice in the matter, I suppose. Growing up with lenses since before I could remember." She chuckled at this, though Liam was hard-pressed to see anything funny in the situation. "Maybe it's just something I picked up at an early age from my parents, as they tried to justify leaving their infant daughter in the care of what essentially amounted to one of the old TV screens stuck onto her eyes."

Liam shifted in his seat. He wasn't used to this role, the silent confidant. But he figured he could shut up and listen with the best of them.

"So it comes as a bit of a shock to have to face the conclusion I've been hiding from for so long. Forget about the physical health concerns. The important cancer isn't the one in Azar Acquah's brain. The real cancer caused by our brave new Augmented world is everywhere, in everyone's brain. It's a corruption, twisting everything good and wholesome about people just being people into greed, consumerism, lies. Selfishness, and the belief that selfishness is all there is, all there ever could be. Everything these days certainly seems to prove them right."

Liam opened his mouth to say something, but was cut short by a sudden fierce look from Azar.

"Everything. Tell me, Liam. Honestly, just between the two of us. No lenses involved. Was I really voted off the show tonight?"

The lie rose to Liam's lips as naturally as the can of premium-grade bachelor sludge had the night before, toward the end of the bottle of gin. Also like last night, it somehow seemed to get stuck in his throat, and not want to come fully out.

Why was lying to Azar face to face somehow different, more difficult even, than lying to literally billions of people across the world? It made no rational sense—or, at least, none he was ready to admit to himself just yet.

He floundered, choking in silence on words he desperately did not want to utter—for some reason, it felt as if his life depended on it. It was silly, stupid even, but the seconds went on and still Liam could do nothing but sit there, flapping his lips more uselessly than a muted politician. Azar looked sick, watching him. After what seemed like at least 1.7 eternities, she looked away, lowered her head, and broke the tense silence.

"It's okay. It's okay," she repeated, as if convincing herself of the fact. "I shouldn't have asked. Forget all about it."

Liam cleared his throat, but his voice still sounded hoarse when he replied. "Azar, you know the rules of the show—"

"Please, Liam. Forget everything I said." She was messing with what was left of her hair, so Liam couldn't really tell, but she sounded like she might be about to start crying again.

"Well, on the bright side," said Liam, desperate to change the subject and lift the pall[1] which seemed to have fallen over the car, "it looks like we're coming up on a promising patch of lens shops." He stopped and chuckled to himself. "That's something I never thought I'd hear myself say."

Azar didn't seem amused.

"Well, then, my dear damsel in distress. Are you ready for this knight gallant to escort you to complete our epic quest?"

It took Liam's most ham-fisted routine—a strange expression, when you think about, since pigs have trotters and can't even form fists—to get a half-smile out of Azar and pull her out of her funk, but

---

[1] "Cloth spread over a coffin"

he was glad for it nonetheless. The car pulled to a stop in the designated area outside of what bright AR signs proclaimed to be a slightly more trendy and lively part of town, and Liam slid out, holding the door open for Azar.

"Onwards, my lady! Your scrying bowls await!"

Encouraged by the odd look he got from Azar, he took her arm to help her out of the vehicle—she was so damned light.

"Yes, it is a little known fact that modern AR lenses are just the latest in a long line of divination tools, going all the way back to the ancient augurs, who would tell the future by observing the movements of birds."

He hooked her arm in his to prevent her from blowing off into the flow of automated traffic, and they set off down the walkway to the pedestrian commercial streets.

"Of course, that became a lot easier when they invented Twitter."

47

As they searched for lenses, Liam tried to keep his enthusiasm and his optimism intact. However, four closed shops later, both lay as tarnished and battered as an uneaten portion of fish and chips.

Liam shook his head and made to push on to the next shop on the AR map, even though it was obvious by now that they were all closed to business this late on a Sunday night and any poor unconnected slob wanting a physical shop to buy lenses from would have to wait until morning. Above them, the ring road overpass loomed like a cathedral, and the vehicles created a general buzz about them, mocking Liam and his pretentions.

Out of sheer pigheadedness, Liam refused to give in to the whims of so-called "reality," and it was Azar who had to grab him by the arm and pull him back, as best she could.

"Liam, there's no point. They're all closed." From her tone, she had probably been saying this for some time now—Liam must have blocked her out in his hubris to help.

"Well, if the shops around here don't want our business, then I'll take you to one of the big commercial areas outside of town! The Hyper-mart will have stacks and stacks of lenses. Sure, they'll be the disposable kind, but at least they're open 24/7. What do you say?"

Liam flashed her his best professional smile, but apparently, she had nothing to say, regardless. She just lowered her eyes.

"Come on, Azar," Liam said eventually, cheesy smile still plastered across his face. "Don't leave me hanging here."

Liam was mortified—his attempt to lighten up the situation backfired terribly, and Azar broke out into sobs again. He leaned forward, as if to console her once more, and this time she broke off, pushing him away.

"It's no good, Liam. Just... just leave it, all right?" She cut back her sobs and backed away from him. "Just leave it," she repeated one final time, before turning tail and running off down the pavement.

Liam stood, dumbstruck, as the feeble excuse for an urban London breeze failed to move any of the smog, or even Liam's trenchcoat, which draped like a damp flag in the mid-afternoon sunlight created by Liam's AR lightning settings.

"Hey, wait up," Liam eventually shouted, taking a few half-hearted steps in the direction of Azar, who was already halfway up the little overpass arching over the ring road expressway, of all things. "Azar! Where do you think you're headed? Be reasonable about this!" Cursing himself for something he couldn't quite name but felt vaguely guilty about, he took up the chase, hoping to bring his former contestant to her senses.

Liam certainly wasn't in the best physical shape, but he didn't expect to take anywhere near as long as it did to catch up with malady-ridden Azar Acquah. The frail woman, aged beyond her years, now seemed possessed by some sort of desperate speed. Liam was panting and sweat-covered by the time he caught up with her at the apex of the overpass and grabbed her arm, bringing her to a spinning stop.

She turned to face him, and for an instant, her eyes burned with an intensity Liam had never seen outside of the worst kind of dramatic soap opera. If he didn't know better, he would have thought it was hatred—loathing, even. Whatever emotion was behind it, the strength of the gaze, especially coming from his meek damsel-in-distress, was enough to cut Liam short and leave him wordless, yet again.

The scene froze for a second or two, like a lagging video, while below them the pilotless vehicles sang the incessant, general buzz of modern life. The car lights sent the shadow of the scant overpass railings dancing across the two figures. Above them, not a single star pierced the urban gloom, not that this would have surprised any of the twelve million people huddled in Greater London, most of whom had never seen an actual star shine in their lives.

Liam looked down at his hand, which was still gripping Azar's ragged army surplus shirt sleeve. He let go, and shook his mind back into gear.

"What do you think you're doing, Azar?" he asked, pretending for propriety's sake that he had only been waiting to catch his breath.

Azar smiled, but instead of her usual, long-suffering grin, this was a rictus; it sent a chill down Liam's spine.

"Think? No, no more thinking, Liam. I've done enough of that. Finding reasons for everything—excuses more like. Putting up and shutting up."

Liam tried to interject, to tell Azar she was making no sense, but her gaze flared again in the passing headlights and stopped him in his tracks.

"I don't just 'think,' I know exactly what I'm doing, for once. I'm doing what I should have done a long time ago, instead of buying, mind and body, into the lie, the collective sham, the con behind our conformity, our confusion..." She trailed off and turned to lean over the handrail, her gaze locked on the lights coming toward her in steady, central computer-regulated waves.

"Listen," said Liam, with a nervous gulp, "it's been a long day for you, what with the lenses, and the elimination show, obviously—"

Azar cut him off with a cackle ripped straight out of the latest *Wizard of Oz* remake. "Elimination show? Yes, a show. Just like everything else. And what a show you put on. Isn't that right, Liam?"

Scared into honesty, Liam said, "Azar, I'm sorry about the voting, okay? You were right earlier, of course. It was completely rigged." It felt good just saying it, but Azar kept her back turned to him and just leaned a bit lower across the rail, waiting in silence for him to offer more. How dare she judge him?

"It wasn't my fault though, you know! It was all the Editor's doing, and some exec or another up at Corporate calling the shots, I suppose. I tried to stop him." He had, hadn't he? "There was nothing I could do." That, at least, was true enough. If only she would say something, or at least react, instead of just flopping over the edge of the rail like that. "Tonight was just your time to go."

This, at last, got a reaction from Azar. She flipped around like a snake on speed and, still leaning against the handrail, hit Liam with her full, teary-eyed glare.

"You know what, Liam Argyle?" She trembled as she said the words. "You're right. It was my time to go, and there was nothing you could do. It wasn't your fault, and there's no reason why you should beat yourself up about it."

"I'm glad you see it that way," said Liam, flummoxed.

"Yes, I'm glad I see things this way now, too," said Azar, with a ghost of her former, genial smile returning to her face. "I see a lot of things more clearly now. All it took was forty years of radiation to the eyeballs, and a brain tumour the size of a ripe damson." She paused, chuckling. Liam didn't dare interrupt. "You shouldn't feel bad about the show, Liam, and I hope you won't feel bad about this, either. It really has nothing to do with you, or with anybody, truth be told."

"What are you talking about?" asked Liam, in a near-perfect imitation of an Angus cow presented with a differential calculus problem. Azar, however, seemed beyond caring about him or anything he might have to say.

"I wonder if it'll look any different, without the lenses?" she said to herself.

And with that, she flopped in a boneless, graceless dive over the top of the overpass handrail. Her fall into the passing automated traffic took little more than a blink of an eye, far longer than it took for Liam's brain to register and process what had just happened before him.

There was a muffled thud, something like a pile of slightly damp laundry hitting the floor, followed by a series of shorter, sharper thumps and squelches. By the time Liam started moving and peered over the rail, it was all over, other than a few patches of unqualifiable gore which described a surprisingly neat semi-circle upon the asphalt, when seen from above.

The vehicles quickly identified a potential road hazard, at least for their flashy nano-paint jobs, and started avoiding the lane altogether, passing through the new chokepoint in a sedate, orderly fashion, not entirely unlike mourners at a funeral.

"Fuck," commented Liam, and he pushed himself away from the handrail before he sent his cheap, studio trolley excuse for a supper down to join Azar's earthly remains on the expressway below.

"Fuck me," he added, covering his mouth with a hand and pulling down, as if making his face resemble one of those masks from *Scream* would somehow make the situation any less real.

"Fucking shit," came the conclusion, and Liam started to move back toward the rail, as if to check to make sure this was really happening, before stopping himself. Of course it was real, and he had no desire to subject himself to that sight again.

It was real, and the consequences would be as well. So, what was he doing, still standing around at what could, under a certain light, be viewed as a murder scene by anyone—such as a police officer, to take a random example—who might not take Liam's word as gospel[i] under the circumstances?

Biting his lip, Liam flicked his thumb out, triggering the AR interface to send his car to pick him up. He walked as fast as he dared back down the overpass and onto the street below, and waited for his car, shivering in the suddenly chilly evening.

When the car finally did arrive, a little pop-up message appeared,

---

[i] Literally "good spell," in the sense of "story."

apologising in copy-pasted terms for the delay, caused by adverse road conditions due to a "human accident." Fighting back another bout of vomit, Liam slid into the car's air-conditioned interior and set off for the liquid comforts of home.

48

There were no corporate rent-a-cops banging at the door of his new house the following morning, no incoming calls for him to stress over and ignore, not a single message or report. It was as if not a single person cared that Azar Acquah had committed suicide the previous night. Looking at himself in the mirror, Liam wondered if that wasn't the truth of it.

Upon arriving at the Mews, the dreaded shitstorm also failed to materialise, and everything was business as usual, except, perhaps, for a look from the Editor that might have been a little too knowing— but who could judge, with a man like Ed?

Just as he was relaxing into his chair and had decided to allow himself to let his guard down a little, a terrible thought struck Liam, and he quickly pulled up the logs from Jill's live feed. Had she been called in to deal with Azar's little "human accident" the previous night? Thank Mars, no: right after the show, she had been called to a run-of-the-mill incident in a tube station on the complete opposite side of town.

Other than a few irate calls from publicists who were angry at having to find some other flavour-of-the-week to replace the scheduled interviews lined up for the latest eliminated *Grass is Greener* candidate, there was a shocking absence of consequence for Azar

Acquah disappearing off the face of the Earth—other than a specific patch of the A406, of course.

A few hours earlier, her every movement was followed, live, by millions of people around the world. Now, nobody even cared to see if she were still alive or not. There was probably a lesson of some sort for Liam there, but he was distracted by work before he had a chance to reflect upon it.

Not that the following week brought any sort of drama. In fact, that was the problem.

Brad was busy combing the city, single-handedly fighting a decidedly unphotogenic gastrointestinal outbreak and saving England's economy from a sick day epidemic—if you listened to him, which nobody seemed to want to do.

Jill was sulking after Azar's elimination and refusing to provide any interesting social commentary whatsoever on her feed.

And as for Juliette, she had started ditching work and any other social activity, preferring to hide in her apartment bedroom, with all the lights off. Since she knew perfectly well about the night optics which were a core feature of the GiG lens, this behaviour mystified Liam and everyone else at the Mews; it hid nothing from the viewers. Liam figured anything that helped Juliette keep her sanity together while counting down the hours until the next elimination show was probably a good thing.

Usnavi was at least back on his feet, but being between medical trials, his daily exploits were no more interesting than any else's, and less than most.

At week's end, Juliette's entirely unsurprising elimination was the anticlimactic cherry on top a bland Sunday. To Liam, even the joy in Juliette's face when her name was called seemed subdued, if not downright perfunctory.

The problem, as ever, was ratings.

The slump over the past two weeks was big enough for the RedCorp Marketing division to edge in and try to take over the feed, suggesting a new flashy host, home-sculpted by their own resident team of crack plastic surgeons.

Ms. Heath came down on Liam and the Editor hard and heavy. They needed to do something drastic to get the ratings back up, if only temporarily. By this, of course, she meant Liam had to do something drastic, and probably highly degrading on a personal level.

His suspicions were not disappointed. The News department execs were not long in planning a scandal for him, one tailored for maximum sensationalism while carefully minimising damage with the prude socio-demographic.

And so, that Tuesday morning, even in the wee pre-sunrise hours, Liam found himself under the trees in a secluded pond-side clearing in Hampstead Heath. As he watched the hired crew install the "candid" podcameras and wheel in all the hardware—including his partner for the upcoming performance. He wondered what he'd done in a previous life to deserve this.

Turning to Ms. Heath, he rubbed his arms to fight off the cold and said, "Is this absolutely necessary?"

"Do you want Marketing to take over the GiG and fire your weather-announcing ass?" replied Ms. Heath, tapping an expensive-shoed foot. "Didn't think so. So be a good boy and strip for me."

"But it's so cold." Despite his best efforts, Liam spoke in a whine as he buttoned down his suit jacket, wishing the whole time he could get his teeth to chatter the way his deep-frozen skin was telling him they should.

Ms. Heath was ostensibly above answering such a plea. She busied herself with checking that the crew weren't about damaging any of the equipment, until Liam was down to his checkerboard briefs. She then came over to inspect him one last time. With a curt nod his way, she turned and gave a signal to the burly temp staffers standing by the largest crate of equipment.

As one, they reached in and unceremoniously pulled out a rigidlimbed but anatomically perfect replica of Liam himself. Right down to the most intimate, and entirely exposed, details.

Under the fascinated gaze of all present, they manhandled—or rather, android-handled—the Liam Argyle-shaped Erobot model into position next to its shivering, flesh-and-blood counterpart, and started booting it up.

"This is ridiculous," Liam whispered to Ms. Heath, if only to get her eyes off his silicon-cast member's member. "How is it going to look for the show, having its Host sneak off to have early morning intercourse with his own damn Erobot in Hampstead Heath?"

"It'll look exactly the way we need it to look. Fresh and scandalous enough to give the ratings a boost for a week or two. And just murky enough from a moral point of view that we won't put off the small fraction of our viewers who still have principles about this sort of thing. Plus, it'll make great advertising for our new line of celebrity-model Erobots."

Liam opened his mouth to protest further, but Ms. Heath's stare chilled him more deeply than the freezing winter morning wind swirling about his nether regions.

"You are in no posture to complain, Argyle," she said loud enough for everyone to hear, further withering his already weather- and shame-withered manhood with her glare. "This is a favour we're doing you, you know. Now buck up and take one for the Company."

The Argyle model Erobot finished booting up right then, turned toward Ms. Heath, and asked for instructions. Soon, the sordid little scenario cooked up in the fevered and reality-starved minds of the News division execs played out before the podcams set up to mimic candid com-footage.

The pretence of candidness ensured the cameras stayed far enough away—and somewhat obscured by foliage—so that "below the belt" action could be simulated rather than performed, which seemed to greatly confuse the android's pre-programmed enthusiasm for its function. It was only when Liam was acting out his finale that it occurred to him that the use of two Liam Argyle Erobots would have negated the need for his participation at all.

"Don't be ridiculous," said Ms. Heath, when Liam offered his belated suggestion once the entire affair, as it were, was over. "You come much cheaper than these damn robots do."

Was... was that a pun?

"You know I didn't actually..."

The chill from Ms. Heath's glare once again shut Liam's mouth for him, a Pavlovian response that felt as degrading[i] as anything else that morning.

Of course, not a single soul in the pod-feeding world had let him forget these events ever since—not a single moment's respite, but plenty of spite, spite and more spite. Over and over again they had shown the footage, claiming he had been caught unawares after a night of binging and debauchery[ii]. The blitz lasted even longer than Ms. Heath had hoped for, well over a month in fact, pushed on by a Corporate media machine that would not let up sales of the Liam Argyle Erobot finally tailed off, so to speak.

Still the painful contrivance had fulfilled its mission well enough—Marketing backed off, knowing a losing fight when they saw it. Sometimes, Liam wondered whether saving his job was really such a good thing after all. However, every time his thoughts turned to what he would or could be doing were he no longer "the *Grass is Greener* guy," he came up against an abyss.

The week's one saving grace was Usnavi.

A working synaptic interface had been in the works for decades, always announced as being "only five years away." So-called tech experts had founded entire media careers on explaining why full

---

[i] "To knock down a step," hence the Universal Declaration of Human Rights-based worldwide ban in 2046 of all Snakes and Ladders games.

[ii] "Enticing from work or duty"—idle hands and whatnot.

synaptic Virtual Reality was a lovely idea, but impossible in practice. And so, the Editor's excitement when he told the team about the idea he had cooked up with Usnavi's doctors was perfectly understandable, and highly contagious.

"This is the big one, guys," Ed said with a drawl, leaning over the conference table, which had been cleared of most of its usual pile of cardboard boxes. "Launching a show, that's easy with enough publicity. Seeing it through to a second season, that's the real trick." He gave them his trademark wink, cocking his finger at them like a very poorly maintained pistol. Liam, Lee, and Carpentiere all kept a wise, seasoned silence. "Well, let me tell you one thing. When the entertainment history fellers tell the story of *Always Greener*'s rise to glory, they'll point to Usnavi's live operation on the Saturday before our season finale as the moment our show achieved greatness."

Ed closed his eyes, seeming to pause to physically savour said greatness, in some sort of strange, self-serving synaesthesia.[1] The pause went on and soon became uncomfortable. The others shifted in their seats and made thoughtful "hmm" sounds, but there was no sign the Editor was paying them the least bit of attention. As senior employee, it fell to Liam to break the silence, after an opening cough.

"That's great news, Ed. So, how are we going to go about it, exactly?"

As icebreakers went, it was about on par with the Titanic, but the Editor seemed content enough as he opened his eyes and a wide grin spread across his features.

"That's the best part. We don't have to do anything. The hospital's PR department has already planned it all out, including the advertisement campaign—targeted AR pop-ins, forum trolls, the works—and all kicking in this afternoon." He paused again, but only snickered a little this time. "Of course, it helps that DynaMed, who owns the new synaptic chip patents, is also a fellow RedCorp subsidiary. They'll be opening the VR chip pre-orders right there

---

[1] My deepest apologies to any eventual audiobook narrators.

and then, during the show. All we had to do is provide them with a bit of stock footage for the ad campaign, and everybody wins!"

Ms. Lee nodded more enthusiastically than a pump above a dry well, while Carpentiere was a bit more reserved—as he always seemed to be of late. But after Azar, Liam was determined to keep a smile on his face and show everyone how good he felt about Life, the Show, and Everything; he couldn't afford to show any doubts.

"Incredible, Ed. And even Usnavi will come out of this a hero. The first human to be connected to full Virtual Reality. Thanks to us, he'll go down in history!"

"Like Neil Armstrong!" chimed in Ms. Lee, always proud to find appropriate uses for ancient trivia.

"Or Dolly the Sheep," added Carpentiere, in a half-mutter. Liam felt the man had somehow missed the point, here.

"It'll go down in ratings history, that's for certain," said the Editor. "It'll do us a world of good—although, if it turns out to be the commercial success DynaMed's PR people are hoping for, it might not be so great for the kid's chances of winning the show." The Editor made a big show of shrugging, as if he didn't care, really, but he seemed somewhat pleased at the idea. "Oh well, you know what they say. You can't make a reality show without breaking a few eggs."

The man knew damn well nobody in the history of showbusiness had ever said that, and also that none of them sitting around the conference table like so many network-connected potted plants would dare to point that out. Liam seethed in impotent silence.

Surely, somebody around here could bring him a drink.

49

Roughly three-and-a-half bottles of prime scotch later, Liam stood in the virtual limelight once again. His glassy-eyed stare was fixed on the free-floating AR window playing the highlight clips from the last week's feeds.

"These calls are always the hardest," narrated Brad Leigh for the benefit of the millions of viewers around the globe watching through his eyes as his patrol vehicle cruised down a quaint, tree-lined suburban street. His gaze lingered on the tidy lawns and immaculate doorsteps a bit longer than was comfortable.

"These people," he nearly spat. "Pensioners, self-employed workers, stay-at-home parents… Too good to be part of something bigger, like the rest of us. Oh, they're happy to know the poor disease control man in the street is keeping them safe. But only when he's far away, in the city. As if disease couldn't possibly spread to their gated slice of suburban paradise."

He let out a long-suffering sigh.

"My job is hard enough without having to explain to people that the Law isn't just for other people."

The disease control patrol vehicle coasted to a silent, electric halt outside a neat white-panelled cottage, indistinguishable from any of the hundreds it had passed along the way. Brad pulled his treatment kit together, hauled both it and himself out of the vehicle, and marched over to pound at the door, sending an orange-leafed autumn wreath swinging under the shock.

"Disease Monitoring and Prevention Corps! Open up!" he bellowed, loud enough for the whole street to hear. But only silence followed, other than a tense shuffling from behind the door.

"Typical," grunted Brad under his voice, for the benefit of the viewers, before raising his tone once more. "Under articles 5 through 11 septies of the World Health Convention and article 8 of the UK Disease Prevention Act, 2048, I am entitled to your obedience and—"

"There must be some mistake, officer!" interrupted a warbling male voice from the other side of the door. "There's no emergency here. There's only the two of us here, and we keep a close eye on all our health apps."

The feed gave a stomach-churning swing as Brad rolled his eyes. "If you persist in refusing to comply, I am entitled to enter the premises and administer treatment by force. This is your only warning."

"But we don't—"

"Right then!" cut in Brad, anger and glee competing in his voice. It took him no more than a few seconds to whip out little pads of sticky putty from his belt, stick them to door above the hinges and lock mechanism, and step back.

"Here we go!" he shouted, breaking from script in his eagerness to trigger the flashing "Detonate" button in his AR overlay.

The explosion of the microcharges was an underwhelming muffled thump, completely drowned out by the geriatric screams from inside the house as the door fell inward. Brad marched in, opening his kit with expert ease at the same time while scanning the dust-filled hallway for his targets.

Back on the *Grass is Greener* main stage, Liam's own, horrified gaze was drawn to the russet-furred cat that dodged around Brad's legs to run out the now permanently open door. He hadn't seen one with those colours in a while, and any excuse was good enough to avoid looking at Brad's undoubtedly joyful face in the hallway mirror as he walked past.

The hallway opened onto an open, cosy living area, and that's where the human residents of the house stood huddled—two elderly gentlemen in matching green sweater vests, clinging to each other for support in the middle of a thick Persian-style rug.

"We've got a reported C. Diff. outbreak in this house, gentlemen. Got to nip buggers like that in the bud," Brad drawled, his invisible grin loud and clear in his voice. He lifted a nozzle-ended tube attached to a brimming tank of khaki-green sludge labelled "faecal bacteriotherapy."

"You know how this goes. C. Diff. is so contagious I need to treat everyone in the house. So don't make this any more difficult for us all than it needs to be," he added, advancing on the wide-eyed and blubbering owners of the home.

The taller of the pair managed to find his wits first. "You can't be serious. We're perfectly healthy! You can't use that on us," he protested, as they both backed away from Brad. Soon, they were up against the ornamental brickwork fireplace and could back away no further.

"Ho-ho, I think we've got ourselves a volunteer! Unless stool transplant therapy too good for you?" spat Brad. "I make this myself, you know. All in a day's work in the Disease Corps. And a damn sight more effective than antibiotics too! So don't be a baby about this. Whip 'em down, bend over, and let's get this done with, shall we?" He gave the nozzle's trigger a playful pump to illustrate his point, sending the brown slurry halfway up the tube, then back down again.

The shorter of the two men twisted to grab an iron poker from beside the fireplace and brandished it before him, less like a weapon and more like a talisman that could banish the demon from their home.

Brad laughed outright, this time around. "That looks a lot like a weapon to me," he said, reaching around to a clip on the left of his belt. "Protocol Four it is, then!"

His hand, when he lifted it back up, was clutching an ugly yellow box with metal darts protruding from the end. It crackled with electric energy at his touch.

"Wha—What's Protocol F—" started to mumble the taller of the two men. But Brad clearly had no intention of letting him finish his thought and fired off the taser, with prongs hitting both men squarely in the chests. They fell to the ground in a jerking, sweater-clad mess, and the scent of scorched printshop wool wafted through the air.

Brad stepped toward them, flipped them over onto their stomachs, one after the other, and started fumbling with their trousers, complaining about entitled babies and irresponsible treatment dodgers the whole time.

The Grass is Greener studio went deathly quiet, all the usual background chatter during a pause in the live feed fading away. Everyone turned to watch through Brad's eyes, with uniformly haunted expressions, as he provided both pacified gentlemen with their complimentary stool transplant enemas.

Once again, Liam wished he'd found the nerve to demand the Editor not replay this whole scene again in this week's primetime show. Or the nerve to say anything about it whatsoever, for that matter. But what good would it have done?

He put his smile back on as the treatment reached its nauseating end and they gave him the five-second warning before the return to live feed. The clip ended—at long last—and the light on the cameras went red again.

"Quite the in-depth look into the work of our brave Disease Corps men and women," he said, cursing himself at the ridiculous attempt at making light of such a fundamental[i] violation of privacy and human rights. "Anything to add about what we've all just watched there, Brad?"

Sitting in his bright red, plush hotseat, Brad Leigh sulked like a toddler hit by a growth ray. "Listen, it ain't easy being on the

---

[i] Yet again, quite literally.

frontlines, protecting all you lot from diseases you couldn't even imagine. And in my defence, it's not my fault the standard bathroom sensors aren't calibrated to tell the difference between a C. Diff. infection in humans or a damn pet. A spore's a spore; they would probably have gotten infected anyway. And what were those two fogeys doing taking in stray cats in the first place, that's what I'd like to know! Bloody bleeding hearts."

Liam wasn't sure their hearts were the bleeding bits they should be worried about here, but he bit back the retort and kept his silence.

Brad shuffled uneasily in his seat, before adding, "They got free treatment, and the Corps prevented contagion as usual, is all I'm trying to say."

Liam beamed at him for the cameras. If only smiles could kill. "And I'm sure the voters will take that into consideration as we move into the last minutes of—" He paused for effect, stepping into the centre of the stage and raising his voice to a carnival shout. "This week's final vote tally!"

From there on, all that was left were the camera smiles, the screams at the announcement of Brad's landslide elimination, and the fake tears and even faker sympathy as Usnavi and Jill said goodbye.

Brad was escorted off the stage in sullen silence, muttering something about ingrates to the security agents. Liam cast aside his sudden questions about when the show had acquired security agents and announced, with great piped-in fanfare, the two finalists of *The Grass is Greener*, Season One.

At the post-show wrap-up meeting, the Editor stood rubbing his brow while the team waited in uncomfortable silence.

"We managed to keep the last week entertaining enough," he said at last, in a low moan, "but I don't know how they expect us to keep the feed lively for a whole one-hundred-sixty-eight hours until the big finale with only two contestants left. We aren't miracle makers, damnit."

Norma Lee rose out of her slump to sit straight as an oversized schoolroom ruler. "Luckily, we already have the Usnavi Musibay live operation event set up with DynaMed. As long as Jill gets another juicy suicide or two to mop up, that should give us a solid base to mount up to the finale, right?"

"No, it is not 'right,' Ms. Lee," answered the Editor. "It's a start, but we will have to bend matters even further than usual in order to produce anything close to the build-up of viewer attention we need for a successful finale to our opening season."

He paused, and his grin reminded Liam of those two poor men, home invaded, tasered, and enema'ed with their assaulter's own faeces, due to an error in medical sensor diagnosis.

"Luckily, I have just the thing in mind," drawled the Editor.

50

The enclosed garden area inside the Elysian Fields private mental rehabilitation facility was highly photogenic. It made for a great backdrop for Liam's interview with patient Juliette Binns.

Not to mention a welcome distraction from the woman's sunken eyes and dilated pupils.

"Thank you for agreeing to see us on such short notice, Juliette," said Liam, trying to put the woman at ease, both for her benefit and his own. He couldn't reconcile the twitchy, broken woman in the blue hospital gown sitting on the other side of the little plastic table with the defiant woman that he'd come to know over the first few weeks of the show. Perhaps more intimately than he was comfortable to admit.

At the sound of his voice, her eyes stopped flicking between the plants in the gently lit solarium, Carpentiere's recording equipment, and the white-suited orderlies always passing nearby. Her gaze fixed on Liam at last.

"I guess I should be the one thanking you, for coming to visit. After the stunts I pulled on the show, the last thing I expected was more cameras."

Liam smiled and shook his head, every inch the understanding host the viewers back home wanted to see.

"Being part of a show like *The Grass is Greener* is an adventure, and a lot of stress. It's enough to make anyone act a little kooky[i] now and again."

Liam's grin became a little strained as the seconds went by. Juliette made no response, simply staring at him with those pitted eyes, as if debating something internally.

"You're a welcome break from routine here, that's for sure," she said at last. "Normally, at this time of day, they've got me wired into some VR therapy scenario or another. I'd almost forgotten what eleven o'clock sunlight looks like."

Here we were: the meat of what the Editor wanted from the interview. Showing off the state-of-the-art rehabilitation facilities eyeNet had generously—and compulsorily—provided for Ms. Binns after her little breakdown and her elimination from the show.

"Tell me a bit more about the facilities here, and your daily routine," asked Liam, all smile and saccharin for the sake of the live podcameras.

Juliette blanched an even paler shade of white, which Liam hadn't thought was possible. "I'm not sure—I mean, I wouldn't want to bore[ii] you, is all," she said, her eyes shooting toward something off behind Liam's shoulder.

"Please," insisted Liam, resisting the urge to turn to see what was so intriguing behind him. "We've had an outpouring of viewer comments since you left the show, all wanting to make sure you're okay. Just like us," he added, trying not to make it sound like the afterthought it was. "You said something about VR therapy? That sounds fancy."

"Oh, they've got all the best resources here, that's for sure." Juliette actually smiled as she spoke and let out a relieved chuckle. Maybe

---

[i] Early 1900s U.S. slang abbreviation of "cuckoo," which itself comes from "cocu," which is both old and current French for a cuckold.

[ii] The verdict is out on whether or not being "boring" originally meant slow and painful discourse that "bores" into your mind. But it's funny to note that the original "bore" was a tool, not unlike many boring people.

this was a safer subject than whatever was worrying her a minute ago. "The doctors and the staff are nice and all, but treatment here is really all about retraining the brain with the VR scenarios they run you through."

"That's amazing," Liam said, nodding thoughtfully so they had something to cut to when editing the highlight clip. "If it's not too private, can you share some examples with us?"

Juliette chuckled at this—a slightly harsh, out-of-practice sound. "I think we're a bit beyond privacy considerations by now, Mr. Argyle. But there are so many different scenarios, I wouldn't know where to start. They're very proud of their in-house developed psychiatric software, but they do tend to all blur together after the first day or two." She paused, wrestling with her thoughts. "In this one program they—"

"Now now, Ms. Binns," boomed a voice so close to Liam's ear he thought he had forgotten to block his incoming calls for the interview. Juliette went instantly silent as the speaker, a tall, silver-haired orderly in a spotless white uniform, stepped out from behind Liam. "You know we don't talk about psychiatry here. What we do is brain training. Oh, sorry if I've interrupted," the man added, as if he had only just realised he'd barged in on a recording, "but I was just passing by and overheard Ms. Binns's little error in terminology."

He turned to smile at Liam, ignoring the recording equipment and the hulking Carpentiere as naturally as if he'd been born in front of the camera. "Ms. Binns is still very new here, of course, and it takes some time for our clients to really come to grips with the nuances of their individualised brain training program. Speaking of which, I think Ms. Binns is late for her next session today. VR room number five, if I'm not mistaken," he added, eyes glazing over as he read something from his personal AR display. "That's just down the hallway. I don't suppose you'd like to see the room before Ms. Binns begins, Mr. Argyle?"

Liam had to fight back a smile. He remembered a time not so long ago when he would have been surprised if a stranger knew his name.

"That would be lovely. And might it be possible to ask you a few questions as well before we wrap up the visit?" he asked.

The orderly smiled, and his identity tag, labelling him as "Felix Reiter, Client Facilitator" above the green rolling hills logo of Elysian Fields Rehabilitation Centre, finally loaded into Liam's display.

"It would be our pleasure. This way, please."

Liam stood, leaving Carpentiere to fumble with the recording equipment as he followed Reiter and a demure Juliette Binns through the pastel corridors, with their comfy chairs that seemed to have been dropped in random places by half-hearted movers and their AR-broadcast copies of inoffensive classical paintings and pop art works.

"Here's VR room five on the left," half-whispered Reiter, like a GPS navigation app with the volume turned too low, as they approached a closet-sized door.

Liam couldn't have told it apart from any of the other half-dozen identical, baby blue doors they'd passed.

Reiter pushed the door, and all three of them, including the panting and filming Carpentiere, followed him into a tiny, dim-lit room dominated by what looked like a high-end fridge set against the far wall. A single, padded chair in the near corner was the only other furnishing in the dark cubbyhole.

"This is where the self-improvement begins," declared Reiter, his white smock darkened to a mute grey without the bright sunlight from the solarium. "Inside this chamber, we can simulate any situation, probe any moral quandary, push any boundaries the client wishes to overcome with our help. And our guidance, of course."

Leaning forward, Liam stepped up to the glass-fronted unit and peered inside. It was even darker than the rest of the room in there, but he could make out a running mill-type floor and various nozzles set into the inner lining of the unit. It was just big enough in there for a person to stand, with enough room to swing arms and legs.

"The science is still rudimentary, of course, with a need for physical simulation of sensations of cold, heat, wet, and such, along with nebulised chemical stimulant delivery. But it serves our clients' purposes for the present," said Reiter, his thoughts trailing away into silence for a moment. "Regardless, our success rates are phenomenal. But privacy during brain training sessions is vital to success, so I unfortunately must ask you to follow me out after I load Ms. Binns's agoraphobia program."

He popped open the front of the unit, ushered an unresisting and stoop-shouldered Juliette inside, and shut it exactly like Liam did his fridge door back home after grabbing a drink. The orderly flicked his fingers through an AR menu, and the lights inside the unit flared to blinding life. Inside, Juliette stood in the glare like a museum specimen in her hospital gown.

"Perfect," said Reiter, turning away to open the door back out to the corridor. "That's all set for the next few hours. If you'll follow me, gentlemen, I'll be happy to answer any questions you'd like. There might even be coffee and biscuits in it for you," he added, conspiratorially, as he ushered them out of the tiny room.

As he emerged into the diffused sunlight, Liam turned to cast one last look past Carpentiere, at Juliette Binns. His former contestant stared straight back at him, mouth pursed shut and eyes like gaping skull-holes in the bottom-lit VR unit.

She didn't mouth a word, and neither did Liam.

There were biscuits and coffee, but neither did anything to wash the sour taste out of Liam's mouth. Reiter lounged in his seat in the bright, leaf-filled solarium area and smiled for the camera above his steaming mug.

"Our dream is that, someday, we'll be able to do away with all that clunky apparatus you saw back there," he said. "Direct sensory immersion is making leaps and bounds, and the therapeutic potential is enormous. In ten or twenty years' time, we'll be able to control every single sense within the simulations—we may even be able to make the client forget they're within a simulation entirely. Imagine the brain training possibilities!"

A shiver ran down Liam's spine. Something wrong with the temperature control in here, maybe? Whatever it was, the podcamera was recording, and he couldn't afford to take his mind off business. Liam made sure his smile was still in place before turning toward the orderly.

"And how would you describe Ms. Binns's progress and outlook, if it isn't a breach of confidentiality for me to ask? The viewers are dying to know."

The white-gowned man swept his hand through the air. "I'd be happy to. We're under instructions to provide you with any assistance we càn for this interview, Mr. Argyle. And once again, we aren't, strictly speaking, a medical institution. We simply provide software and facilities to help our clients retrain their own brains. As for Ms. Binns, there was some initial resistance at first. Not that unusual really, and I'm sure you can relate to that after what she put you through on that show of yours. We're all big fans here, by the way," added Reiter, with an embarrassed chuckle.

Liam chuckled back, mostly to cover the sinking feeling deep in his internal plumbing. "The show wouldn't be anything without its fans. But as for Juliette, you'd say she's making progress toward a full recovery, then?"

"Oh, absolutely," replied Reiter, all smiles. "Our simulations are the best, allowing the clients to face their ethical dilemmas and personal trauma in a safe, controlled environment. Now that she's fully compliant, Ms. Binns's successful rehabilitation is only a matter of time."

The orderly paused, taking a pensive sip from a mug bearing the presumably humorous statement "Allow me to introduce my selves" before continuing.

"Of course, calling it a 'full recovery' might be a bit misleading. The brain is a wily beast, Mr. Argyle, and maintaining the desired personality traits takes more than a one-time fix. It's a constant work upon the self, and our clients never truly leave us. They always come back for more, if only for a few psyche touch-ups every now and again. And that's for people who've never had a breakdown like Ms. Binns."

Liam took an audible gulp and started speaking the question on his mind before his good sense caught up with him and killed the words before they left his lips. "But don't you think this sort of immersive VR therapy, as powerful as it clearly is, could be dangerous for someone like Ms. Binns? Given the nature of her trauma, that is? I mean, she's here because she rejected her implants and the show's immersive technology. Isn't there a risk exposing her to more of the same could do more harm than good?"

Shocked silence descended on all three men—interviewer, interviewee, and cameraman alike. Liam swore at himself. When would he learn to keep his damn thoughts to himself?

Then Reiter chuckled again and broke the spell. "Your concern does you credit, Mr. Argyle, and your contestants are lucky to have such a caring host. But have no fear. Every therapy program here is tailored for and approved by the client. When she leaves our care here, Ms. Binns will be a new woman, free from her crippling and pathogenic anxieties."

After seeing the broken shell of what used to be Juliette Binns, Liam didn't know how the man could spout such blatant lies and keep a straight face. Then again, maybe it took a hypocrite to know one. The people here didn't care about Juliette. They were probably just happy for the paying subject, and the publicity.

"Well, our time here is up. Thank you so much for all your help today, Mr. Reiter, and we look forward to hearing great things from you in the future."

"Likewise, Mr. Argyle," said the orderly, his fake smile never wavering.

51

Suicide Jill's feed the next day promised to live up to the Editor's wildest hopes for sensationalism and filler content to see the show through the last three days until Usnavi's big live operation and the finale the following day. And like every time the shit hit the fan, Liam was the one stuck on live feed monitoring duty.

"Dispatch, I can't go in there," she said in deadpan tones, standing stone-still at the low, rusted iron gate to a dilapidated terraced house in the eastern suburbs of the city. The hose of her multipurpose industrial cleaning unit lay limp in her hand. "I know the lady who lives here. I can't take this clean-up job, chief. Personal conflict."

"Jill, it's already been over a day since the rent-a-cops flagged this one for us," replied the bored voice over her comms, relayed in real-time to the monitoring Liam and, thirty seconds later, viewers around world. "If we leave it any longer, we'll have Disease Control on our asses for endangering public health. And you know the tender's coming back up for grabs in six months. This is more than both of our jobs are worth, Jill."

She cursed into the cold evening air, and Liam flagged this segment as vulgar for the rare viewer out there who may not have turned off their profanity filters yet.

"Don't fuck around with me, man. This is my ex-girlfriend's house. I've been doing this job for three years now, and I know you can't force me to do a clean-up when there's personal conflict. Send somebody else."

"Damnit, Jill. You know we've already got everyone working double shifts, and we still haven't gotten over the Monday hump. There's nobody else to send. So get your shit together, load up your Funfilter, and get in there. Or resign right now and enjoy spending the next week in queue at the Job Placement centre. Your call. I'm covered either way."

"Man, could you at least try to give a shit? For appearance's sake?"

"I don't get paid to care, Jill. But you know, it might not even be your ex or whoever in there. All the Secufax report says is that's it's a single-sized clean-up, sex female. They didn't bother identifying. So sure, that could be your ex, but it could also be someone else. A visitor, a squatter, who knows? Are you even sure she still lives here? I mean, as far as registered addresses go," added the man on dispatch, in an embarrassed rush.

Jill was clearly beyond caring about poor word choice. "It's true, I haven't spoken with Jamila in ages. Almost a year now. I suppose she could have moved on by now."

"Well, one way or the other, I'd say she has," chimed in the dispatch man.

"You're not helping here, Rodrigo."

"My brilliant and underappreciated wit isn't the question here. So are you gonna stand there all night or are you going to do your job? I bet it isn't getting any warmer out there, either."

A cloud of condensed exhalation betrayed Jill's exasperated sigh to the millions viewing through her eyes. Then the AR filters fell over her eyes, and bright virtual sunlight replaced the grey, early evening gloom all around. The broken-windowed, crumbling-bricked terraced house before her was suddenly a charming, flower-decked cosy little home.

"That's my girl," said the dispatch man. "That's one hell of a Funfilter, by the way."

"Shit," swore Jill. "I guess I shouldn't be surprised you're watching this live as well."

Rodrigo chuckled. "Can you blame me? Oh, and hey everybody! Go listen to my DJ mixes at—"

Shaking his head, Liam edited the pathetic attempt at a plug out of the live feed. Trying to get free advertisement on the feed was a far worse offense than any profanity they could come up with.

"You silly shit," said Jill, half-chuckling as she steeled herself and stepped up to the front door. The security lock responded to her AR system's ping, and then both her and her bulky cleaning unit were inside the house.

In the rosy Funfilter glow, the house looked amazing, and about as unlikely a scene for a post-suicide clean-up as could be.

Jill rolled her equipment down the cheery corridor, lit by bright sunlight that made no objective sense, but was welcome regardless. Walking with the certainty of someone well-acquainted with the house, she cast a cursory glance through the wrapped parcel-filled kitchen at the end of the hall, filled with little buzzing fairy-bugs, but otherwise empty. Passing an equally empty sitting room, she marched up a bright green-painted staircase.

As she set foot on the landing, the thick, yellow carpet squelched slightly under Jill's boot—a sensation her Funfilter, after a few seconds' processing, translated by placing puddles of water along the left side of the landing, shimmering invitingly and begging to be splashed about in.

Heedless, Jill followed them down the landing, all the way to the house's only bathroom. The door had a giant yellow smiley face plastered over it and lay half open. Pausing only slightly, Jill stepped forward and swung it open with the touch of a rubber-gloved hand.

Inside, the ancient freestanding bathtub was filled to the brim with water. It shimmered with such impossible clarity and brilliance that the Funfilter must have been working overtime to hide something particularly unpleasant. Bobbing gently in the water, a fully-dressed female clown lay relaxed and stretched out, by all appearances fast asleep despite the large, goofy grin painted on her face, and untouched by the water all around. Little bonbon tubes were scattered within arm's reach at the base of the tub.

"Oh fuck, Jamila," whispered Jill, her swear at complete odds with the bright, cheerful scene. Dropping her cleaning hose, she rushed forward to plunge a hand into the water and grip at the clown's wrinkled, loose-fitting lapel. She gave it a shake, peering at the smiling, painted face for a reaction.

But the eyes stayed shut, the body unmoving, and the only reward for her efforts was when the lapel she was gripping ripped loose with a wet tearing sound. The body fell back into the bath, sending a wave of impossibly fresh water gushing over the rim and onto Jill's legs.

"Fuck!" she yelled this time, winning no points for originality, and jumped back, raising her hand to gaze in horror at the ripped "clown suit" still in her hand.

The edges of the fabric oozed with sluggish frayed strings, which flowed outward before dripping onto the gleaming tiles at Jill's feet.

Dropping the ripped bit out of suddenly limp fingers, Jill rushed past the recumbent form in the bathtub and bent down above the toilet in the far corner, heaving.

Liam and all the viewers around the world, in their homes or out and about, were treated to the live feed of Suicide Jill puking out a seemingly endless flow of colourful party streamers into the rapidly-filling toilet bowl.

"Oh shit," said Jill in a low, throaty moan, when the last bits of confetti were finally out of her innards. "Fuck this right off. I can't."

And without further ado, she pushed herself away from the party supply-filled toilet bowl and rushed out the door, across the squelching landing carpet, and down the cheerful stairs, hardly stumbling at all as she made it to the bottom step.

"You know I'm sympathetic and all," came the voice of Rodrigo from dispatch over her comms, as she laid her wet, gloved hand on the front door handle. "But it's my job to remind you that refusing to do your job there, whatever the reason, is the same thing as a resignation. No severance or benefits. Are you sure that's what you want?"

Jill stood uncharacteristically silent for a moment, staring at the bright Funfiltered paint of the house's front door.

"What I want?" she said at last, with a nervous chuckle. "What I want is for you to add 'Jamila Lewis' as the confirmed identity on that file. Then I want you to find your manager and tell them Jill Nowicki says they can go fuck themselves for thinking they can treat people this way. And their own bosses along with them."

Jill cut off her comms at that, swung the door open with filter-jarring violence, and stomped out of the house. Leaving the company vehicle behind her, she flicked off the Funfilter and marched on down the suddenly dark, smoke-filled road toward the nearest bus stop.

Leaning back in his swivel seat, Liam nibbled on a thumbnail, lost in thought, then reached a decision and called up the Editor with a flick through his heads-up display.

"Yes, Argyle?" replied a grumbling Editor, answering only at the sixth ring, and with the sound of other people speaking fading into the background. "I hope this is worth interrupting a meeting at Central."

Despite himself, Liam gulped. "It's Suicide Jill, sir. Have you been watching the feed?"

"Argyle," the Editor growled in Liam's ear, "assume I am always watching the feed. And assuming that you are calling about Jill's resignation from her job, I really wish you hadn't."

"But isn't having Jill badmouth her employer live a problem for the show?"

"People quit their jobs all the time. Do you know the number of applicants any company, even a suicide clean-up contractor, will have for any sort of menial labour position? They'll be beyond caring, trust me. And so should you."

"Yes sir," replied Liam, not knowing how else to answer that.

"As ever, Jill's timing is perfect," carried on the Editor. "We couldn't have hoped for a better show from her in the run-up to the Finale. And now we have a good explanation to give for her victory on Sunday, despite little Usnavi's big night with his live operation on Saturday. So chin up, Argyle, and back to the grindstone!"

The Editor cut off the call without waiting for a reply, which saved Liam the trouble of having to piece one together from the confused swirl that was his mind.

52

"Whoa, is all this for me?" asked Usnavi, his gaze swinging around the bright-lit operating theatre, from the blinking podcameras to the science and tabloid journalists rubbing shoulders against the far wall. His eyes finally rested on the operating table set under a bright spotlight in the exact centre of the circular room, with a hulking brain-imaging unit and a gleaming forest of specialised robotic arms at its head, and surgical tool trolleys on either side.

When he didn't get a reply, Usnavi turned to face the chisel-faced and smiling DynaMed doctor ushering him into the room. "It's just that, normally, it's all waiting around until the researchers are ready for me, then five minutes in a backroom, and I'm lucky if I get an Elastoplast afterward. This is swanky."

The DynaMed doctor carried on manoeuvring the boy in the freshly printed and ill-fitting grey suit into position, sitting him on the edge of the padded green operating table, moulded to human shape and segmented like a caterpillar. The overhead spotlights blinded Usnavi as he looked up at his assigned guide.

At last the doctor answered, "That's because what we're accomplishing here today, together, is something nobody has ever done before. You're going to be the first person to receive our patented new full-immersion brain interface implant, Usnavi. The first to enter the world of tomorrow, where everyone can access information and interact with the world of tech at the speed of thought, using all of our senses and not just a clumsy AR interface or unreliable external sensors."

The doctor smiled, an indistinguishable clean-shaven face half-hidden by the overhead glare, and put his hands on Usnavi's shoulders. "You're going to make history, young man! A modern-day Neil Armstrong!"

The view from Usnavi's eyes shivered, and back at the Mews, Liam wondered if it was excitement, fear, or both.

"That's amazing."

And a nice consolation prize for not winning tomorrow, added Liam in silence.

"But are you sure it's safe?"

Usnavi's eyes wandered from the doctor's face down to the tray already in place by the operating table, with its saw-like instruments, drills, clamps, forceps… "If you haven't ever done this on a person before, how can you know there isn't any danger?"

"There's nothing to worry about, Mr. Musibay," replied the doctor, all smiles as he used his grip on Usnavi's shoulders to guide the unresisting boy down into a horizontal position atop the operating table. "The interface has been tested extensively. AI simulations, live animals, cloned human tissue, you name it. And the success rates, with no impairment of vital functions whatsoever, were much higher than expected."

Usnavi nodded, reacting to the doctor's smooth, placating tone, then stopped suddenly. "Wait, what do you mean 'impairment of vital f—'"

"Oh look, here comes the operating team," cut in the doctor, finishing his adjustments of the seat to Usnavi's diminutive size and moving to strap his arms against the curved green armrests. "No need to worry about these, either," he added, pre-emptively. "Just like everything else, it's only for your comfort and security. Always a safe precaution when dealing with the ol' noggin wiring, you know."

Usnavi squinted into the glare of the overhead lights, trying to make out the emerald-green scrub-clad forms appearing all around the operating table. He started pulling himself back up.

"Doctor! I don't think—I don't think I want to do this anymore. I want to stop!" he cried.

"Shh," said the doctor, reappearing beside his head and giving him a gentle yet irresistible push back down onto the operating table. "That's just your nerves talking. And we'll soon have those sorted out," he added, with a bit of a chuckle he quickly cut short. "But seriously, you've already signed on for this, and everyone is here for you. There's no backing out now. You're going to make history, Usnavi!"

The camera gave a sharp jerk as Usnavi craned to look at his arm, where a no-nonsense nurse had just inserted an IV feed. It instantly started dripping with a clear liquid.

"There's nothing to worry about," cooed the doctor, easing Usnavi back down into a resting position once again. "That's just to make sure you don't feel any pain during the operation, so you can stay awake, see how the operation progresses, and share your impressions as the first human in history to enter the new, full-immersion digital world."

Let alone share the experience with a few hundred million non-squeamish viewers back home, added Liam. The Editor had been adamant that it would either be awake surgery, or nothing at all.

"Well, as long as I'm awake and can tell you if something feels like it's going wrong..." Usnavi said in a low, sleepy voice. The anaesthetic was already starting to take effect.

"That's the spirit," beamed the doctor. "And I'll be right here, standing next to you the whole time, if you need me for anything, Usnavi. You're an amazing young man, you know," he added, sounding genuine to Liam's ears for the first time.

Usnavi simply nodded in response, as much as the operating table's formed headrest allowed him to.

The doctors and nurses busied themselves in the glare surrounding Usnavi. They hooked up electrodes to various parts of his body, and it was strange to think that he probably couldn't even feel those bits anymore—no more than the millions of spectators watching through his eyes. Somewhere to his side, a monitor started bleeping; it rang like a stream of censored expletives in Liam's show-addled mind.

He winced in instinctive fear as the whirr of a drill started up in his ear and the head-clamps fastened into place. The view from behind Usnavi's eyes started vibrating as the robotic arms pulled in closer, but the boy himself didn't seem to mind in the least.

"You're doing great," cooed the boy's handler doctor, along with a dozen other sweet nothings, while the machines got to work opening his skull and exposing his living brain. "How do you feel?" he eventually asked, when the silence got too heavy.

"A bit foggy, if that makes any sense," replied Usnavi, the clamps keeping him frozen in place as he spoke. "But okay otherwise. No pain or anything."

"Perfect," the doctor said in absent tones as he peered around the busy robotic arms at whatever was going on at the top of the boy's head. At the edges of Usnavi's locked-down field of view, beyond the glare of the lights, the various spectators jostled for position, all craning for a view of what was going on at the top of his head a well. There was a slow pneumatic *whirr*, and then a small *whump* of pressurised air.

"Weyhey, there we go," said the doctor, his eyes sparkling in the spotlights. "The first relay implant is in! Congratulations, Usnavi, and well done!"

The boy giggled as best he could under the restraints. "I should be congratulating you guys. You're the ones who've done all the work. I'm just lying here."

"All our work is only to help you make history, my boy," replied the doctor, patting Usnavi on a strapped-down arm. Somewhere behind Usnavi's ears, the faintest of scratching sounds grew faster and faster.

"We're almost there now," the doctor said, carrying on his running commentary, both for Usnavi's sake and for the millions of viewers around the globe. "The nanoscopic manipulators are hooking up the artificial neurons to the key hubs in your visual cortex, so you might start receiving our test input any moment now." His voice trembled. "Make sure to tell us as soon as you see anyth—"

"Doctor, I think I see something!" interrupted Usnavi, a laugh escaping his lips. "There's a green shape. And it doesn't move when I move my eyes!"

Sure enough, the feed flicked from left to right as Usnavi tested his theory. However, all he was succeeding in doing, as far as the show was concerned, was make Liam and the viewers feel sick. They could only see what the ocular implants recorded and not this new signal coming directly from inside the boy's brain.

One of the scrub-clad people behind Usnavi's head started to cheer but was quickly shushed by their colleagues. "That's great, Usnavi," said his handler, in guarded tones, "but we need to you to try to focus on the green shape. Can you describe it to us?"

The feed finally stopped moving as the boy focused on the green shape only he could see.

"It's long. And it looks like it's bigger at the end."

Someone sniggered in the crowd and was quickly shuffled off to the back row. Usnavi carried on, unphased.

"I think—I think it could be an arrow. A green arrow, with some other shapes in front of it. And inside it. They might be letters."

The doctor leaned in over Usnavi. "I need you to concentrate now. Can you read the letters and tell us what they say?"

"I don't think I can," Usnavi said, shaking his head gently. "It's too fuzzy."

"Please," urged the Doctor. "You can do this. Just concentrate on the picture."

Doctors and spectators alike, both in the room and around the world, all held their breath as the boy strained to decipher the signals from the implant.

"It's getting clearer now! I can almost read it. The bit inside the arrow says 'Med,' and the bit in front is... Oh, of course. DynaMed! That's you guys, right?"

"Right you are," answered the doctor, a finger dabbing at the corner of his eye. "And can you see anything else?"

"Yes! There's something written underneath the DynaMed arrow, in little letters. It says, 'A Red Company—Blazing Trails Since 2034.'"

Another cheer went up from the doctors and nurses at Usnavi's exposed head, and this time nobody cut it short.

"That's amazing, Usnavi. Well done!" said the doctor, squeezing the boy's arm in celebration.

Back in *The Grass is Greener* control room, Liam shook his head, marvelling at the simple beauty of the publicity stunt. Usnavi could see the company logo, but no one else could. It was the end of the world of physical AR. From here on in, it would all be about direct stimulation of the relevant brain centres. Talk about advertising: denying the viewers the same view as Usnavi was the best way to make them all desperate for their own implants.

"There's more here, too," said Usnavi, eagerness to please oozing from his tone.

The hand on his arm froze mid-grip. "More? What do you mean, more?"

"There's something else underneath it now. A big box, with lots of letters," answered Usnavi, squinting to read the invisible new signal from the implant.

The boy's handler turned his still chiselled but no longer smiling face to someone behind Usnavi. "What the hell is he talking about?"

Silence reigned for a few tense seconds as someone busied themselves conferring with the monitoring machinery.

"He's right," replied a young and trembling male voice. "There's something else coming in over the implant. Something we didn't put there."

"I think I can read some of it," said Usnavi, who was completely ignored by the assembly.

"Whatever it is, get rid of it," hissed the PR doctor. "It's messing up our event."

"I'm not certain that's wise, sir. Or even possible," replied the technician. "At this stage, with the implant connected, any interference could have serious repercussions, both for the equipment and the host."

"Oh," interrupted Usnavi, with a laugh that brought all attention back onto him. "It's just someone's public network profile. Millie Shardlow," he read. "Works at eyeNet Stream 4 Entertainment News, single, likes Thai food and science fiction comedies, dislikes 'haters,' whatever that means, and—"

"Where the hell is this coming from?" demanded Usnavi's handler, ignoring the boy completely.

Someone whacked a machine out of Usnavi's line of sight. "From somewhere outside of the system, sir. That's all I can tell for sure. There's a lot going on here."

"Ooh, there's something else now," said the boy strapped to the operating table, slurring his words ever so slightly. "It's moving this time—looks like an ad. There's no sound, but I think it's the MediCalc health insurance mascot, Timmy the Turtle. I've always loved that guy."

Looming above Usnavi, the doctor's face had turned a bright, apoplectic red, like an irate harvest moon. "There must be something we can do to stop it!" he spat, gripping one of the technicians by the sleeve.

"Powdered eggs!" Usnavi shouted, saving the tech lady from having to find a response. "Two cartons, twelve per. Satsumas, four large. Cultured yeast, five hundred gram jar," he spouted on, not even stopping for a breath. "Erectile stimulant—Doctor, why can't I stop reading this? Fourteen gels, generic by preference. Help me, doctor! Water filtration tablets, one-kilogram box—"

"Do something, damn it!" shouted the PR doctor one last time, before leaning in to loom over Usnavi once again. A bead of sweat dripped down from his now frazzle-haired temple. "And you hang in there now, young man. Do you hear me? We're going to sort this out! Nothing can stop progress!"

"You—" whispered Usnavi. "Y—Y—You…"

He stuttered, then stopped, the words so eager to rush out of his throat they were jamming in his brain.

"Yes?" asked the doctor, leaning in even closer.

"You can finally make your neighbours green with envy," he shouted into the man's startled face, "as you ride to work in style and comfort in the brand new 2073 Lagrange Imperial! Available at employee prices with no money down and easy monthly payments of five hundred eighty-eight credits!"

His voice dropped at the end of this. Then he added, in little more than a whisper once again, "No credit check required."

Back in the control room, Liam sat transfixed, watching the screen. Was this good for their advertisers or not? Was it good for the show? Or, you know, morally decent, he added as an afterthought?

One of the monitors outside of the feed's field of view started bleeping a whole lot faster.

"Shit, we're losing him here!" shouted the female techie. The PR doctor's genial façade crumbled faster than Usnavi's brain cell count.

The sound of journalists dictating article snippets to their AR interfaces drowned out the frantic work of the medical team, and Usnavi's ever-weakening drivel—until the mad bleeping turned into a single, drawn-out, spine-chilling note.

"Shit," repeated the medical technician, no longer having to shout in the hush that fell on the operating theatre.

Usnavi's now redundant handler shook his head and backed away from the boy. "Brain-death recorded at 17:33 hours," he said, the same way a puppy-owner might say, "Oh, another mess on the kitchen floor." He spun on his heel and left Usnavi altogether, marching over toward the crowd of spectators at the back of the room.

That's when Liam realised that, while Usnavi was dead, the feed was still very much live. He, and the millions of viewers around the world, were looking out through the eyes of a dead boy.

Some vestigial shred of decency deep within him sent his hand shooting out toward the big red button in his interface that would kill the feed. But it didn't even make it halfway there before a priority call came in from the Editor.

"Argyle!" he shouted in all his bone-conducted glory straight into Liam's eardrums. "I hope you aren't even considering interrupting this feed!"

"But, sir," protested Liam, before he could stop himself, "Usnavi died! And the feed is still live! This is terrible!"

"This is no time to worry about the PR impact for our biotech sponsors," scolded the Editor, not unkindly, but completely missing the point of Liam's half-hearted protests. "You've got to see the bigger picture. Here, let me send it to you."

Sure enough, a picture file came through, and a speechless Liam displayed it on his AR desktop. It was a close-up screen save of *The Grass is Greener* live viewer count, and not unlike a radiation-belt construction worker's baby, it had at least one or two digits too many.

"You see those numbers?" asked the Editor. "They don't lie. The feed is now the number one trend on social media. People are sharing the link like crazy. They lap up this macabre nonsense."

At the edge of Usnavi's dead gaze, medical staff wearing disappointed frowns started cleaning up the equipment, while the PR doctor was shouting something along the lines of "All right, time to fess up! Who did this?" at the assembled scientific and entertainment journalists.

Liam couldn't find the words to express the conflicting ideas raging through his mind. "But it's just not… I don't know…" He cast about for a term to latch onto. "Decent."

The Editor paused for a full three seconds, before muttering something that sounded like, "I don't have time for this crap." In the background of his audio feed, someone laughed.

"Liam, my boy," returned the Editor's voice at last, cold and calculated. "I thought we were long past this. You need to stop thinking about things in terms of 'decency.'" The sneer on his lips was obvious in his voice as he spoke the word. "Think about what we do in terms of public service, yes? We bring people a direct glimpse into the lives of those who, for whatever reason, can be seen as less fortunate than themselves. Someone they can look down at, so to speak, providing them with a vital boost to their self-esteem, their mental well-being. Just the thing to help someone who might otherwise feel unsatisfied accept their lot in modern society."

Liam mulled over this novel way of looking at the show, in silence.

Meanwhile, on the still-running feed, the implants behind Usnavi's still and rapidly cooling eyes caught the PR doctor's voice.

"Do you mean to say not a single one of you bothered to read the sign outside the door and turn off broadcasting on your devices before entering the operating theatre?" he yelled.

There was an indignant and in no way repentant collective outburst from the assembled journalists. One voice eventually emerged from the babble as a spokesman for the rest. "Well, yes, we all read it. But we didn't think you were serious," stated the man, as if this should be obvious to anyone with half a brain. "These are the '70s, man. And we're journalists. Why don't you just ask us to rip out our eyeballs and chop off our fingers before entering?"

The doctor grumbled, told the journalists to stay put so he could deliver an official statement from DynaMed, and stomped back over toward Usnavi's strapped-in corpse, where the medical and technical team was still packing away the equipment, whispering amongst themselves, and waiting.

As was the Editor, Liam realised with a shock that brought him out of his feed-induced reverie.

"Yes, I think I see what you mean," he replied, eyes still riveted on the view through young Usnavi's open lids. "If we're helping people around the world feel happier with their own daily lives, then that has to be a worthy endeavour, right, Ed?"

"That's the spirit!" boomed the voice in Liam's inner ear. "And it certainly beats the alternative, which is unemployment, eh, Argyle?" he added, with a half-convincing attempt at a laugh.

Liam gulped. On screen, one of the medical technicians jostled the operating table as they reached for a piece of equipment, and Usnavi's head tilted, his eyes sliding blissfully shut, at long last. "You've got that right," he said.

Though the feed's visual feed was almost completely covered by Usnavi's eyelids, the sound was still coming through loud and clear.

"So what's the official takeaway here?" said the PR doctor, in a tense whisper.

"Well, from a technical standpoint, the operation was still a complete success," answered the female technician from earlier, also whispering. "It's still the first operational human synaptic link in history. Just a little too operational, that's all."

"You know, I think that could work," mused the PR man. "Historic success, dramatic sacrifice, crucial data learned, all that jazz. And crucial changes will be implemented as DynaMed moves on toward full commercial release, of course."

"Yes. A touch less open connectivity, for one."

"Well then, I guess celebration is in order after all," said the PR doctor, no longer feeling the need to whisper. "Pass me that champagne bottle. Here's to success!"

The pop of the cork was deafening over Usnavi's forever blind-eyed feed.

"And scene," said the Editor into Liam's inner ear. He'd forgotten the call was still active. "You can stop the feed now, Liam," he added, and Liam pushed the button before he'd even consciously registered the instruction.

Usnavi's live feed went dark, for the last time.

"Now that's entertainment," the Editor purred. "And I don't think I'm giving too much away when I say we may have a new winner for tomorrow's big finale."

53

The full moon above the special outdoor finale set loomed large and bright, despite the set's bright lights. *Must be something about being up so high in the Andes,* mused Liam. *So much closer to the heavens.*

If only the altitude and Quito valley pollution didn't join forces to wreak havoc on his sinuses, he might actually be enjoying getting out of the Mews for the big finish to *The Grass is Greener*'s first season. As it was, he just had to grin, take his place on the set built at the base of the squat Equator Monument tower, read the words in the AR teleprompter, and fake it. For just one more show.

"An overwhelming four-point-six billion have voted in this, the final round of *The Grass is Greener*, Season One." His own voice boomed through the speakers set all around Quito's *Ciudad Mitad del Mundo*, the commercial buildings and the sphere-topped Monument tower brightly lit in the show's floodlights, but dwarfed by the already soaring spire base of the future Quito Space Elevator.

"It's been a wild ride, and we couldn't have done it without you, folks. Thank you all so very much!"

On cue, the live audience of curious Quiteños and visiting GiGalos—as *The Grass is Greener*'s ever-growing number of diehard fans called each other—broke into wild cheer. Liam let it play out the pre-defined five seconds, enjoying real, non-canned applause for a change, before signalling for silence with a casual wave of his hand.

"So many votes, and in just a few moments, we'll be ushering your two finalists in for the last, teary goodbyes—and the results we've all been waiting for. But first, I'd like to take the opportunity of this special show, broadcast live across the world from Quito's beautiful Equator Monument, to draw your attention to our magnificent surroundings."

Liam swept his arm upward, guiding the eye past the balled tip of the Equator Monument and all the way up the black, floodlit cathedral lines of the Space Elevator base. High above the upturned heads, little constructor drones were hard at work in the skeletal upper reaches of the spire, pumping out heat-absorbent polymers to build Elevator crawler rails and support beams for the cable itself— whenever it finally got down here from the hollowed-out asteroid that'd serve as ball at the end of the nanocarbon assembly chain.

"Take a moment to appreciate the sight, everyone. Really let it sink in. because what you're seeing here tonight is the Future. And I know that sounds cheesy," Liam added, wishing the bosses hadn't forced him to go through with the PR spiel—it was part of the deal with the other Corporations partnered in the Elevator Initiative so they could get permission to use the site for the finale, apparently. "But I really mean it. Once the Elevator is in place, it'll be cheaper and safer to get cargo and people up and down from space than it is to cross an ocean today. The next great step in humankind's expansion out into the Cosmos. Hell, maybe someday soon, everyone will be able to have their own private Paradise Mars, and we'll have to find another prize for the show!"

Once again on perfect, docile cue, the crowd laughed at his feeble attempt at humour. Liam didn't know if it were possible to loathe himself any more than he did at that instant—but he grit his teeth, smiled, and resigned himself to find out.

"What I know for sure is that, between the Elevator work and the tourism boom, business in Quito has never been better—isn't that right, Quiteños?"

This time, a weirdly tame roar of local pride met his scripted call, all according to plan.

"I'd like to thank you fine folk of Quito for welcoming us here tonight for this very special show. And for making it possible, too, by letting us use your fine Space Launch Tube to send your chosen winner on their way to their reward in Paradise Mars."

In perfect timing, a capsule finished its constant 1G acceleration through the maglev tube network woven around the Andes valleys and up to the launch point at the end of the half-built Space Elevator base tower, kilometres above. There was a dramatic flash of light as the air ignited under the capsule's escape velocity speed, quickly quashed as the smart materials absorbed and harnessed the energy to feed the onboard systems on their way to rendezvous with the interplanetary laser thrust railway.

Back down on Earth, Liam crossed the stage in pre-calculated steps and stopped before a swanky, gold-accented, advertisement-filled train terminal. A shiny green pill-shaped capsule bearing *The Grass is Greener* logo lay waiting, snug in the groove of the maglev track.

"A lot of viewers out there may never have even seen a picture of a Space Launch Tube station before, and that makes me sad. So, before we get started, I wanted to give you all a little glimpse at what humanity can achieve when we all band together and work as one united planet.

"Sure, a Launch Tube like this is expensive to run, and very few people can afford to use it today," he added, trading his manic host's smile for a solemn look. "But soon, with the Elevator, everyone will be able to get to Space if they want to. I call that real progress!"

Liam grinned his false grin again and walked forward toward the audience. "And until that happy day, *The Grass is Greener* is here to make Space dreams come true! So, without further ado, please give a warm round of applause for your 2072 *Grass is Greener* grand finalists!"

As the deep bass fanfare of the show's theme song blared from every speaker, and in the ears of viewers around the globe, the two final contestants were ushered onto the stage—so to speak. No-Longer-Suicide Jill entered on her own two legs, scowling like never before, while on the other side of the stage the show's ever-exploitable temp service worker Mary carried in a little urn, a tasteful black lacquered affair with gold highlights. Liam suspected the urn had cost the show more than the boy whose incinerated remains rested inside had earned in a year.

Above their heads, free-floating AR windows played each finalist's highlight reel—Jill's live suicide clean-up escapades, leading up to and including her last misadventure, on the left; Usnavi's smiling face and willing participation in his medical experiments, on the right. The latter finished off with pictures of spontaneous vigils organised by GiGalos around the world in the last twenty-four hours, since his death live on feed.

Liam tried to ignore it all and focus on what he was supposed to say next, once both contestants were, each in their own way, safely ensconced in their seats. Mary shrank into the background, ignored by all.

"It's been a long road, folks, and again, if we're here tonight, it's only thanks to you faithful viewers and voters back home. So let's hear a big round of applause for you guys!"

The audience broke into applause even more energetic than before, and Liam could only assume the cheers were echoed by viewers around the world. A planet united in obliviousness to how ridiculous it is to applaud yourself.

Next to him on stage, Usnavi's urn gleamed in the spotlight, and Jill hung her head.

"There's someone else I want to thank before we close the voting and check the final tally—so get those last-minute votes in, folks!" smarmed Liam, hating every second of it. "While you do, I'd like to take a moment to remember the contestants who weren't quite so bad off as our finalists, but who were brave enough to open their lives up to the world and help make the show the amazing phenomenon it has become. Let's hear it for the grateful eliminated!"

A spattering of applause greeted the new AR display that opened up at Liam's words, and all eyes watched the last highlight reel of the night, a hodgepodge of sepia-toned moments ranging from Professor Ali Fourka's brief tenure on the show to Spike Bighorn's robo-pornographic sexcapades, from Brad Leigh's heavy-handed public service to Juliette Binns's fearful submission to the live ocular implant operation.

Liam watched along with everyone else, not even turning away when Azar Acquah's haunting face smiled at him from the screen. Yet he seethed in silence. Why wouldn't the Editor even listen to his idea of getting live commentary, or at least fresh footage, from the eliminated contestants? Granted, when you started making a list, you soon realised how few contestants were physically able to make a recording for the finale. But even without intruding on Juliette's VR therapy again, they could have tracked down Professor Fourka, wherever he was now. And surely Spike Bighorn must have recovered enough to make a recording by now. The fans would have loved that.

But the Editor had been firm. A brief "best of" montage and then straight on to the final sequence. Who was Liam to argue? And what did it matter, anyway. The sooner he got on with this, the sooner it would be finished, and he could go hide in his trailer, where a non-judgmental and non-demanding one-litre bottle of aguardiente waited for him on chill.

"Wow, that sure takes me back," he resumed, as the reel finished and the teleprompter in his retina started scrolling again. "The votes are still coming in, so we'll leave them open just a few moments longer. Just long enough to hear from Jill."

Liam strode over to where the now-unemployed finalist formerly known as Suicide Jill sat glowering at him, daring him to ask her anything. But the teleprompter wouldn't have it any other way, so Liam gulped and soldiered on.

"So, my dear," he said, despite the evidence of his eyes, "how does it feel to have made it all the way to the grand finale?"

"Well, if you really need to know, it feels fucking ridiculous, Liam."

Liam laughed, a touch nervously to his own ears. "I suppose so, if you mean how ridiculously amazing the possibility of a lifetime of luxury on Paradise Mars is, and so close to hand, right, Jill?"

Jill's only response was to rise to her feet, barge past Liam with a sad shake of her head, and walk over to speak directly to the assembled spectators.

"How can you lot stand there and cheer on this nonsense?" she shouted, squinting into the floodlight glare, trying to make out the people in the crowd. "This show is a monster! It takes people, spreads their lives wide open, grinds them into nothing, and then spits out whatever is left. And you people, all you people watching, are what powers it. It's a consumer product, and your brains are the commodity it's selling!"

This wasn't quite on script, and Liam stood smiling and paralysed. Maybe the Editor had a point about avoiding live input you couldn't control.

As if summoned by the very thought, a priority text message from the Editor appeared in Liam's display. *Well played from Jill, but that's enough. Get her back in her seat.*

Easier said than done. She was in full tilt now, and even if Liam could somehow strongarm the woman back into her seat—which he doubted—he couldn't very well do it live in front of billions of viewers. He cast about for some solution to the problem and, seizing the first idea to come to mind, strode forward to stand beside Jill, cutting into her rant.

"That's the Jill we know and love. Strong and frank-spoken as ever. And the viewers can't get enough of it. The live comments keep pouring in. Let's have a look!"

Liam waved his hand, and a new AR window appeared in mid-air, with a streaming flow of live comments from viewers.

lul who does she think she is?
someone forgot their pill
salty

There was just enough time for Jill to get the gist of the viewers' reactions before the chat delay caught up with the live show and ruined the effect.

we're on the show!
hi Mom!
Best show evar!

Jill stared at the cascade of words, at a loss for any of her own.

"Is this really what you all think?" she finally said, in tones lower than her chances of winning the show, now that the Editor had decided otherwise. "Is this all just fun and games for you?"

The crowd responded with spattered applause, which turned into full-out cheering and hooting when Liam stepped forward and cocked an ear, urging them on. Jill's tense, confrontational stance melted as the seconds went on and the cheering showed no sign of dying down.

"Wow, you guys are amazing," said Liam, eventually, and it was only then the crowd stopped cheering. "And I've just had word that voting is now officially closed! We should have the results any second now, folks, so don't leave your seats!"

He ushered the unresisting and downcast Jill back into her own chair on stage and took his designated position in the very centre. A gleaming new window appeared above his head—the largest one yet—with both Jill and Usnavi's names appearing in sparkling green letters.

"The time is finally here!" he announced, voice echoing between the Andes peaks. "After months of hopes and fears, of smiles and tears, it's all come down to this one vote. Who has it the worst? Who deserves the ticket to Paradise Mars the most? It's time to find out— right after this brief word from our sponsors. Don't go anywhere!"

54

Standing, eyes shut, in the floodlights while the precious seconds of the commercial break wasted away, Liam didn't know which was more depressing: the votes coming in or the comments on the show's live chat from the voters.

Not that he was surprised at the final tally displayed against the canvas of his shut eyelids. After the... incident with Usnavi's operation, the Editor had all but decreed that the boy would be the winner. And Liam knew the man would always end up right, one way or the other.

No—what depressed him was his growing suspicion that Ed didn't even need to doctor the results this time around. Surely the man couldn't have faked the messages scrolling down the live chat window. Not all of them, at least.

Vote 2 to pay respects to Usnavi!
RIP little man! Now you can live forever among the stars!
Usnavi wins or riot!

One million votes after the next, the tally overwhelmingly declared Usnavi the winner, the worst off of all the victims of modern life and the most deserving of the one-way trip to Paradise Mars.

The prize was supposed to involve a lifetime of luxury at the end of the trip, but in Usnavi's case... Well, at least there wasn't any doubt about the Editor's motivation in pushing Usnavi to win.

"One minute to air," bellowed Ms. Lee's voice from somewhere beyond the comforting veil of Liam's shut eyelids.

He chuckled to himself. He'd spent the first forty-odd years of his life cursing how long advertisements lasted. Now that he was on the other side of the screen, they never lasted long enough.

Time to face the music. Announce that the collective wisdom of the human race has decided to send an urn full of ashes to Mars instead of a living person. The ashes of a poor neglected boy murdered in the name of science.

No, Liam told himself. This was no time for half-truths. Science had nothing to do with it.

Usnavi was murdered in the name of entertainment.

And here were the viewers, the ones his brain got fried for, acting like they were doing the boy some sort of favour by giving him the win. As if it'd make any difference to him now. Or to Azar. Or Juliette Binns, for that matter. After all, what was left of her in that chemical and virtual haze could hardly be called living.

"Thirty seconds!" Carpentiere shouted in a low rumble.

There was no escaping it. The second Liam declared Usnavi the winner, it would all be done and dusted. He would have added his rubber stamp to everything RedCorp had done to demolish the lives of these people. What he himself had done to these people. His people.

Eyes downcast, he stumbled out of the spotlight and off to the side of the stage. He made it right to the edge of the set before anybody took any notice of him.

"Liam, my boy," said the Editor, grabbing Liam by the arm. "Here, I think this is what you're looking for." Liam looked up, taking in the stiff drink in the shorter man's free hand, and the even stiffer smile on his hairless face.

A peace offering, unquestionably, but held in a hand of steel. The Editor saw right through Liam. There would be no smiles whatsoever if he gave into his doubts and didn't go back up there to do his job. The moment of truth.

There was the slightest of pauses. A lump caught in Liam's throat, stealing his voice. Then he swallowed it down and drew in a deep breath.

Fuck it all. What difference would it make, anyway? Would any grand gesture from him make Usnavi or Azar any less dead? Spike or Juliette any less messed up? It wasn't as if one man could make any sort of difference.

Filled with new resolve, Liam nodded in silent thanks to the Editor, took the offered glass, belted it down without even wasting time on figuring out what it was, and trotted back into position at the centre of the set. Without a second to spare.

"The people have spoken!" he shouted, with a glee that no longer felt difficult to fake. "We have a winner!"

Under Jill's sulking stare, he stepped over to Usnavi's chair, grabbed the little urn in both hands, and lifted it high above his head.

"I give you your grand prize winner, your choice by a landslide— Usnavi Musibay!"

Liam paused for applause. The clapping and hooting from the crowd cheered him up to no end. He marvelled at how beautiful the urn above his head looked, its gold accents glinting in the spotlights.

The show's upbeat theme song started playing, and Liam stuck to the game plan. He stepped over, smiling, to wrap an arm around a shrunken, disabused Jill. With the urn still under his other arm, he hugged both finalists for one last, photogenic, front-page-worthy shot. Then he rushed over to the waiting shuttle, trying not to stumble at the edge of the set and scatter grand winner ashes all over the rubbery launch station floor.

"Come on, everyone," he shouted, and waved in mock spontaneity, the second he reached the open door of the maglev shuttle. The barriers holding back the spectators flipped down, just like the script said they would, and the crowd surged forward, carrying Carpentiere, Lee, and the set's mobile podcameras along with them.

Hands, faces, and squashed bodies crowded against the shuttle's transparent shielding, with everyone desperate to get their own touch of the moment before the shuttle and Usnavi went on their way down the tube, up the launch plume, and off to Mars.

Ignoring the somewhat nightmarish sight and smiling for the cameras inside the shuttle itself, Liam carefully placed the no-longer-glimmering urn in the lone plush green seat and strapped it in snug, thanks to the convenient, urn-sized straps someone had thoughtfully planned for.

"Thank you, young man," he said, just low enough for the viewers to get a sense of privacy and intimacy. "And congratulations. Couldn't have happened to a better person."

His hostly duty dispensed with, he backed out of the shuttle and turned back toward the crowd. Behind him, there was a *whir* of alarm, and the door began to slide shut with carefully programmed and dramatic slowness.

Liam waved his arms, shooing the crowd away from the shuttle. "Back up, folks! Back up! It's preparing to launch!"

The door finally sealed shut with a hiss, and the deep bone throb of the maglev track powering up produced the effect Liam's warnings alone could not. The crowd backed away, and it was with mixed cheers and sobs that all assembled watched the little craft slide onto the maglev track and float into launch position. With a high-tension crackle, it set into motion and was soon speeding down the station track, before being swallowed by the tube, on its way to frictionless acceleration and launch into space.

That, of course, wouldn't be for another hour or so, after it had gained enough acceleration zipping through the warren of tubes dug through the local mountains and valleys. Some of the spectators might stick around to watch Usnavi's little departing flare, but Liam sure as hell wasn't going to. He had no time for that, and neither did the crew. There was work to do to tidy up the set. And as for Liam, he had a celebrity after-party to attend in downtown Quito.

He was surprisingly at peace with the outcome of the show. This was good. Everything about the finale and Usnavi's big send-off felt, somehow, pretty great. He really wished someone had told him sooner how much simpler all your problems became when you just gave up, put your trials and tribulations into their proper perspective, and stopped taking everything so personally. If he'd known, he would have stopped giving a crap years ago.

"A huge thanks once again to all you folks back home for setting Usnavi on his journey to Paradise Mars," he shouted over the hoots and roars of a crowd eager to have their animal grunts heard around the world. "And thank you for accompanying us on our journey, the first of many, to find where—" he paused for effect one last time— "the grass is greener! See you soon for Season Two, everybody!

EPILOGUE

The men and women in the designer casual suits lounged in their easy chairs and gazed through the low-G club's extravagantly large viewing port. Watching the local photonic thrust relay tease the latest shuttle into docking position at Paradise Mars always drew a few spectators. It was a reliable way to kill an idle afternoon cycle.

But this shuttle contained neither crates full of luxury goods from Old Smoggy nor queasy-looking fresh arrivals to size up before anyone else could get their hands on them.

"What's this about, then?" said one silicone-faced man to the grand dame sitting across the aisle from him. "Are we taking on genies now?"

The lady shook her head and smiled, quickly dismissing the search window she'd pulled up to find the answer to the question. "Don't be silly. It's just the shuttle from that show. You know, the one with the low-class people and the man with the ears. They found a way to give the grand prize to a dead person and avoid having to send anyone here at all, dontchaknow?"

"Well, it's a handsome enough urn, I suppose," grunted the first speaker, a man of keen aesthetic sensibilities.

The lady reached over to rest a hand on his arm as they watched the robot workers empty out the shuttle, urn and all. "Oh, isn't it just? I think it will look marvellous on the lounge mantelpiece. A real conversation piece."

Liam Argyle will return
to take on the corporate dystopia in
The Rude Eye of Rebellion.

SPOILER ALERT: It does not go well.

Read the first chapter now at:
LawlessAuthor.com

Coming in Fall 2020

ACKNOWLEDGEMENTS

It's been a long road for *Always Greener*, from the shadows of a twelfth century abbey in rural England all the way to your eyes today, some twelve years later. None of it would have possible without my long-suffering travelling companions and the new friends met along the way.

My editor at Uproar Books, Rick, has put so much work and inspiration into this series, his name should by all rights be on the front as well. Thank you for seeing the potential at the core of my rambling mess, prescribing the harsh love it required, adding your own sheen of brilliance to the bits that still stuck out, and then wrapping it all up to get it out into the world. If you didn't enjoy this book, then the blame is entirely mine.

Marisa, my time travel-loving motivational star of an agent, has also been dedicated to helping this book reach its full potential, and I can't thank her enough for it. Her and her team at the Corvisiero Literary Agency do amazing work; I highly recommend you do yourself a favor and check them out.

And an enormous, Flare-ridden thank you to agent brother James Dashner, whose words of praise after reading the advance copy of the book I would never have believed possible, if his sincerity hadn't shone through at every turn.

Speaking of fellow authors, the team at PitchWars, the annual online mentoring competition, deserve every bit of praise and thanks I could possibly give them. From the organizers all the way to my personal PitchWars heroes, they've all taught me so much throughout my participation in the events. The writing community is incredibly lucky to have an event like PitchWars happening every year. Don't miss out on the vast amounts of volunteer support the mentoring competition channels.

My own personal mentor will always be my mother. Along with my father, the values, the caring, the wisdom, and the deep-seated love for humanity she has passed on to me are the foundation everything I write is built upon. As for my beloved sister and brother, I hope you enjoy this pile of words—you were both firmly in my mind, listening, as I wrote them.

And, finally, it almost seems silly to put into words how much neither I nor this book could ever have existed as we are today without the love and joy of my three amazing children and the unwavering support and guidance of my mighty pillar of strength, my constant critique partner, my first and forever reader—in short, my amazing wife. Without her wisdom and innate sense for quality, the manuscript would never have reached a presentable state in the first place. This book belongs to her just as much as it does to me.

ABOUT THE AUTHOR

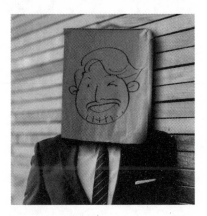

Born in Newfoundland, Canada, raised in France, and come into his own as an author while living in rural England, J.R.H. Lawless is an attorney by day and a speculative fiction author by night, mostly adult science fiction with a sharply humorous and occasionally political edge. He now lives and writes in Atlantic Canada with his beautiful family.

Also from Uproar Books:

ASPERFELL by Jamie Thomas (Gothic Fantasy)

When a sharp-tongued young woman is sentenced to an otherworldly prison for magic she never knew she possessed, she must rescue a lost prince to prevent a civil war.

SAND DANCER by Trudie Skies (YA Fantasy)

In a desert kingdom where fire magic is a sin, a half-starved peasant girl must disguise herself as a nobleman's son to find her father's killer.

THE WAY OUT by Armond Boudreaux (Sci-Fi Thriller)

When natural human reproduction is outlawed in favor of artificial wombs, two women discover a conspiracy to prevent telepathic children from ever being born.

WILD SUN by Ehsan Ahmad & Shakil Ahmad (Epic Sci-Fi)

On a world enslaved, a fierce young woman sparks an uprising against the soldiers of the interstellar empire that conquered her people.

Discover more great books at UproarBooks.com